A cobra's bite doesn't hurt

A cobra's bite doesn't hurt

Published by The Conrad Press in the United Kingdom 2020

Tel: +44(0)1227 472 874
www.theconradpress.com
info@theconradpress.com

ISBN 978-1-911546-96-2

Typesetting and Cover Design by: Charlotte Mouncey, www.bookstyle.co.uk

The Conrad Press logo was designed by Maria Priestley.

A cobra's bite doesn't hurt

Anil Nijhawan

My inspiration, my sons, Kavin and Rohit

Chapter 1

Your Highness Mr Narendra Modi,
   You are the Prime Minister of India, one of the largest democracies of the world. They say you know many famous people, like Xi Jinpi, Obama, Putin, Merkel and Trump. They invite you to their countries and welcome you like a VIP. When they come to India, you wear your best suit stitched by tailors in London and go to the airport to greet them with garlands of flowers. I have heard you even gift them beautiful marble replicas of our Taj Mahal. Once I saw you in a big black car rushing to Kolkata airport for one such visit. I ran forward between two policemen and waved to you. However, did you wave back? No. Another time I saw you on NDTV 9 o'clock news. You were giving a speech to thousands of people assembled at the *maidan.* They were listening to you as if it was the most important thing in their lives. I was very impressed. However, my friend Sanju was not. He said it was all a political *tamasha* organised with rent-a-crowd audience. Promise these people hundred rupees and cup of chai they will go anywhere, do anything for you. For two hundred rupees, they will even start a riot.

   You said many things that day which did not interest me. However, when you started talking about children, I asked Sanju to turn up the volume. You were saying every child in India is like your own son or daughter; you will give them the education they deserve and help them achieve their ambitions in life. You went on to say children were the future of the country; no child should live in poverty, fear or ignorance.

That is when I said to myself, Kalu you must write to Mr Modi, tell him all about yourself. If anyone knows about living in poverty, fear, ignorance, it is I. With due respects sir, however good your intentions, you will not succeed in this noble venture unless you look deeper into why there are so many abandoned children in this country. Do you know what happens to them? I can tell you. Many end up living on pavements, railway stations or bus shelters. The lucky ones end up in orphanages, like the one I was in, until some gangsters kidnapped me at the age of fourteen.

I will tell you absolutely everything about me, including how often I go to the toilet and at what time. I hope you are not of delicate nature sir, not easily offended by violence and bad language. That is because I am going to be brutally honest. Like you, I am a man who likes to speak his mind.

When I said I would write to you, I did not mean literally. That is because I cannot write, though I can read a little. I am going to dictate everything to a Sanyo voice-recording machine. About twenty years old, made in Japan, it still works like a dream. My friend Sanju has promised to type the story on his HP 250 laptop.

Sanju went to school in Dhule village, studied to class VI. He said he had to leave school when his father died of *bhang* overdose. Then the mother kicked him out saying she did not want a man in the house anymore. She said she had had enough of men; they are all lazy fuckers. She did not use that word exactly, but something similar in Marathi. You will never catch me use bad language. Well almost never. Once I did. That is because someone had made me very angry and sad. Let me tell you about that.

At the time, I was in Bangalore. I had a steady job working as a pickpocket. Now Mr Modiji sir, please do not be mad with me. I had to do what a man has to do to survive. I had no choice in the matter. If you meet Babu Bajrang and Father Petre, you will understand. Big, powerful gangsters they are. You may be interested to learn they are also your *bhakts*, devotees. They said they have big reach in the BJP party and that nobody can touch them. It may be true because once I saw them send a bundle of thousand-rupee notes to a very important man in the government, whose name I forget now. However, I have seen him on television a few times, a small man with greasy hair and blob of saffron *tilak* on forehead, bowing and doing *namaste* to the camera like a very moral and saintly human being.

So, when they offered me the job of *phoketmar* how could I refuse? I was not alone though. There were four of us in the team, Ramesh, Gokul, Bhushan and myself. My name is Kalu, though I am also called Kalu Cobra. Why Cobra? You will find out later. Ramesh was my best friend. I loved him like a brother. One night he went missing from the house. It was a surprise because no one had heard him leave. We assumed he had left early to work the crowd that had gathered in Cubborn Park for Guru Ramdev's *darshan* and learn yoga from him. In the evening back home, we found Babu sitting on the white leather sofa, drinking Black Label. However, Ramesh was not there. That is when I began feeling uneasy, as if something bad had happened to him. I just could not shake off the fear that he may have come to some harm. Have you ever faced this kind of dilemma sir?

'Ramesh has run away. We have looked for him everywhere. He can't be found,' Babu said just like that, casually, as if announcing tomorrow we are going to eat mutton biryani for dinner.

My heart stopped. I knew Ramesh so well. He never went anywhere without first telling me. If he was unhappy and wanted to leave Bangalore, I definitely would have known.

I said to Babu, 'boss no way he would have run away. Something bad must have happened to him.' Ramesh's favourite song, *oye Raju pyar na kariya kariyo - dil toot jata hai*, began ringing in my ears. He often sang it to me, replacing Raju with Kalu.

However, Babu was adamant Ramesh had gone of his own free will. 'Forget about that double crossing *sarak ka kuta*,' he said. Calling my brother a dirty wild dog was out of order. That is when I swore at Babu, sir. I called him *bahnchoot*, sister-fucker. Luckily, he did not hear me, or I would not be here dictating this letter to you.

Chapter 2

So, I will begin from the first time I met Ramesh. That was four years ago. I was sitting quietly at my favourite spot, the alcove of the first floor window, looking out into the lane below. The angle of the window afforded a clear view of the half-tarmacked dirt track for a quarter of a mile. I saw a man turn into the lane. He was walking with a limp, as if his legs were of different lengths. A little boy was with him. As they came closer, I could see they were holding hands and the boy was crying. I assumed they were city folks by the way they were dressed. Why are they coming here? Visitors were rare to our orphanage called Durga Bhabi Bal Kalyan, founded by Prime Minister Indira Gandhi many years ago. She said it was in memory of her personal astrologer, Durga Bhabi. However, few people knew of its existence or of the small village nearby, neither appeared on any maps nor in government records.

That afternoon I saw the boy again in my ward, this time he was holding nannie Urmila *didi's* hand. The first thing I noticed was his long face and big ears. He was also very short. The shirt and grey trousers he wore were brand new. How classy they looked. It made us all jealous for we had never worn anything new.

'Boys this is Ramesh Banika, he is going to stay with us,' Urmila *didi* announced. The boys rushed forward and surrounded Ramesh; some were touching him to see if he was real, not a *pharishta*, an alien descended from the sky;

others were talking to him, asking where he was from, if he had mama and papa. Another was admiring his shirt, asking if he could borrow it once. Yet another wanted to know if he would like to be his friend. I could see all this attention was making Ramesh very uncomfortable. He hid his face in *didi's* sari and began crying. When *didi* asked for a volunteer to show Ramesh around I threw my hand up fast.

Early next morning I went to the bed allocated to Ramesh. He was lying on his back, nervously scanning the room with wide-open eyes.

I took him on a guided tour of the four wards. First was the infant ward for six year olds where most of the children were still asleep. Some were awake, sitting up on old metal cots arranged back to back, staring at us with sunken blank eyes as we walked past. Sheets on the cots were shit stained and threadbare. The windows draped with very thin material, did nothing to stop sun's rays falling on the cots. The grime on walls stood exposed where the sun light fell. As always, the air smelled of urine and shit. We were used to it, but I could see Ramesh was holding his breath.

I took him to the dining hall at the back. It was dark and damp as always. Of the three windows on the south side, one was sealed with plywood, ever since someone had smashed its glass. Rows of long wooden tables stood crammed from end to end. In the kitchen, cooks were rattling pots and pans, shouting and screaming at each other.

'Are you hungry?' I asked.

He did not reply but stared at a boy walking past. The boy was tugging at his very loose trousers to stop them from slipping, while the shirt he was wearing was so tight it was biting into his armpits. I knew what Ramesh was thinking. I told him, '*yaar* this is normal. We wear what *didis* give us. Nobody cares about the size. You will even see little boys in frocks or girls in boys' shorts. Who cares?' I showed him the massive pile of clothes taller than me lying next to another hill of dirty laundry.

He refused to speak. His eyes were darting around nervously as if he was about to burst into tears again. I took him back to the upper floor, to the alcove of the front window.

'Come on sit here,' I told him, 'this is my favourite spot. You can see the whole street from here.'

He did sit down on the old wooden seat. But would not look out of the window as if he knew out there was nothing but a long dirt track, wide enough for tractors and small cars, wasteland on either side. Rats and dogs outnumbered the farm workers who passed by on foot, bicycles or Bajaj scooters. The nearest village of Tehri Nagar was three miles away and the bus stop a mile away in Bahadrabad. In the mornings and evenings, you could see thick mist over the entire area like smoke of a burnt out fire. No one from the village ever came this way.

When he relaxed a little, I asked him about the man who had come to drop him.

'My papa,' Ramesh replied tapping the wooden panel under his legs. The way he pronounced papa, I knew he was a city boy.

'So why did he leave you here?'

'He had something to do in Mumbai. He will come back soon to take me home.'

'Hah, Bhagu's *dadima* had left him here. She was going to come back too.'

'My papa isn't like that,' he retorted sharply.

Two boys nearby were listening. 'You were lucky your old

man left you here,' interjected one of the boys, skinny and sickly looking, two lines of green snot ran permanently from his nose. 'My baba used to get drunk, beat us all the time. You want to see something. Look at this.' He pulled up his shirt, revealing thin quarter moon shaped scars on his chest. 'Hot iron. He was a *dhobi* laundryman.'

'That's nothing. My papa killed himself. He cut his head off with an electric saw,' the second boy said running a thumb across his throat and dropped his head sideways and let his tongue hang loose. We had nicknamed this boy *natakbaz* because of his habit of dramatizing everything he said.

Ramesh looked enquiringly at him.

'He used to bring a friend, aunty Sindhu, home in the afternoons. They always locked themselves in the room. One day ma came home early and found them in bed together. They had a big fight and my ma threatened to kill papa. He said she need not bother he would do it himself. Next day our neighbour found him hanging from a tree. The electric saw on the floor was still doing buzz, buzz, buzz.'

'What's wrong with lying down together on the bed?' the first boy asked.

Natakbaz laughed exposing his chipped front tooth and slapped his friend on the head. '*Bilkul chutia hai,* you are an utter fool.' He pulled his loose pyjama down and exposed his penis.

A month later *natakbaz* was gone, adopted by a couple from Jaipur who were going away to live in Texas. No one knew where Texas was, but it felt like an exciting faraway place. The news spread, very fast. Every heart was burning with jealousy. Everybody wishing they were next for adoption. Have a mama and papa of his or her own, maybe even a brother or sister. I used to dream of having my own special family - brothers, sisters, cousins, uncles and aunts - living together in a big, big house.

One day we were seated at the table, squeezed four abreast on benches meant for two. *Didis* were tossing battered aluminium bowls, half-filled with runny porridge, on the tables. All around us children were screaming, complaining they did not like the food or it was not enough. Nannies were yelling at them to keep the noise down. Pots and pans were clashing in the kitchen. The heat of bodies was sweating up the room. I asked Ramesh, 'what do you think of this place?'

'Shit house,' he replied without hesitation in that upper class way and pinched his nose shut with two fingers.

Normally this sort of thing did not bother me. However, coming from Ramesh I felt insulted, as if he was blaming me this place was rubbish. It made me think. Perhaps he was right. I started noticing things around me, doors and windows, the fading grey walls, as if they were staring back at me, mocking me: you fool now you see us, how many years have you been rotting here?

I started fantasising about the village nearby, sauntering into the chai shop for a cup of milky tea and samosa with tomato ketchup. Then my thoughts turned to Haridwar, only a few miles away. How exciting it would be to live in a big city. But how could I leave this place. I had no relatives or friends outside. Whom could I ask for help and advice? I trusted very few people. The only person I thought might help me was nannie Bela *didi*.

'Where are you from Kalu?' she had once asked me. We were

in the kitchen helping the staff with cleaning the stoves, walls and ceilings, coated in layers of soot and grease.

'I don't know,' I said, poking the blocked drain with a pole. A thick smell of burnt oil and rotting food filled the room.

'What's your family name?' she asked.

'Don't know.' I pushed the pole again. This time the drain cleared. A gurgling sound rumbled upward as if coming from deep within the earth. I stood the pole in a corner, ready for use the next time the drain was blocked.

'Do you know your caste?'

'No.' I did not know who I was, but I had always assumed I was of a lower caste, a *dalit*, *chamar* or from a travelling community. I had taken it for granted that children of upper caste families never came to a *yateemkhana* like ours.

'Is Kalu your real name?' she asked.

'Yes,' I said.

'No.'

'What do you mean no?'

'It is a pet name. Like I am called Bela, but my proper name is Balakrishna.'

I was stumped.

She began telling me about her past. She was from a *jat* family of farmers. They did not have their own land but rented a plot from a rich landowner. As a young girl, she started working as a domestic at the landowner household. She worked like that for many years out of a sense of duty to her father. After he died, she ran away from the landowner and came to work at Durga Bhabi Bal Kalyan.

I had decided to speak to her after breakfast. However, as usual luck was against me. Poor Bela died that very day. I remember so well, how it happened. It was a very cold day. Snow had fallen on the mountains a few miles up. Some said it might travel south to Haridwar. Can you imagine snow falling on us? It was unheard of.

However, snow or no snow, nannies were determined to uphold the routine. Early morning bath was a familiar daily ritual, quick splash of water from a big drum; scrub and dry with a shared towel. Bela was clapping her hands noisily, screaming at us to join the queue. 'We are short staffed today. I don't want any trouble.'

Malka *didi* was at it too, 'do as y'er told or I'll snap every one of y'er bones – you nasty little creatures.'

We came out into the corridors to wait our turn for the bathrooms, leaning against stained walls or squatting on frozen concrete floor littered with garments left out for washing which had been there for three days and puddles of urine here and there. During the night some of the little ones, too scared to run to toilets, often lowered their pants and relieved themselves in the corridor, sometimes even shit.

While we waited with clattering teeth, one of the girls began crying. She could not bear the cold anymore. Soon a few more joined in and then everybody was howling or weeping. It was an amazing sight.

Madam Dhruvya, the manager of the orphanage, came running. Her sandals clip clopping noisily.

'*Oh, oh*, what is going on here?' she appeared startled and then began pacing up and down the corridor, clipping us on the head, 'be quiet, be quiet, it will be over soon.'

A boy wrapped himself around her leg, refusing to let go. 'Madam, today I don't want to have bath.' His name was Nicu, a former rubbish tip scavenger. He was used to going without a bath for days at a time. I remember seeing his hands scoured with rat bites and long scratches on the day he had arrived.

'Shut up Nicu, shut up, good boy, it will be over soon.' Madam was trying to reason with him. Nicu just would not stop howling.

Finally, she went red with anger, her dagger eyes piercing Nicu's flesh. 'Do you want it? Do you?' she hissed with clenched fists.

Some of us gasped in horror, for we knew what she meant.

'Right then,' she said and stormed out to the storeroom. She returned clutching a white tin box with a red cross painted on the lid. I recognised the box instantly as she slammed it on the table and raised the lid, exposing an assortment of pills, ointments and injection syringes. She took out a vial and a syringe with an attached needle. Working methodically, she inserted the needle in the vial, sucked the liquid out. Once the procedure was complete, she tapped the needle twice and raised it up in the air for all to see. It had the desired effect of shutting everyone up. Nicu too became quiet. However, Dhruvya took no notice. She grabbed the poor boy's right arm, squeezed the flesh between her forefinger and thumb and jabbed the needle in.

Ramesh tugged at my shirt from behind. 'Did you see that?'

I had seen it and experienced it all before. Sometimes they forced us to swallow a large white pill. Both had the same effect, made us weak and sleepy, as if we were dreaming with our eyes open. Later, we would feel very sick, unable to eat or drink for hours, even days.

Seeing Nicu get the 'needle' I was beginning to feel sick too when we heard a terrifying shriek. I turned just in time to see the bathroom door fly open. Bela *didi* came stumbling out and slumped to the floor in a heap. The door behind her, dislodged from the frame, came to rest at a precarious angle. She rolled to facedown position, legs straight behind, her large bosoms spread out under the chest. At the same time, an electric kettle fell clanging to the floor. The chord was stretched full length, while the socket appeared yanked off the wall.

Sir, if you are wondering, what a humble kettle was doing in the bathroom, let me tell you. The management had decided to pour boiling water in the drums to make the bathwater less cold. A useless exercise if you ask me. It made no difference.

Madam Dhruvya came running, dropped to the floor beside Bela, patted her cheeks and began rocking her body with both hands. More nannies arrived.

'*O, hari ram.* Oh my God. What has happened here?' Malka *didi*, a skinny woman who always wore orange saris, cried and locked her wild eyes on the body, as if trying to memorise its contours. Rakshas Bhai, the handyman arrived soon after, out of breath, puffing like a steam engine. He declared the bathroom out of bound. Rakshas had been a resident of the orphanage from a very young age. As he grew older, he had taken on the job of a handyman and security man. A round, stumpy man, he had hideously large feet. The toes with scaly skin stuck out of the *chappals* at a strange upward angle. We used to tease him. 'Why have you got elephant feet Rakshas Bhai?'

He would retort sharply, 'so I can crush you under them if you don't behave.'

Later seeing a stretcher carried away by two men, a white sheet shrouding the body, some of the children began crying again. I found Bhagu sitting huddled on the floor, shaking like a leaf.

'Probably missing his mother,' I overheard a *didi* whisper as she picked him up off the floor, 'she was beaten to death by the moneylender and the poor boy had witnessed it all.' I remember well when Bhagu came with his grandmother. When she left, he began howling. He had cried for a whole week. Did not eat or utter a word and refused to sleep on the bed, insisting on crawling under it. In the end, they had to give in, spread a sheet for him under the bed. When he did speak, a thin wobbling voice, the first thing he said to me was, 'I am only here for a few days. My grandmother is coming to take me home.' That was three years ago sir.

Next day two *pandits* arrived to say prayers and perform *havan*. As if, she needed blessing by the potbellied men of God who chewed *pan* and *gutka* while chanting *slokas*. All paid for by Madam, who stood with all the assembled staff, hands folded in *namaste*, 'bless the departed soul'. Then she tilted her face to the ceiling where house lizards were darting around hunting insects.

From then on, I began to fear having a bath, not because I found the task difficult, nor was I afraid of being carried away by some mysterious being, but because I had realised the extent of my own helplessness. Death was already in the house. It hovered everywhere, from room to room, between my bed and the next. Though I knew my life would never be the same, I had no option but to stay put. I began seeing myself a permanent member of Durga Bhabi Bal Kalyan and at some stage stepping into Rakshas Bhai's size ten shoes.

Months went by. One day I noticed the grocery delivery van

had started backing deep into the side entrance. A thought sparked in my head, why do not I slip onto the van's roof and hitch a ride to the city. I knew the city was near. I began planning my departure again.

'Let's get out of here,' I suggested to Ramesh. We had become good friends by then.

'Oh, how is that possible?' Ramesh said in his usual high-brow accent.

'I have worked it out. But first I want to know if you will come with me.'

'I am ready,' he said.

I took him to the bathroom on the first floor, stood on a wooden crate to reach the two-by-two square window and forced the latch free. 'See that drain-pipe. All we have to do is slip down to the kitchen roof. The side entrance is just there, on the left. It is easy to jump from there, about eight feet. We will go down in the dark and wait for the van.'

Ramesh whistled and rubbed his big ears. 'Are you sure about this?'

'Yes, yes stop worrying. I will tell you when we leave. Meanwhile just act natural. Don't tell anyone.'

CHAPTER 3

Modiji, do you know how many different types of chocolates are sold in India? There are mouth-watering brands like Lotus Suzy, Eclairs, Ferrero Roches, Amul Dark, ChocOn, Campco, Melody, Mars, and Dairy Milk. I could go on. However, did you know the 250 boys and girls of our orphanage could only dream of holding these delicacies in their hands? They saw them advertised on television and drooled foolishly. Now I will admit to you something sir. Around the time I was planning my escape I found a source for regular supply of Amul Dark and Mars bars. I kept the source secret and filled my stomach every day like a hungry pig. I thought I was the only lucky one, until one day I discovered there was someone else receiving the same Amul Dark.

For some reason I had gone to the walk-in storage cupboard on the lower floor. This is where all the brooms, mops, liquid soap, buckets and drums were kept stored. Who do I see sitting on a stool with his legs wide apart? It was old Rakshas Bhai. His penis was sticking out of the flies. Twelve-year-old Marku was standing in front; his little hand around the base of the erect member and Rakshas's hand on Marku's, both were moving up and down. Rakshas's chin tucked into his neck; face pulled hard back, mouth open as if in pain.

'You, you,' Rakshas bhai mouthed when he saw me, as if he could not think of anything else to say. The look on his flushed red face - of horror, regrets and shames - all three emotions surfacing simultaneously. 'You, you.' I stood and stared. I did not know if I was angry or relieved to see Marku standing where I had stood regularly for several weeks; Rakshas's yuck spreading over my hand while all the while I am thinking of nothing but Mars bar. Waiting, waiting, waiting for Rakshas to whip them out of his shirt pocket and throw them at me. He always gave me a piece of rag to wipe my hands and place a finger on his lips. It meant I was not to tell anyone. He had threatened to kill me if I did. I kept it to myself, for I did not want to die before I had found my mother. Yes, I dreamt of her all the time. I wondered what she looked like and indulged in wild day dreams, visualised her as beautiful as a film star but never as any of the *didis* around me. I would spin stories of her coming for me, taking me away to a big house where my father, uncles, aunts, brothers, sisters are all waiting. They start embracing me as soon as I arrive: Kalu where have you been, we were so worried for you.

Are you horrified, sir? I can tell you stuff that will make the hair on your chest stand on edge, if you have any hair that is. However, I will spare you the details. I am sure you are a very busy man. Running a country like India, it cannot be easy. My friend Sanju says it is not you but RSS who are in charge. You are just the front man with a big chest.

Ha, ha, ha, that was a joke sir – about the chest. See, I can be funny too.

Sanju says RSS are going to make a mess of it, as have all previous governments. Even the British tried. 'For three hundred years they were at it until they gave up, stole our Kohinoor and an ancient recipe book for chicken biryani and fucked off back home,' he said. I told Sanju to shut up, do not say anything against Modiji. He is a very capable man. Am I right, sir?

Anyway, I want to tell you about one of our nannies, Padmawati, a very nasty woman. Everybody hated her. We had named her Panu because she was always chewing on a *paan*, her lips permanently stained red. In the afternoon, when everyone was taking a siesta with windows shuttered to block the sun's heat, she would lie on the bed, under a fast spinning ceiling fan and call a girl over. Usually it was eleven-year-old Sita, who was mute and partially blind. '*Beti* can you give your *didi* a massage on the legs,' she would say, 'they are hurting badly.' She would give the girl a small bottle of mustard oil with thread tied to the neck in a loop for easy carrying. She would raise her sari to the knees, exposing bow shaped thin legs with taut dark skin and ask Sita to massage from the feet up. Every few minutes she would say, 'up a bit *beti*, up a bit,' until the girl was squeezing her knees with all her strength. Now and then, she would raise her head and direct a red stream into a spittoon. 'Up a bit.' The girl's hands would disappear under the sari. Soon they were all the way up. Panu would spread her legs wider, groaning and going, 'woo, woo, woo,' as if she was finding it very pleasing. One time I saw her pulling Sita's head inside the sari. Later, I found Sita sitting alone in the pantry, weeping. I wanted to talk to her, but it was difficult because she could not speak. I offered her half of a Mars bar. To my surprise, she refused to take it showing me her own bar of Amul dark and pointed at the bed where Marku slept. I understood instantly. Marku was sharing his Amul with her. Now this is a strange thing sir, even though I knew what Marku was doing to get his supplies. Like me, Rakshas Bhai, to keep his mouth shut, had probably threatened the poor fellow with death. Yet I was mad with him for I considered myself the king of chocolates. How dare he try to wrestle the crown off me?

I went to have it out with Marku. He was standing by the bed in his usual dirty pyjamas, drawstring hanging down the front and the crotch stained with dribbled urine, drooling at the corners of his mouth. As I approached him, his grin broadened and he pulled something out from behind his back. It was a plank of wood. I could not believe what I was seeing. He had pinned a mouse to the plank with legs spread out, as if crucified like Jesus Christ. Rusting nails pushed into all four feet and one through the head.

'What's that?'

'Can't you see? It is a mouse. I caught it yesterday.' He beamed with pride. 'You should have seen the fucker struggle. It was difficult to drive the pins into its paws.'

'You're mad.'

'You want to hold it?'

'No, get away from me. I'll tell Madam.'

'You do that, you know what'll happen?'

'What.'

'I will release them in your bed, big fat ones? I have a collection of cockroaches too.'

A shiver ran through me visualising a cluster of mice and cockroaches warming up to me under the sheet. I stepped back from him. His grin broadened as if he had won. But there was something strange about his eyes. It was not that they were big or the whites of them were much too white. It was that deep down there was no expression in them. If there were a door between us, I would have locked it. It disturbed

25

me to see the mindless torture and death he was inflicting on the little creatures.

Chapter 4

Sir, it is eleven o'clock. I must stop speaking to my trusted Sanyo for now. Roby has just returned to his room. His real name is Robindro, but he prefers Roby. If he hears me, he will think I am talking to myself again. *Rasgulla pagal ho gya hai*, I have gone mad, he will hoot and thump his guitar wildly. He has started calling me *rasgulla* because I am partial to these Bengali sweets. Have you ever tried them, sir? You should. They are delicious. The wall dividing our rooms is so thin, made of cheap plywood; we can hear each other all the time. I can even hear him cough and snore. Even his fart travels through the wall, so clear I am convinced I can smell the odour. He does it a lot, especially after he has had a few kebabs from Nizam, which he says he gets free because he knows the proprietor. He keeps his long hair tied with a rubber band and wears trainers that are probably as old as my Sanyo. You may have guessed it sir, yes, he is a musician, plays an electric guitar. Very good guitarist I have to tell you. However, as you may know these musicians can be very eccentric. He comes from a rich, respectable family, Bengali *bhadralok*, as they say. His lineage goes back to wealthy landowners of eastern Bengal. He told me his family still has photographs of his great grandfather seated next to an Englishman, Viceroy of India. In spite of a good home and a family business, Roby chooses to live like me. Not that he knows I make my living stealing wallets from rich people. People like his family. What a fucking paradox that is.

I like Roby though, but I also despise him for I know he is playing a game. Game of 'Let's do Poverty' which children of the rich and powerful like to play, safe in the knowledge if they get bored, they can always go back to their wealthy daddies. They do not understand us poor folks. We do not have the option of folding up the board game, put away the dice, and go for a car ride. We are the dice and pawns of the game.

Chapter 5

Good morning, Mr Modiji. I have just pressed the ON button on the Sanyo. It is ten o'clock and already the heat is unbearable. Today being the market day there is so much noise on the street, as if the entire population of Chitpur is on the move. The fruit vendors with new consignment of guavas are screaming the loudest. Somewhere down the road, a loudspeaker is blaring out religious songs. A barking dog under my window has suddenly turned to yelping in pain. Someone must have struck it with a stick.

Going back four years, to Durga Bhabi Bal Kalyan, near the city of Haridwar in Uttarakhand state; soon after my encounter with Marku, I had a dream. I am in a dark alleyway. There are rats everywhere, under my feet, by my side, in front. I am trying to get away from them. However, I just cannot run fast enough. One lands on my head. I begin dancing, lashing out with both hands to dislodge it from my hair. More rats are scuttling up my legs, stampeding. I feel the pricks of thousands of little claws on my skin. I hear one sniffing in my ear. Convinced first blood will come from my earhole I scream.

When I opened my eyes, the ugly face of Panu *didi* came into view. She was looking down at me with intense irritation. Her small triangular face with hooked nose set in permanent frown. Even at that time of the night, her lips were red from the *paan* she chewed all day long. For a moment, I thought she was part of the dream. 'Wake up Kalu, wake up.' She was prodding my ribs. 'Wake up, wake up. Bhagat is not well. I want you to sit with him.'

'But, its middle of the night,' I protested.

'I said get up,' she whacked me across the head, 'middle of the night or middle of the day, go sit with Bhagat. He has a fever. I want you to keep an eye on him.'

What to do. I had to sit with poor Bhagat. He had a wheezing chest, rasping like a broken harmonium.

'Don't sleep, or else,' she said showing me a stumpy forefinger as she went and lay down on my bed, yes my bed. Within minutes, the bitch began snoring, drowning out Bhagat's harmonium.

I must have fallen asleep too sometime during the night. I woke with a start as I felt someone shaking me. 'Didn't I tell you not to sleep – didn't I?' Panu screamed in my ear and slapped me across the face.

'Sorry,' I said.

'You are answering me back?' She slapped me again, harder this time. I tried to move out of her hands reach, accidently fell off the chair onto the floor. She became even more irate. 'You have the audacity of falling off the chair when I am talking to you?'

'*Saali*, hit me,' I said to Ramesh later, 'I am going to tell madam Dhruvya.'

Ramesh shook his head like a sage. 'No good complaining.'

'Why not?'

'Think about it. Will your word stand against her?'

'No, no, you should complain,' a boy sitting nearby said, tearing a roti with just two fingers. The other three fingers of his right hand were missing.

There were others willing to back me up but when it came to it, I knew no one would. That is because they expected outright dismissal or receive more beating. Slap, slap, slap. Now what are you going to do? Tell your mum and dad? Bah, you do not have any. So shut up, and bugger off.

Now Mr Modiji, please hear me out on this before you accuse me of talking nonsense.

Beating, kicking, and slapping were common in the home. *Didis* beat children; older children beat younger ones and so on. It was kind of a chain of command, the stronger wanting to assert authority over the weaker. It is human nature. I suspect it happens in every orphanage across the country. Now hear this. One time Madam Dhruvya's husband had assaulted a junior *didi's* husband. You might wonder what husbands had to do with it. Simply that *didis* considered it unbecoming to be seen fighting each other so they used their husbands as proxies.

In case you still do not believe me, sir, I have evidence to prove it. If we meet, I will show you the three-inch scar on my forehead above the right eye. Once, an older girl hit me on the head with a steel cooking pot. That was because I had refused to run an errand for her. When Madam came to investigate the girl said I had self-inflicted the injury in order to blame her.

'Is that true?' Madam asked me.

'Yes, it is,' I said, because I did not want to receive another crack on the head with a pot.

One day I was sitting at the window watching a flock of birds circling a tree, disturbing the leaves as if by a strong breeze and then taking off, flying high in the blue sky in a formation. A smaller flock of green parakeets were hungrily picking berries of another tree. A fascinating sight, I could sit and watch for hours. I saw a car speeding towards us, a white Maruti Ertiga. It came to a stop in front of our building and then I saw Uttarakhand police emblem painted on the side. Two men in khaki uniform stepped out. I thought they had stopped to relieve themselves in the bushes by the side of the road. Instead of going to the bushes, they started up the path to our front door. Their manner suggested they had come on an urgent business.

Someone let the police officers in and took them to Madam's office. I stood at the top of the stairs watching discreetly. I could hear muffled angry voices. Fifteen minutes later the office door flew open. The bigger policeman came out first, followed by Madam and then the second policeman. She was protesting, refusing to go with them. The policemen were egging her to come with them. This went on for a while, pushing and shoving. Eventually she gave in. I saw her deflated figure slipping into the back seat of the car. What crimes she had committed? Was she being victimised unjustly? What will they do to her? So many thoughts were churning in my head. Life without madam Dhruva was unthinkable. She had many faults but was still preferable to any of the other nannies. Ramesh was of the same opinion, calling her Dhruv *masi*. He had said she reminded him of his dead mother's sister who had gone off to live in Canada.

I ran to look for Ramesh, to let him know two police officers had taken his *masi* away. The rascal was with Maria, sitting on her bed, hand in hand. He was singing her a Bollywood love song while she was swaying from side to side, enjoying the attention. Maria was a big girl for her age. A Christian from Kerala, how she came to be in Uttarakhand no one was sure. Someone said her family had deliberately dumped her in Haridwar because it was a holy place. God will look after her. A loner, she was often seen curled up on the floor in dirty white frock, wrists between her knees. She would hold conversation with unseen people, or laugh for no reason. Sometimes she slapped her own face and rocked, back and forth or claw at her throat until rubies of blood opened-up, bright red against the brown skin.

'Come on, sing,' Ramesh said when he saw me.

Sing? Hah. The only thing I could recite was the national anthem, Vandematram. Once a week we assembled under Mahatma Gandhi's poster to recite the anthem. Nannies occasionally hummed under their breath, but never indulged in singsong with children, as if entertaining them was not in their remit.

Some of the boys joined in with Ramesh. Others started dancing, swinging arms and stamping feet.

Slowly, slowly, shedding inhibition, Maria opened her mouth, a rare grin, exposing yellowish teeth. She began clapping and swaying. No one had ever seen her so happy.

Old metal trays appeared from somewhere and turned into drums. There was no rhythm, but it did not matter. Then the younger crowd came running from the lower floor. Within minutes, a melee of small bodies was shifting, shuffling, jumping and laughing. A boy tripped, fell and rolled over laughing. Under the combined weight of so many dancing feet, the floor boomed. A *didi* came running to investigate. She stood open mouthed, did not know what to do, join in or stop the merrymaking. She went away. Two boys began mimicking her, hands on hips, open mouth and wide eyes. Others howled with laughter watching the caricature, encouraging the boys to do more, strut her walk, 'like this'. Suddenly Ramesh gave Maria a kiss on the lips. Maria blushed and lowered her head.

After the fun was over, I took Ramesh to the washroom and told him about the police. 'Were they carrying guns? I wish I was there,' he said, regretting he had missed an opportunity to be close to a policeman.

'Don't be a fool,' I said, 'they don't take guns everywhere.'

'What will they do to Madam?' Ramesh said peeing, unaware he was missing the urinal.

'I don't know and don't care. But it's time.'

Ramesh sat down on the cracked toilet seat. 'When?'

'Tomorrow, early, in the dark to get a better start.'

'*Nahi yaar*,' he said, 'better to wait for daylight when people are around, that way we will not be noticed.'

'After breakfast then. Meet me in the upstairs washroom. We will not take anything with us, just as we are. Meanwhile keep your head down.'

'What about Maria. Can we take her with us?' Ramesh said.

'No, don't be a fool, we can't take her.'

'Oh, oh, I can't leave her here.'

'You mad? You haven't even asked her if she wants to come and if she says no, what then?'

'Please Kalu.'

'It will be difficult to get her out of the window and then there is the eight feet jump. Even if she comes out what are we going to do with her, take her where?'

'I will ask my papa. He will take care of her.'

'Alright. Two of us leave now and then we come back for her later, as soon as we can.'

On the way back to our ward, I saw the door to the Manager's office was ajar. Normally we were terrified of entering uninvited, but we sneaked in now that there was no manager. Ramesh plonked his backside on the sofa. It was a sweet luxury despite its broken spring and because it was pilfered. I sat on manager's swivelling chair and swung myself around, a sensation I had never experienced before. Ramesh was giggling snuggled in the cushions, determined to pilfer maximum pleasure.

Something else I had to do before leaving this place. I wanted to expose Marku as the animal torturer that he was. Stop him brutalising innocent creatures. That night, after everyone had gone to sleep, I got up and crept down to the corridor. From there I went to the outhouse. The odour of rotting kitchen waste rising to the ceiling. It appeared more intense at night. I set to work looking for Marku's mice. I knew they were behind the big metal bins. I went down on my knees on the greasy floor. It was not long before I spotted four lengths of wood lying side by side. I raised the one nearest to me. A different kind of stench hit me. I found a hole covered in plastic sheeting. As soon as I raised the sheet, something darted across my face. I sprang backwards. A cardboard box was lying in the hole, containing several dead mice. They had been laid out side-by-side, equal distance apart, as if for some kind of black magic ritual. I picked up the cardboard box and dropped it to one side, to make it visible to anyone passing by. The plan was to implicate Marku with the mice.

I went back to bed and began rehearsing the escape. Through the small window, scale the drainpipe, cross the flat roof; slip over to the van roof. It seemed simple. What could go wrong? Then a thought entered my head, alarming me. Why would

Ramesh's dad be happy to see him? He had not been back for so long.

Fingers were prodding me, someone yelling my name. I thought it was a dream. When I opened my eyes, I saw Malka *didi* and her faded green sari. 'Where is Ramesh?' she was asking. I did not understand why she had woken me to ask such a stupid question.

'He sleeps over there, in that bed,' I said, pointing.

'I know where his bed is you fool. Do you know where he is?'

I shot up. My ears attuned to the commotion. Someone was yelling across the hall. Lights were coming on in rapid succession. Bastard, he has left without me. How could he? I ran to the washroom. The latch on the casement window was undisturbed. I forced it open. In the darkness, I could barely see the drainpipe or the edge of the flat roof. I checked all the windows. They were all secure.

He is hiding somewhere or playing a joke. It was not out of character for Ramesh to do things like that, sometimes for his amusement or to annoy someone. On a night like this? I conducted my own search; looked under each bed, raised every curtain, scrutinised broom cupboards, washrooms. I questioned everyone in the wards, even threatened them with a good beating if they did not tell the truth.

Sushila *didi* held my face between her palms. I have to tell you about Sushila here. Unlike others, she was always dressed in simple but clean clothes, mostly a sari, and smelled fresh as if she had just had a bath. Even in the middle of a sweltering hot day, she managed to radiate calm. 'Look at me Kalu, look at me,' she said, 'now take a deep breath, calm down.'

I refused to look at her. All I wanted was my friend with me.

Half an hour later, air thick with shouts and recriminations, I heard the van outside, the cankerous roar of its engine as it reversed into the side entrance. My heart scorched with disappointment. So close – so close to starting a new life - and now it was over. Looking out the window, I had not even noticed the day had already broken. Another thing I had not noticed - Harshna had already arrived, her high-pitched voice bouncing off the walls. Slowly, in fearful silence, children spilled out of their wards. They began strolling towards the washrooms, to stand in line for bathing, even though no one had called them out. Perhaps they felt sorry for *didis*. I went to Ramesh's bed. Third in a row of twenty, all crammed together, yet no one had heard or seen him get up and leave. How could this have happened?

Call went out for all nannies and older children to assemble in the dining hall.

Two tables pushed together. Cooks, seven *didis*, Rakshas and Harshna sat around it. Harshna was the catering manager, about forty years old, always smartly dressed. She placed her arms on the table, like a queen presiding over her court. It was her manner, her self-confidence that made her look like a leader even without trying. 'Someone has to take charge as Dhruvya unfortunately is not with us. Any volunteers?' she asked.

There was some nodding of heads, but no one spoke. Harshna looked at each face in turn. 'Do you want me to take charge?'

Still there was silence.

'Alright, I will,' she said, all grave and concerned, 'but I need your support. Let us pray for Ramesh and hope he is unharmed. We will do everything possible to find him.'

Panu arrived wearing a cardigan over the sari. 'I want to know who was in charge of the ward. How did the boy slip out from under her nose?'

All eyes turned to Malka. Malka shook her shoulders and returned Panu's glare. 'I cannot be blamed. I was managing two wards.'

'Managing two wards, eh,' Panu made a face, 'why don't you tell them you were asleep.'

'So, so, you were here last night. Were you? Watching me ...,' Malka shot back, half rising from the stool.

'Now, now,' Harshna interrupted, 'this is no time to quarrel. Right now, I want you to pray – pray that no harm comes to Ramesh, wherever he is. The rest will come later.'

'Yes, but someone must accept responsibility. This would never have happened if I was on night duty,' Panu said to Harshna, 'this pray, pray rubbish isn't going to bring the boy back. Who put you in charge here anyway?'

'We did,' Gayatri *didi* said in her customary soft voice, her fingers folding and unfolding a piece of rag that she kept tucked in a pocket.

'I have been here the longest. I should be the manager,' Panu snapped, jabbing a finger in her chest as if testing the strength of her own ribs.

As if a hot poker was been shoved in my arse, I sprang up. I wanted to scream, No, No, do not allow the bitch to take over from Dhruvya. I looked at Harshna, shooting warning signals with my eyes, do not let her bully you, do not let her bully you.

There was a knock on the front door. All heads gyrated in the direction of the main entrance. 'Ramesh?' it slipped out of Gayatri's mouth and she clamped it shut, as if she had blasphemed.

Even I felt briefly elated. Then I cast the thought aside. I realised Ramesh has been taken, probably gagged and bound. That was the only possibility. Only Rakshas and senior staff had the keys to exit doors.

'Police,' Rakshas said and got up, his hips labouring under the weight as he walked to the front door. He returned with four police officers behind him, all taller by at least four inches. Harshna took them to the office.

Back in the ward, children surrounded me, shocked, seeking answers. 'Don't worry,' I said, trying to lift their spirits, 'they will find big ears now that police are here.'

'Do they have pistols?' someone asked.

'No, they have left them in the car.' I pretended to know police procedures.

A little boy hobbled over to me. 'What is a pistol?' he asked, and everyone burst out giggling.

I explained, 'pistol is that thing with which police shoot robbers and bad people. Haven't you ever seen one?'

The boy shook his head. Besides being a cripple, he was also half-blind, the good eye only good enough to see six feet ahead. Television pictures were just colours and shapes. They said a farm donkey had trampled him when he was five years old. His family, instead of beating the donkey, punished him by handing him over to the orphanage.

That night I cried in secret and asked Ramesh for forgiveness, for not being there in time of need. My heart squeezed tighter in guilt the more I tried to rationalise. Convinced it was an inside job; I tried to pick the culprit – Rakshas, Harshna, Malka or Panu – they were the only ones with keys. Panu appeared the most likely candidate. Of course, she would not have done it by herself. She must have had outside assistance.

I gave up all hope of leaving and went back to sitting at the window for hours. A spider had laced a nest in the corner. It never appeared to move, as if it was dead. I knew it was alive, as it had grown over the weeks. There were more spiders of same size nearby. I imagined they were brothers and sisters. Everybody has somebody, why not me. Why, why, why.

Later I overheard a conversation between nannies Bhartidevi and Khushi. They were sitting on a bench in the front hall behind a long wooden desk, under a rusty framed picture of Baba Ramdev, smiling from behind a beard.

'… but I have found out the reason for Dhruvya's arrest,' Bhartidevi was saying.

'You do?'

'Well, you remember when they said a proper hot water boiler will be installed for the bathrooms and the kitchen. Also, an extension will be built so they could take in more children.'

'Yes, of course I do.'

'Dhruvya had asked for funding.'

'Yes … and I told you nothing will happen.'

'You were wrong. The request for funding had been approved.'

'So why didn't she do anything?'

'She did. With help from someone high up, a contractor was bribed and asked to submit invoices and papers without ever setting foot in the building. She approved the documents and sent them off for payment. When the contractor received the money, he took his cut, and handed over the rest. She must have been laughing, believing she had executed a perfect scam and will be long gone by the time it was discovered.'

'Aha, I understand now. However, she had not anticipated Bela would unravel her beautifully planned fraud. She must have panicked when police turned up and started investigating.'

There was a brief silence and then Khushi said gravely, 'it's the curse of two.'

'… what's that?'

'It always happens in twos. One calamity is followed very quickly by another.'

'And what are you expecting?'

'Ramesh has been kidnapped. Another one will go soon. You will see.'

I ran back to my room convinced the kidnapper was Panu. Who will she take next? The choice was endless, with so many vulnerable boys and girls, ready for picking, like summer berries on trees. It could be anyone with competent mental capacity, with arms and legs fit for the purpose.

Sunderlal Bhagwan was the new manager. A six-footer, fair complexion, he always wore a white short sleeved shirt and khaki trousers. His walking style reminded one of a movie gangster, the way he yanked the left shoulder and took long strides.

White shirt, khaki trousers, a thick orange *tilak* on the forehead – what does he remind you of, sir?

Sanju stopped punching the keys on his HP 250. He said one word only, 'RSS.'

'What do you mean?'

'He must have been a Sanghvi.'

I was still mystified.

'Have you got only dung in the head? Don't you know RSS,' he said, 'it's a right-wing Hindu organisation. It wants to turn India into a Hindu Rashtra, a bit like Taliban who want to create a Muslim state.'

This RSS fellow had installed a small statue of Lord Ganesha in his office, along with an assortment of incense holders, candles, earthen pots containing red and yellow powder, a jar of mustard oil, cotton wool.

For all the godliness, his manner irritated the women. '*Ye admi bhang pike atta hai*. He must be high on *bhang*.' *Didis* mocked him, making faces behind his back.

However, he seemed determined to improve conditions in the orphanage. Two women with skinny stick like legs and arms arrived each morning to mop floors with rags. Then he did something, which took everyone by surprise. He had two LG top loading washing machines installed in an outhouse. No hand washing any more. He gave Panu free hand to do whatever was necessary so all beds had a change of sheets once a month.

One day I bumped into her coming out of the bathroom. She snapped her fingers at me, flaunting her newfound authority. 'Strip all the beds in your ward and bring the sheets down to the washroom,' she ordered.

It was a terrifying thought, being alone with this woman in a steam-filled room away from the main building. However, I had no choice. I rolled the sheets into a bundle and dragged it down, hoping to deposit it on the floor and run out. I entered the room silently. The bitch was leaning against a rumbling machine, facing away from me, talking to someone on a mobile phone.

'…yes, there are some good boys here.' I heard her say in a conspiratorial tone. '…when …how much?'

Shit, she is planning another kidnapping. I placed the

bundle on the floor and sneaked out. In the hallway, I had seen Rakshas's tools lying to one side. I picked up his rusty saw. Ran a finger on the serrated edge and crept back to the laundry room. She was still on the phone facing away. I saw the softness of the flesh on her shoulder between the hairline and white blouse. I raised the saw like a sword and crept closer.

'Leave them on the floor,' she said without looking back.

I froze.

'I said leave them anywhere and get out.'

I dropped the saw on the floor and ran. On the way out, I came across a cockroach crawling on the floor. One thing I detested and feared more than Panu was those horrible little creatures. Rainy season was the time when they came out of hiding, scattering their droppings everywhere. You stepped on one accidently, heard the 'plup, plop' sound and the gluey feel under your feet, stench of ammonia, the revulsion you felt afterwards. I hated it but the boys had turned squashing cockroaches into a sport. They would compete happily, keeping a tally of who had killed or maimed most.

Chapter 6

Mr Modiji, three days ago I was on Southern Avenue near Dhakuria Lake, sitting on a stool outside a chai shop, a cup of sweet tea in my hand, listening to the radio on a shelf above the tea seller's head. As it happened, you were giving a speech in a radio programme called Chai aur Charcha. Again, you were saying how much you value the life of every child, whether born to a beggar or millionaire. On hearing those words, the fellow sitting opposite me took an appreciative sip of the tea and made loud sucking noise. 'This man has a big heart,' he said pointing at the radio.

'Absolutely correct,' someone else agreed.

Another man with thick moustache, poking his ear with a toothpick, posed a question to no one in particular, 'does anyone know why Modiji's chest is fifty-six inches?'

All heads turned to him in query.

'*Are bhai*, it stands to reason, one needs a big chest to accommodate a big ....' The man had not finished the sentence when a scream drowned out his voice.

I swung around just in time to see a black Mercedes come to a screeching halt. A little girl of ten or twelve lying sprawled face down in the middle of the road. At first, I could not understand how she came to be there and then realised she had been hit by the car. I was mere eight feet from the car. There were five occupants including the driver in white uniform. Two women at the back, dressed smartly in expensive saris were arching their heads as if trying to see where the child lay. The men in suits looked at each other and then out at the people who were arriving at the scene. I was expecting the driver and the men to jump out of the car to see to the girl, pick her up and rush her to the hospital. The girl was probably the child of one of the labourer families living under the arches of the flyover. The driver, a young fellow with handsome face was looking at his masters for instructions. I scrutinised the faces of these rich people, probably going to a party or an important function. I was expecting to see horror, panic, pity, and fear in their middle class, upper income eyes.

Here is the irony Mr Modiji, what I saw on their faces was nothing of the sort. There was no pity for the dead or dying, no fear of police or courts. Instead, I was seeing revulsion and annoyance of inconvenience. It took me back to DBBK (Durga Bhabi Bal Kalyan), to the accidental crunching of cockroaches under our feet.

CHAPTER 7

Marku's behaviour had changed again. He was going back to the old ways, spending more time in dust and rocks and discarded furniture in the back yard. No one was paying much attention, taking him for a fool and a loner. Only I knew what he was planning. One day Sunderlal handed me a broom. 'Kalu I want you to go down to the bins and give the place a thorough clean. Take Ghanshyam and Bhagu with you.'

My heart leapt with dread at the thought of uncovering dead mice, cockroaches or other creatures in the filthy dark corner covered in black slurry, liquid seeping from cracks in bins. Our locality was home to many insects and things with legs. There were a variety of spiders known locally as *makadis,* beetles, lizards and geckos called *chhipakalees* and there were the crickets with their nightly racket. However, do you know what I feared most? Yes, you have guessed it sir – cockroaches.

I did not want to disobey Sunderlal. Ghanshyam and Bhagu behind me with their brooms and buckets of water, I began prodding the rubbish with a long-handled broom. We were making small heaps to be scooped up later. I went deeper in, behind a metal bin. On the very first swipe, I felt a flicker of movement. I froze for a moment wondering if I had disturbed a mouse. I stood still for a few more moments and when I lifted the broom again something moved so fast, I did not see it until it was about two feet off the ground. Then I saw the head of the cobra splayed out like a banyan tree leaf. Its lower body on the ground, curled into a round circle. Its eyes, shining like two jewels, locked onto mine. It was flicking its tongue in and out, the head swaying from side to side.

Sir, if you ever come across a cobra unexpectedly, my advice is not to stare directly into its eyes. I made the mistake of doing just that and found myself powerless to move, as if I had been hypnotised. I heard Ghanshyam calling me, 'Kalu, Kalu, what's the matter with you?'

I could not respond. And then I heard him scream, 'samp, samp.' Both the boys ran out. I tell you there is no lie in this sir, when the boys returned good two minutes later with Sunderlal; they found me still standing in the same position. The snake had not shifted either, though it was no longer swaying from side to side.

Sunderlal pushed me out of the way and took a swipe at the snake with a pole, as if he was taking a goal shot with a hockey stick.

Hence the name Kalu Cobra. It just stuck, like glue to paper. People I met later assumed it was my real name. The boys would not stop laughing, teasing me by making their bodies stiff, like a *sadhu* meditating. Sometimes they hissed in my ears or shape cobra's head with the palm and fingers of a hand. You see what I had to put up with those days. However, I never told anyone why the cobra was there in the first instance. It had come to feed on Marku's collection of mice.

One day, after lunch I was sitting at my window seat. It was a hot day. I spotted a cat lying on the dirt track outside. From head up it was just a smear of pink pulp imprinted with a tyre tread. Sign of bad luck I was convinced. 'Bad luck. Something dreadful is going to happen tonight,' I told Bhagu.

He peered out of the window, cupped a hand over his eyes to shield them from sun. 'Lomri,' he cried.

'What are you saying? There are no foxes around here,' I insisted.

'*Hanh, hanh*, I am telling you that is a fox, *yar, batcha hai,* a baby. Look at the tail.'

'Does that mean no bad luck?'

'On the contrary, it means big bad luck,' he said gravely, 'there is only one way to stop the curse.'

'How?'

'Spit on it,' he said.

'Spit, you crazy?'

'*Are hanh*, that's the only way. Move back.' He opened the window wide, summoned a big blob of phlegm in his mouth and spat, falling short by several feet.

'Let me try,' I said, and spat out with all my strength.

We were still taking turns coughing and spitting harder and harder and not succeeding to reach the carcass when Maria came over and announced, 'Sunderlal wants everyone in *khana ghar.*'

Sunderlal was standing at the top of the table, a hand raised in the familiar thoughtful manner, the other hand in the khaki trouser pocket. He cleared his throat very loud, looked from left to right and back, cleared the throat again. I recognised the gesture. He was going to announce something important.

'A party of Germans are coming next week to visit us. I want you all to behave.'

'What is German?' Maria whispered.

'Germany is a country. People of that country are called Germans.'

She scratched her head. 'Why are they coming here?'

I had met a foreigner only once, five years ago. A man and a woman from Sweden had come bearing gifts. When they left, they had taken Bhola and his sister with them.

Now the news of the Germans visit was causing a lot of excitement. Each one of us convinced we were next for adoption.

A few days later, on a Sunday, I was sitting on the floor in the front hall, sheltering from the sun. Maria came over and sat down beside me. I sensed she was thinking of Ramesh.

'Kalu, Maria, *chalo, chalo*, I need help. Germans are coming this afternoon,' Mayabhen *didi* came running.

In no time, the place was buzzing, people pushing furniture, shoving clutter into cupboards. Rakshas with broom in hand worked with uncharacteristic speed, shifting dirt from one place to another. Two girls were on their haunches wiping the floor with a rag soaked in Lezol and water. Sunderlal, in a crisp white shirt, black trouser and shiny black shoes came clapping and shouting, urging everyone to move faster, complaining we were slow, 'even a three-legged donkey with fever can move faster than you.'

'They are here, they are here,' someone yelled.

Rakshas Bhai shuffling, stooping went to open the door. We waited in silent suspense to see who would walk in through the door. First person to enter was a man with thick beard, jeans and t-shirt. Two more men came in. Two women in long skirts followed behind.

Younger ones were to stand by their beds. The older boys and girls were to stand in line as a welcoming committee. Sunderlal met them with folded hands and did the introductions, naming each *didi* individually. Then they set off on a guided tour,

Sunderlal leading the Germans and then every member of staff.

The Germans entered the first ward, strolling along crammed aisles, too slow or too fast, unable to keep a steady pace. The smiles on their faces disappeared. Now they were staring in amazement. Children were staring back. The tallest of the three men knelt down and stretched his hand out, attempting to engage with a seven-year-old boy. The boy instantly burst into tears. Sunderlal stepped in quickly. 'I'm sorry. They have never seen a European with facial hair before.'

The men laughed. 'Next time we will leave the hair behind.' The big German ran his fingers across the beard in a mock snipping action.

They moved to the next ward. This one was bigger and noisier. The woman with strange orange hair did a kind of dance routine, twirling round and round. 'Alo, Alo, Alo,' she said. With a dramatic gesture, she raised the lid off a large tin box, exposing the contents for all to see. It contained sweets and chocolates in colourful wrappers. 'Ta-ra,' she said and started dishing out the sweets in handfuls. The other woman opened another tin. Children hesitated first and then came running, tugging at the women's dresses, begging for more, scavenging sweets that fell to the floor. I was at the back, feeling left out. Another German came in with an enormous cardboard box. Behind him, Rakshas Bhai appeared with a similar cardboard box on his head, labouring under the weight.

'Presents,' someone shouted over the din. There was a momentary silence and then the children at the front screamed and ran towards the box. Now the nannies were straining their necks over each other to see what was going on ahead. I could see they were itching to dive into the fray. On my left Panu started elbowing her way towards the front. Even that ogre Rakshas was looking on with greedy eyes, barely able to restrain himself from diving into the melee.

A German produced a knife, ready to slit the box open. Harshna poked a finger in my side and whispered something in my ear.

'Yes, Harshna,' I said and ran the length of the corridor, taking double steps down the stairs to the deserted dining hall. I picked up the nearest chair and hoisted it over my head to take it back up to Harshna. I was about to leave when the kitchen doors burst open. I turned around to find two men I had never seen before standing in the doorway. At first, they said nothing, just glared at me.

'What do you want?' I said.

They did not reply. The taller one started walking towards the door to the corridor while keeping an eye on me.

'Why are you here?' I asked and then the taller one spoke. 'You are coming with us,' he said, his voice strangely deep and heavy.

'Go where.' I thought of Ramesh and my heart began pumping madly.

'We want you to come with us,' he said, casual as if it was a done deal and there was no question of me refusing. He put his hand out, urging me to take it. I saw the fat greasy fingers, tuft of black hair above the knuckles, a gold ring. I looked up at his face. He was smiling at me, but his eyes looked so sinister. Instinctively I flung the chair at him and ran towards the door.

'I will scream,' I said.

'No point, they will not hear you,' he said in an even deeper voice.

How does he know the noise will not travel that far? His companion came forward and slammed a tobacco smelling hand on my mouth. He had a very round oily face and black moustache.

They picked me up and carried me through the kitchen to the yard at the rear. I noticed the back door was already open. They clearly had the key. Finally, they put me down and pushed my head between the knees. I heard the door slam shut and the clunk of the key; a feeling of absolute separation hit me as if I would never see my friends again.

They had already cut an opening in the fence. On the other side were weeds and bushes, trees in full bloom, *khnor, bhoj patra* and others, taller than the building we had just left. I thought of the mongrel dogs and scanned the bushes, hoping they will create a ruckus, go on the attack for trespassing on their patch. However, the dogs had slinked away. It seemed that even they were scared of the evil man with deep voice. I managed a backward glance. Only the upper part of the building was visible now. A strange sight; I had never imagined my home of fifteen years would look like a big impregnable prison.

Round Face kept pushing and kneeing me in the back. 'Walk faster, walk faster.' Hidden ditches and fallen logs, as if deliberately placed obstacles. I tripped several times. 'What's the matter? Is your leg broken? Walk faster or I will break the other one too.'

We went over a little hill and suddenly arrived at a farm. My heart fluttered at the sight of symmetrical rows of plants with yellow flowers all facing the sun. However, there was not a soul around.

Further, ahead we came across a cluster of ten or twelve small houses and shacks. Cows in muddy soil, goats tethered to trees, a lamb bleating for its mother. Now or never I thought and started screaming, making a racket, hoping to attract attention.

'Shut up you fool.' Round Face struck me on the head. 'I am going to teach you a lesson.'

'Go on, do your best,' I yelled. A dog was crossing the path. He glanced briefly at us. I willed him to bark, raise the roof. However, he turned and walked on, as if he had no business interfering in affairs of squabbling humans.

They dragged me to a tree trunk, tied my hands with some sticky tape. My thighs made immobile, Round Face walking around the trunk of the tree several times with the roll of sticky tape. Deep Voice stood facing me. '*Ab me thikhaoonga,*' he said, 'I will show you how to respect authority.'

He ripped my shirt open. I could see his hands shaking as he unbuckled his trouser belt and with one full swing pulled it out. Taking a step back, he swung the belt in the air like a whip, producing a terrifying crack. He took five steps back, his booted feet disturbing dust at each footfall. As his arm shot up, I saw the belt silhouetted against the blue sky and instantly shut my eyes. Convinced I was going to die I started thinking of my friends. Will they miss me? I saw them grinning instead. Thank God, he has gone; he cannot boss over us anymore. I saw Marku, saw his frightened drooping eyelids, and saw his hand on crotch. Regret threaded my heart. Why was I so nasty to him? While I was thinking of my friends, I heard the whip crack and then felt a stinging sensation on the chest. The belt cracked again and then a second, third and fourth time. One missed my face by an inch. It set off bells ringing in my ear.

I must stop here, sir. There is a lump in my throat and I am finding it difficult to speak. I will now press the STOP button on my Sanyo. Good night.

CHAPTER 8

The heat, fear, and pain was so intense, I thought I was going to pass out. Maybe that was their plan, to kill me by slow torture. Round Face made me sit down on a flat rock directly under the sun. 'The car is on the way,' he said standing over me, smelling of stale tobacco and cheap deodorant. He was wearing a cream safari suit; dirt stains around the chest pocket where he kept a cigarette box. I wondered if I could get him to talk, find out why they had brought me here. I began weeping and in no time, tears came rolling down my cheeks.

Yes sir, I had learned to produce tears at will, an essential survival mechanism in the home. I looked at him with pleading eyes, waiting to see his response. He ignored me. However, I did not relent, continued sobbing and releasing tears. His face twitched finally. 'Are you alright,' he asked. Wham! I had him. 'Uncle, at least tell me where you are taking me.'

However, before he could reply Deep Voice came over, clicked his fingers and pointed at a black Honda approaching at speed, whipping up dust in its wake. Round Face reverted to the hard man persona and pulled me roughly off the rock.

They made me sit on the back seat squeezed between them. We went up a highway that cut through suburban lanes, houses with metal gates, parked cars on drives, ornamental bushes, and guards in uniform sitting on plastic chairs. Some of the houses were under construction. Stacks of bricks, sacks of cement, bamboo scaffolding, shirtless men with shovels, dusty trucks, women in saris hitched to waist huddling bricks - came into view briefly.

I realised we were approaching Haridwar as the lanes became narrower and winding, congested with honking cars, trucks and people on foot. Massive paint store posters, granite-marble-tile business placards, carpentry workshops, garages, every available space covered in hoardings. Shop fronts with neon signs. I had never seen anything like this. Vendors of *alu puri*, *samosa* and *pakoras*, *jalebis* were all across a bus depot. Roadside stalls selling plastic watches, clay statues of Gods and Goddesses, metal locks, toys for children, sandals and t-shirts. Lord Krishna flaunting a flute crudely painted on a temple wall. Rags, newspapers, empty packets of Mother Dairy, broken clay cups strewn all over the paths. This was my first glimpse of the city. I was fascinated.

We came to an open-air market, stalls piled high with household utensils, vegetables, fruits. People were sifting, pushing, shoving and swearing. Our car had to slow down. The driver lowered his window, cursing and spitting. I saw a woman dressed in rags, sitting cross legged, hands cupped, begging. A wet patch between her legs on the ground. It looked suspiciously like urine. Across the road, three policemen were arresting a boy dressed only in a ripped vest and pyjama bottom. An excited crowd had gathered, watching but not interfering. He was my age.

'Prison for the rascal,' Round Face said with a scowl and spat out of the window.

Are they taking me to a prison too? I thought of Panu. She must have organised it all. I looked at Deep Voice on my right, wondering what his connection with the woman was.

'What are you looking at? Am I handing out *ladoos*?' he said.

'Uncle, where are you taking me?' I asked. I could barely speak.

'Silence or I'll cut off your tongue,' he replied.

Another half hour, the car came to a halt. The driver killed the engine and picked up a newspaper. I looked out the window, expecting to see a building with barbed wire fencing, gun totting guards or a house with padded windows so what went on inside stayed a secret. However, what I was seeing was a six-story building, tallest I had ever seen. A metal gate at the front, beautiful flower beds. I held my heart still, afraid to ask why we had stopped. Round Face leaned back in his seat and began mumbling a song. Minutes passed. Still we were waiting. I scanned the street. Palatial houses on both sides. Trees planted on pavements, all were of similar height.

After about fifteen minutes, Deep Voice's phone burst into life. '*Hanh*, yes,' he said into the phone, nodding as if the person he was speaking to could see him. When he had finished, he turned to me. 'We are going in,' he said, 'I don't want any of your monkey business. You understand.' Round Face positioned himself at the rear door with a hand on the roof.

I came out and looked around me, how to get away from these monsters. A quarter of mile on my right, I could see a few people outside the shops. I clutched my stomach as if I was in great pain.

'Come on,' Round Face said and started walking ahead. I dived sideways and took off running towards the shops. I heard footsteps behind me. I was surprised to see the driver. Unlike the other two who were big and muscular, this man was slim and athletic. I speeded up, started waving my arms and yelling to catch the shoppers attention. Just when I thought I had beaten him my foot caught a cracked paving slab, bringing me down on my knees. I tried to get up and run but the driver was already over me, kicking and yelling. The other two arrived thumping their heavy feet. 'Didn't I tell you no *tamasha*, you little motherfucker,' Deep Voice cried.

The driver pulled me up to standing position and rained a few punches, stopping only when he saw the blood on my face.

'Don't make a scene here. Come inside and later we will see about taking you home.'

What could I do? I had to go along with them. We entered the lobby and the first thing I noticed was the elaborate decor, shiny marble floor, framed pictures on the wall, a beautiful flower vase sitting on a desk. Even the air had a flowery fragrance.

Someone pressed a button. A metal door slid open revealing a small chamber, about six by six feet. No windows, just one recessed light in the ceiling. The driver poked me from behind. 'Go in,' he said.

I panicked. Is this my prison cell? I refused to go in.

'It's an elevator you fool,' the driver said and all three began laughing. I stepped inside, held my breath, waiting for the lift off, expecting a rough ride. In no time the doors slid open again revealing a long hallway, ceramic pots with a palm at each end, floor to ceiling windows. There was not a squeak of outdoor noise. I certainly was not expecting this. My visions were of dungeons with padlocked doors and air thick with prisoners' screams. Maybe they are further in. My bladder gave in and I wanted to piss. I could easily have watered the palm if no one was watching.

Deep Voice in front, walking in haste, clicking his heels, as if this was his home turf. At the end of the long corridor he stopped. Still no sign of prisoner cells, maybe this is a false exterior. At the door marked 11 he knocked twice and pushed it open without waiting for a response. For a few moments, there was complete silence. I shut my eyes, not wanting to look inside; convinced this was my prison cell. I began praying to God – please save me, please save me.

'Come in Kalu.' I heard a female voice. It sounded familiar. I could not understand why I was hearing it. Deep Voice stepped aside. There, standing by a sofa, dressed in the same yellow sari she had worn to greet the Germans, was Harshna.

'Harshna … you.' It is hard to describe the feeling of relief I felt then. I rushed in to hug her. Thank God, I am safe. I had taken a few steps when I realised suddenly she had not looked surprised to see me. I stopped and looked behind me. Deep Voice had already settled down on a chair, feet planted firmly on the beige carpet. The Round Face and the driver had disappeared.

'Come, I'll explain everything,' she said taking my right arm and sat me down on the sofa with floral patterned cushions, 'you are safe now Kalu.'

I must have mumbled something for she said shaking me by the shoulder, 'it's alright Kalu, don't worry.'

'What is going on Harshna *didi*? Why I am here?' I asked.

'I will explain everything. Sit down,' she said.

I stayed standing, my head reeling in confusion.

'Are you hungry or thirsty?' she said.

Why is she talking about food at a time like this?

'Are you hungry?' she repeated.

'The chair - you planned it all. Didn't you?' I asked.

'You wanted to leave Durga Bhabi,' she said, 'didn't you?'

'Leave? How do you know what I want?'

'You are growing up. I know you wanted to leave that place.'

'Yes, but what is the meaning of this? They beat me so much. You want to see?' I raised my shirt and showed her the lacerations on my chest.

She gasped and looked away briefly. 'There was no other way, Kalu. From now on no one will touch you,' she said and began fidgeting with a ring on her finger.

'Are you saying I can go now?' I asked though I already knew the answer.

'You are free to go, Kalu. You can walk out of here any time you want.' She pointed at the door. 'But the question is where will you go? You need a home and you need money.'

'As I have no money, can you send me back to Durga Bhabi?'

'But you don't have to go. You will have a job very soon. Once you've money in your pocket you can do anything, buy whatever you like, chocolate, ice-cream, go to a cinema.'

'What kind of work can I do?' I asked in disbelief, 'and who will pay me?'

'You leave it to us. We will train you. If you work hard, you will earn good money. There is no limit.'

Training, work, money – it was beyond my comprehension. I could not understand why anyone would give me money.

She did a signal with her fingers and Deep Voice appeared from a side door carrying a silver tray. On it was a plate of *alu paratha*, a bowl of *curd* sprinkled with salt, pepper and chilli. He placed it on the glass-topped coffee table and straightened with a stiff gesture to show he was not used to these kinds of menial tasks. Oh, the odour of butter paratha. At home, this would have created a sensation, a scramble to the kitchen to grab the first batch. Treats like this were rare, perhaps once every other month.

'Now eat,' she said.

I tried to resist, but it was hopeless. Without another word, I pulled the tray over and started gobbling. Harshna and Deep Voice were watching me amused as if I was a feeding zoo animal. I did not care.

I had only just finished eating; a man appeared at the doorway. A tall imposing figure with drooping moustache, dark greasy hair, a scar down the side of his nose, he was wearing a heavily starched white kurta and pyjama, a dark grey waistcoat with two gold capped pens in the top pocket. He looked at me with piercing eyes. I sprang to my feet, fearing an attack.

Harshna screamed at me, 'arre Kalu what are you doing, this is the boss, sit down, sit down.'

I sat down on the sofa keeping an eye on him. He sat opposite me, legs wide apart and clicked his fingers at Deep Voice without looking at him. Deep Voice moved swiftly to a sideboard and opened the doors, revealing several bottles of foreign liquor. He pulled one bottle out, uncorked it and poured a small amount into a crystal glass, working smartly as if he knew what his master wanted. The master took the glass in his hand, sat with an air of someone who possessed everything around him, including Harshna. It surprised me for I could not imagine Harshna taking orders from anyone. He cross-examined the content of the glass, deep red in colour, held it up to the light, took a sip, rolled it in his mouth, looked at the glass again, took it to his nose and sniffed, drank a bit more.

'So, would you like to work for me?' he asked placing the glass on the table. His speech was lazy and guttural, incongruent to his alert manner.

Why is he asking if I would like to work for him?

'Yes, son … speak.' He waved a finger at me as if impatient for a reply.

'But … but what work can I do?' I said.

'Did I ask you what work you can do?'

I shook my head.

'Then answer my question. Do you want to work for me?'

I said yes. It seemed the right thing to do.

'Good,' he said slapping his thighs with both hands as if he was done. He clicked his fingers again. Deep Voice moved to the leather attaché case lying on the desk and snapped it open. From my position, I could not see what was inside the case. With hands by his side, Deep Voice waited for the next instruction.

'Give it here, what are you staring at,' the boss said, impatiently clicking his fingers.

'Yes,' Deep Voice said and picked up a thick bundle of thousand rupee notes, held together with rubber bands. My eyes popped. I had never seen so much money before. The boss took the bundle, peeled out a few notes at random, fanned them out with flick of his fingers, like a deck of playing cards, and waved them at me. 'Son, have you ever owned this amount of money before?'

'No,' I said.

'Well you do now. Take it,' he said.

I recoiled as if he was offering me something dangerous. It would explode and burn a hole in my hand. I turned to Harshna.

She clicked her tongue and made a face as if she could not believe how stupid I was. 'Take it, take it,' she said.

Can you believe it Modiji? I had never owned any money in my life, not even a few coins. However, fast-forward four years. Today, I can make five thousand rupees in a week. How fortunes change. I heard you yourself were not rolling in it in your younger days, before you entered politics. You were an ordinary *chai- wallah*, selling tea from a market stall. Is that true sir? Some people say its rubbish. You made up the story to win the poor man's vote. I say to these people, shut up and grow up. We understand each other. Don't we sir? We have so much in common.

The boss dropped the rest of the thick bundle on the sofa, casually, as if they were a few coins. You should have seen the speed at which Harshna picked it up, put it in her brown leather handbag and pressed it shut with a firm click.

After the boss left the flat Harshna announced, 'Kalu this is your home from now on. Wonderful ...no.'

'But how can I afford it?'

'Afford it, afford it - what are you saying,' she threw up a hand, '*are baba* you don't have to afford it. It is free. Come with me.'

She took me to a room so lavishly furnished I was afraid to touch anything in case I soiled it with my dirty fingers. There was marble flooring with a Kashmiri rug, thick curtains on windows, and a hardwood wardrobe with pretty carvings. A table lamp with white shade sat on a matching dark wood writing desk. In the top half of the room, two beds lay separated by a small table. The beds had brilliant white cotton sheets on them. 'Why are you showing me this *didi*?' I asked.

'You will be sleeping here,' she said with a half-smile, 'different, no … from Durga Bhabi.'

Wah, how different it was. I had never seen anything like it.

'Yes Kalu, this is home now.'

I looked around the room again, ran a finger on the shining tabletop. How smooth it felt.

'And you?' I asked.

'I don't live here Kalu. My home is two miles away.'

'Then I won't sleep here. I want my friends,' I protested. All my life I had slept in open dormitories with twenty or thirty others. The mere thought of sleeping alone in a strange place terrified me.

'Listen to me. You will not live alone. Munna will be here shortly. You two will be sharing the flat. He is almost same age as you and a good boy, you will see. I will be back in the morning to see everything is alright. You have met Om Prakash, haven't you?'

Deep Voice lowered the magazine from his face and for the first time I saw a hint of smile on the scoundrels face.

'Om Prakash and his men live in the next flat. Their job is to keep an eye on everything.'

I assumed it meant his job was to keep an eye on me.

When Munna arrived, the very first thing he did was hug me as if we were old friends. He showed me around the rest of the flat. There were two more rooms, one with beds in them; the second room had a massive table with ten chairs circling it. 'These are spare rooms,' he said.

Later I asked him a question, one that had been nagging me all afternoon, 'what's to stop me from walking out of here?'

He threw himself on the sofa, sinking into the fabric and clicked a button on the remote control. The television burst into life.

'What do you think?'

'I don't know what to think.'

'First of all, the hallway is kept locked. Om Prakash has the keys. Secondly, Om Praksah and his men live next door. Harshna must have told you that. You cannot leave here without them knowing. What floor are we on?' he asked.

'Sixth.'

'Correct,' he said, 'the top floor. No one comes up here. No one will hear you, even if you are foolish enough to scream.' He switched the channel. A woman in long black dress burst onto the screen, singing a love song. 'Did they beat you bad?' he asked.

I showed him the bruises on my chest.

He gave them a cursory glance. 'I have seen much worse. You were lucky.'

Lucky? God help me, I said to myself.

'You know what happened to the previous boy who tried to run away,' he said, 'they asked him to swim the Ganga.'

'Swim in Ganga … you call that punishment?' I said.

He tapped his forehead. '*Arre bhai*, what have you got in that head, cow dung? The boy had his hands tied behind his back before he was asked to swim.'

I waited for Munna to claim one of the two beds, and then I took the other. Munna fell asleep within minutes. I lay awake staring at the ceiling. '…hands tied behind his back … hands tied behind his back … hands tied behind his back ….' In that moment, I wanted nothing more to do with Harshna, Munna or the Boss. I do not mind admitting I cried whole night, but silently. I just wanted to go back home.

My voice is hoarse now, sir. So much talking into my Sanyo, *oorf*, my head hurts. Before I press the stop button, a clarification is in order: I may have invoked *God* earlier, ask him to save me. It was just a figure of speech. At the time, I did not believe in God. Therefore, I had no reason to thank him, or lick his arse like halwai Baldev does. Baldev is my landlord. A colourful character, you will see more of him later. He is stickler for routine, wakes every morning at six and goes to the temple, which has a massive *peepal* tree at the entrance. He places a hand on the tree trunk, which already has imprints of thousands of other hands. Before entering, he rings a brass bell hanging from the ceiling, as if to warn Lord Krishna: I am coming my Lord, kindly lift your arse a little higher so I won't have to stoop too low to lick it. I have a bad back from all the humping I have been doing with Pryanka the prostitute. Around the deity are three or four Brahmins, bare-chested with enormous potbellies. He bows his head to the dais, does this back and forth movement with his fingers as if touching the feet of the Lord and throws a hundred rupee note. It floats slowly to the donation mat. The Brahmins begin chanting hymns and sprinkle holy water on him as if to absolve him of the sins of the previous day. If he needs an extra, scrub and cleans, he throws two hundred rupee notes. The priests turn up the volume and become more liberal with the holy water.

CHAPTER 9

'Where is your family?' I asked Munna. We were on the steps of Har Ki Pauri, surrounded by hundreds of pilgrims from around the country, stripping to the waist for a dip in river Ganga. Mixed in among them were foreign tourists, vociferously capturing the sights on their cameras. Munna's instructions were to show me the hotspots of the city, commercial district, railway station, bus terminals, temples, shopping centres, so I could take on board the atmosphere and setting of our theatre of operation.

'I don't care about my family,' Munna said with a terse wave of his hand.

'You don't care for your mama and papa?' I was amazed.

'My mother died when I was eight and my step-father used to beat me regularly.'

'Why?'

'*Gaandu* was a drunkard. He used to do things to me, beat me if I refused. I had to go buy whiskey for him.'

'Whiskey? I thought alcohol is banned in Haridwar.'

'Banned? Everything is banned, everything is available. You only have to know where to look, whiskey, gin, rum, brandy, girls, boys, everything.'

'Then you should have fought back?'

'I did. One day I lashed out with the whiskey bottle itself, nearly killed him.' My sister intervened, 'how will you explain his death,' she said.

'What happened then?'

'He recovered that time. But the fucker was the same, still beating me for little little things.'

'What about your sister?'

'He didn't beat her because she was a quiet submissive type. She was getting very fat though.'

'Was she married?' I asked.

'Married? No *yaar*. One day she came home screaming in pain. Help me Munna, help me Munna, the baby is coming. That's when I understood why she was turning into a balloon. What could I do? I had to call him for help. Instead of helping my sister, he asked me to get him some vodka. Why are you thinking of vodka at a time like this. Can you see she is in pain? Now she was kicking, screaming and hugging her stomach. If you won't help papa, you might as well kill me, she was screaming at him, strangle me and my baby to death. He went mad and slapped her across the face. She fell to the floor clutching the stomach and gasping for air. She pulled her sari up which was soaking wet. At first nothing happened then I saw the top of a baby's head and realised she was trying to push the baby out of the womb. So I took the baby's head in my fingers and tried to pull. There was a rope like thing wrapped around its neck. Have you ever seen baby being born?'

'No, never.'

'Good, better you don't. By now, the old man was down beside me, yelling at her to push, push, push. But she was pulling his hair, which she would not let go. This went on for a while, pulling, pushing, and screaming; still the baby would not come out. She was now shaking violently and breathing fast like, as if trying to drink the air. After about ten minutes like this, she appeared to calm down. *Baas*, that was the end.'

Munna went quiet, looked to his left and right as if fearing his father was nearby and then continued, 'I asked him, why you didn't call a doctor, take her to hospital. He just shook his head. I understood then it was he. He had made her pregnant and he was shitting in his trousers in case someone found out.'

I was shocked to hear all this. My limbs went numb at the thought my mother could have suffered similar pain in giving me birth. Who made her pregnant? I had tried and tried, to form a picture of my father in my head. What did he look like? How old was he? For some reason I could never picture him as a human being, as if he had never existed. 'I wish I knew him,' I mumbled.

'*Hah*, he was probably a drunken fool like mine,' Munna said, 'think about it. If he loved you he wouldn't have left you in that dog house and run away.'

'Still, I would have liked to meet him,' I said.

An old man sitting on the bench with us was listening to our conversation. He pointed at some boys in rags begging outside a roadside *chana bhaturas* stall. Hungry dogs and a man without legs were fighting over scraps of food that fell to the ground. In amongst plastic bottles, food wrappings, scattered paving slabs, a boy had lowered his pant to defecate.

'Those beggar boys ...,' he started saying but a cough interrupted his speech.

'What are you saying uncle?' Munna said.

The man gestured for patience by patting the air and continued. 'I am saying son, you should be thankful to God. He has been kind to you, you do not have to beg like them even though you have lost your *ma bap*.'

'Are you saying I should thank God that my father made my sister pregnant and then killed her? Is that what you are saying uncle?'

The old man touched his earlobes with both hands. '*Bap re bap* what kind of language is that son? All I am saying is God is the greatest. He looks after us. Without him we will all be living in hell.'

'Look around you uncle, look around you. What do you see? Heaven or hell.'

The old man rose instantly and started walking away shaking his head.

'Oh uncle, your bag,' Munna called after the man. He picked up a carrier bag from the bench, ran and handed it to the startled old man.

On the way to Chandi Devi temple Munna pointed at a street sign. 'This is where I met the boss.'

'The boss?'

'Yes, the boss, Lal Bahadur Yadav? Everyone knows him. Even the Chief of Police bows down to his feet. I saw him coming out of his car. At the time, I didn't know who he was, but I could tell he was rich. I ran up to him and offered to guard his car, to make sure no one would scratch it. Cost you four cigarettes boss, I said. When he returned his eyes went boom - he was shocked. I had washed and polished his car, shiny like glass. He was so pleased he gave me a whole packet of cigarettes and asked me if I would like to work for him. Yes boss, I said with a salute.'

We went to the railway station next. At the taxi stand a young couple was standing, presumably waiting for their ride. Munna asked me to go and ask the boy for direction to east platform. I will meet you in the café.

I was eager to help. The man and his wife appeared puzzled when I asked were the east platform was. 'There is no such thing as east platform; all platforms are numbered,' he said, 'check with the enquiry office which one is for your train.'

I thanked them and went to the café. Munna was not there. He arrived a few minutes later looking very smug.

'What's up?' I asked.

'You have just had your first hit,' he said winking as he pulled something out of his pocket and let me have a glimpse. It was a ladies purse, dark red in colour. 'Did you notice anything unusual when you were asking the boy for direction?'

I thought for a moment. 'Just the beggar,' I said, 'this woman with a sleeping child in her arms came over to beg from the lady. She was being pushy, very aggressive.'

'Anything else?'

'The lady was getting irritated, kind of stepping back from the beggar.'

'How long did it last?'

'A minute, maybe more.'

'And did you see me?'

'You?' I cried, 'no, but I was not looking for you.'

'I was there - behind the lady.' He summoned the waiter, 'two teas and biscuits, hurry.'

'And the beggar woman?' I asked.

'She works for me. I pay her by the day.'

That was my initiation to the business of pickpocketing Mr Modiji. I was amazed. How simple it seemed.

As we progressed, I started to initiate the process of picking customers and going in for the kill, with Munna acting as my backup. I wondered how many people Lal Bahadur had working for him. 'He has teams in Haridwar and in many other cities,' Munna said, 'but he likes to keep them hidden from each other. He is strict about that.'

Six months later, we had assembled in Lal Bahadur's residence, in his home office in Shivalik Nagar. It was an upmarket neighbourhood, home to all self-respecting gangsters and, of course, businessmen. Sitting relaxed on a leather sofa, a glass of whiskey on the table, Lal Bahadur, the boss, selected a toothpick from an onyx jar and began picking the remnants of a chewed *paan* from between his teeth, working methodically from front to rear, eventually lifting the upper lip with his forefinger and thumb to get to difficult parts. When done, he took a slug of the whiskey and turned to me. 'Are you happy going to Bangalore or Bengaluru as those fools call it?'

The question disoriented me again. Most definitely, I wanted to go. However, I feared there was a catch to it. Only last week Om Prakash had broken the news to me in the kitchen while drying his hands with a towel. He had the habit of rinsing his hands each night with scented soap, as if doing away the odour of crime. Some nights, after taking charge of the proceeds he would butt his head under the tap, gargle and dry himself with a large hand towel that he kept especially for this purpose. He always did it in the kitchen sink. Then clad in a lungi and open shirt he would pull the tab off a can of Vimto. 'Kalu you have been selected to go to Bangalore,' he had declared. At first, I had taken it as a joke.

Lal Bahadur asked again, 'Do you want to go?'

'Yes, whatever you want,' I said dutifully. I knew showing selfless devotion to the boss was essential if you wanted to get anywhere.

'Good, you will get along nicely with Babu Bajrang. He is a reasonable man,' he said and slapped the table. Basha, the family Dalmatian took the slapping as a *come here* signal and came dashing into the room. He began licking his master's face. '*Puthaa* eats a chicken every day,' Lal Bahadur announced proudly while patting the beast all over, 'if he doesn't get two hours of exercise every day in the park, *sale ka mood kharab ho jata hai,* he becomes grumpy.'

We waited for him to finish cuddling the dog. The beast appeared better fed and loved than the servants did.

'OK, now remember this. As soon as you are on the plane, you shut your mouth. Say your name only if asked. If they ask the purpose of your visit, you say holiday. That is all. No bullshit.' He picked up a small parcel and a bundle of notes lying under a crystal orb. 'Here are two thousand rupees and a book. Keep the book in your hand. Act as if you are a college student. Can you manage that?' he said and chuckled. Om Prakash chortled too, dutifully.

Are they really going to put me on an airplane? It was so hard to believe I thought I must have misheard. 'I am to go by airplane?' I asked, expecting ridicule, airplane, ha, ha, ha, do you consider yourself a maharaja or something.

'Yes, yes, you fly. Make sure you behave yourself. There will be respectable people on the plane, you understand, not your *khat pat* type,' Om Prakash said.

Lal Bahadur crooked a finger at me. 'Come near.'

I went closer. He placed a hand on my shoulder, pressed it gently. 'Babu will be waiting for you. I have sent him your details along with a photograph. Do as I tell you. You will be all right. However, if you get into trouble, then you are on your own. Don't expect help from us.'

Bastards, bastards, bastards, they are going to throw me to the lions and walk away. My heart sank and I did not want to go anymore. Why should I leave the comfort of home? Perhaps comfort was not the right word, familiarity of home. Then I tried to console myself. What is the worst that can happen, maybe a few days in jail? I will go back to Lal Bahadur. 'Told you it won't work boss.' Even Munna said I would be a fool not to go.

That evening I went for a walk in the rain. Drops of water were dripping persistently from trees, lampposts and shop awnings. I inhaled scents: charcoal and rotting fruit, gasoline and ammonia, a swirling belch of odour from gutters. The street was buzzing with children, playing, laughing and crying. Women at doorsteps were yelling at them to come away from the rain. I thought of the orphanage: rows of old metal cots in large square rooms with peeling plaster, peeing children and smell of decay. I wondered what was wrong with me that I should miss the orphanage already when I had dreamt of going to big cities for so long.

The flight was at eleven o'clock in the morning from Dehradun. We had to leave early for the two-hour drive to the airport. The car was a gleaming Toyota Land Cruiser. I recognised the driver. The bastard had assaulted and insulted me the first time we had met. Now I was the boss, a privileged member of Lal Bahadur's team. I was determined to exact revenge. 'Driver turn on the AC,' I ordered.

'Yes, sir,' he replied reluctantly. I could see him burning inside.

'Go faster, I have a plane to catch,' I said.

'Yes sir,' he croaked.

I watched him fidget nervously with the gearbox, barging in and out of traffic. If Munna were there, he would have had a laugh too.

Outside the city, he stopped the car suddenly, opened the door and walked away without an explanation. We thought he had gone for pee behind the shops. Five minutes and he had still not returned. That is when Om Prakash saw the keys in the ignition. 'Mother-fucker has run away,' he screamed angrily.

I was not expecting the driver to react this way. I asked Om Prakash what he was going to do about it.

'I know what I am going to do to him,' he lowered the window and spat, 'we know where his family lives.'

A shiver ran down my spine. Later I heard the driver had gone back to Haridwar station after dumping us. From there he went to New Delhi, to Lucknow and finally to Benares. Lal Bahadur's men found him hiding in a temple, masquerading as a priest. Do you want to know what punishment he received Modiji? They hung him upside down from a tree, set alight and a fire demolished his family home. Then they patched over everything to make it look accidental. I must admit I did feel guilty afterwards. Even today the regret that I may have been partly to blame for his death hasn't gone away. The family made homeless. If he had young children, it's possible they are living on the street. What a horrible thought, sir.

As the Toyota approached the airport, Om Prakash driving, the shadowy cross of an aeroplane roared overhead. At the runway perimeter prickly rolls of barbed wire sagged with middle age disappointment. Behind the wires men in uniform laboured on tarmac or on airport machinery. The air in the enclosed dome was thick with peppery scent of perfume, hint of spent jet fuel and discordant announcements of flight departures and arrivals. Om Prakash pointed at an airline desk, which had a long queue.

'Go, join that line.'

'That line?'

'Yes.'

'OK.'

'Goodbye, then,' he said with a long stare. My heart sagged, realising this was the final parting. I took a few steps towards the queue and looked back, hoping for a final word or a nod of reassurance from him. However, he had already gone.

I handed the ticket to the check-in clerk. While she was typing on the computer, I studied my fellow passengers in the queue. There were smartly dressed businessmen. A group of Englishmen were chatting and laughing with no care in the world, expensive suitcases by their side. My suitcase, old and insubstantial, contained nothing but two shirts and jeans. I had an uneasy feeling I did not belong here and not really destined to leave Haridwar. Any moment a stern faced uniformed official would pull me over. Where do you think you are going son? Then thrown out with a stiff warning: Keep away from the airport, this place is not for the likes of you.

On the plane, I was sitting beside a man of European appearance. Om Prakash had instructed me to observe my fellow passengers and copy them like a monkey. When the European fastened his seatbelt, I did the same. A few minutes into the journey, he picked up a book and set the light above to focus on it. I pulled my book out and pretended to read.

Half an hour into the flight, everything was going smoothly. Suddenly the man turned to me. 'Going to Bangalore?' he asked in English. An executive from England, I presumed. Om Prakash had told me Bangalore was home to many Englishmen.

I nodded

'It's a beautiful city,' he said.

I nodded again, politely. Though I understood a little bit of English, there was no way I could have conversation with him.

'And people are very friendly.'

Again, I nodded, mindful of Lal Bahadur's warning: keep your mouth shut at all times.

'I am a padre, priest.' This time he said it in Hindi. 'I am from Romania.'

I looked at him proper for the first time, astonished to hear a Romanian speak Hindi. He was well dressed in a clean white shirt, tall with a prominent broad nose and light brown hair.

'*Unthalis sal mein Hindustan me hoon.* Thirty-nine years I have lived in Hindustan,' he said.

'You speak good Hindi,' I said.

He nodded slowly. 'Yes, it was not hard to learn. Did you know Hindi language and Romanian have a common ancestry? Both originated in what is now Middle East.'

'No,' I said.

'Do you know where Romania is?' he asked.

I nodded emphatically, 'yes.' Though I had never heard of Romania I thought it would be discourteous to say so.

'*Accha*, if you need any help ask me,' he said and settled back on his seat.

By the time the lady came with the drinks trolley the priest had fallen asleep. I got up and went to the toilet, unzipped the fly. However, the pee would not come as if someone had tied a knot in my bladder. I gave up. As soon as I returned to the seat, I wanted to go again. This time I decided to stay put, hold the pee until I was off the plane.

Behind me, a family from Kerala were discussing the merit of a school. They had come to Dehradun to have their son admitted to the prestigious Doon school. The father was complaining, 'ten lakhs, we need an additional ten lakhs'. The mother was saying, 'yes, but what choice we have, the local schools only produce good-for-nothing communists or layabouts.'

I asked my friend Sanju what was a communist. We were sitting in India Coffee House on the upper level, overlooking Presidency College. He was listening to my Sanyo and typing on his HP250.

'Opposite of capitalist,' he said while his fingers danced skilfully on the keyboard.

'What is capitalist?'

'*Oh hoh*, have you heard of democracy,' he asked impatiently.

I said yes, but it does not mean I understand it.

'I will explain it like this: the opposite of capitalism is socialism. Democracy is the opposite of fascism. One might say fascism is really the corporate control of politics. So democracy would be the opposite of capitalism ....'

'Enough, enough, enough,' I said, 'I only asked what is a communist or communism.'

He laughed. '*Arre yaar* I was coming to that ... '

A student sitting at the next table interjected. 'Brother, do you want to know about communism? I will tell you.' He looked like an eccentric intellectual with long hair, a beard and kurta made of cheap khadi fabric.

Go on explain.

'This is the Karl Marx theory – communism is an ideology, a movement covering all aspects of a society – philosophical, social, political and economic. According to him, all the resources and property of a nation must be owned collectively by the people and not by an individual citizen ...'

Another boy butted in, 'communism is both political and economic. It seeks to get rid of capitalism.'

Someone else disagreed, 'no, no socialism is an economic system. It allows capitalism to exist in its midst while communism seeks to destroy it.'

'Don't interfere while I am speaking - .'

'Comrade your explanation is incorrect ...'

Then there was a free for all, everybody joining in, including Sanju and students from a third table, springing off their chairs, gesticulating, shouting to get their points across. It is a Bengali thing, sir. No self-respecting Bengali likes to lose in a debate.

Mr Modiji, are you wondering why my friend Sanju appears so knowledgeable of politics and economy? Let me explain. After his mother kicked him out of the house, he went to Bangalore and got a job as an assistant in a *chai and biscuit* shop. His duties were simply to serve tea to the customers and keep the tables clear. In return he was given food and floor space at the back of the shop to sleep on.

The chai shop was the haunt of domestic servants working in the neighbourhood. They came all hours of the day to gossip about their masters. Sanju always kept his ears open, should there be a vacancy in any of the households. One day he overheard a maid telling someone her madam was looking for a companion for her disabled son. 'There is nothing to it, take the boy to school, bring him home and play with him when he wants to. That's all.'

'I will do it,' Sanju whispered to her in private.

He was at the house the next day. Madam took him on, on the maid's recommendation. Later when madam learned of his personal misfortunes, an interrupted education, a mother who had disowned him, dead father, she asked him if he would like to go to school. 'You will be educated just like my son,' she said. So, the master and servant, as well as playing together, started attending the same school. When Sanju finished school with top class grades, even better than the master's, madam asked him what he would like to do next. 'I will like to go to university *maji,* to study political science,' he said without hesitation. He applied for admission to Presidency College in Kolkata. Two months later, he arrived in the city, homeless but optimistic. As luck would have it, someone had told him about *halwai* Baldev. That he had a room available to rent. That is how Sanju and I met, neighbours in the same building. I do not mind admitting, sir, I was jealous of Sanju. I wish I had gone to school, learned to read and write, do complex mathematical calculations.

CHAPTER 10

I followed the passengers from my flight to the baggage hall with rows and rows of conveyer belts, chugging and clapping, mining and disgorging suitcases, as if from caves under our feet. It was an astonishing sight.

As I was trying to figure out how to find my suitcase, the priest appeared from nowhere and placed a hand on my shoulder. 'That's our conveyer belt, the luggage will arrive from that direction - see the ramp over there? Be ready to grab - like this - as soon as you see your case.' He demonstrated how to lift a case off a fast moving conveyer belt. 'That's fun, hah,' he said laughing and clapped his hands.

'Yes,' I said.

'Is anyone meeting you?' he asked.

'A friend is waiting for me outside.'

'Oh good, good,' he said.

I wondered why he thought it was good.

A very flimsy suitcase, sandwiched between two holdalls and an attaché case, came into view. So rickety and old in comparison to others I felt embarrassed claiming it. Out in the lounge my fellow travellers were falling into the arms of waiting relatives. It was a drama of human emotion, repeated endlessly, every scene identical, except the actors were different. However, for me there were no smiling faces or welcoming arms. I surveyed the hall, searching a face in the crowd, face I had only seen in a 6 x 4 photograph. Hopeless, how am I going to pick him out from this sea of faces? I pushed the trolley to one side and stood on it to make myself visible to Babu. Almost immediately, I spotted the priest, standing by a tall carousal of newspapers and magazines. He saw me too, grinned and waved a rolled-up newspaper, beckoning me to come over. It would be impolite to refuse, I thought. As I reached the carousal, he gestured, asking me to come closer, as if he had something important to tell me in confidence. 'Come, come,' he said, 'don't be afraid, son, nothing to worry.'

I went a little closer. Am I walking into a trap? Suddenly, he threw an arm up in the air, in a very theatrical manner and said, pointing at a man standing beside him, 'here is Babu Bajrang, the friend you are looking for.' Again, he burst into a mischievous laugh.

Babu Bajrang! I was so shocked the suitcase slipped from my grip. I looked at the younger man who was already scrutinizing me intently.

'Kalu … I am Babu,' he said. His words sounded like clash of echoes in a hollow chamber. About thirty years old, like the priest he was wearing dark trousers and white shirt. His words or hand gestures were of no use to me, but I recognised the smile, the curl of the lips and crows' feet wrinkles on the corners of his eyes, which I had seen in the photograph.

'I am Babu,' he repeated, this time more resolutely, as if to dispel any doubts, 'Lal Bahadur has told me everything about you.'

We shook hands, a powerful grip, just like Lal Bahadur's, same confident and relaxed manner. This is what Om Prakash had said about Babu: Look out for a thirty-year-old well-built man with a friendly but hideously ugly face. He has a lovely smile, but do not be fooled by appearances, underneath he is a ruthless sadistic bastard.

So, this is Babu. However, I was still perplexed. Where does the priest fit in with all this?

'I will explain,' Babu said, as if he had read my mind, 'this is Father Petre Antonescu, Lal Bahadur and Petre are very good friends – like brothers. Petre was on the plane to keep an eye, should there be any problems.'

I was astonished Lal Bahadur had sent a priest to accompany me. Why didn't he tell me? It was not as if I would have refused to board the plane.

The taxi took off for the long drive to our destination giving me the first glimpse of a city I had heard of so much. For someone who had spent the whole life confined to an orphanage and then seen briefly the one-dimensional city of Haridwar, which thrived only on religious tourism, coming to Bangalore was a dream comes true. It was like going to a foreign country.

Babu asked the driver to take a longer route so I could do some sightseeing. On Lalbagh Road, I saw a group of young boys and girls laughing and joking. I wished I were with them. I fancied being a student in a university campus, strolling through hallways carrying big books, a different class of person, looking very grand and learned.

We entered a narrow street off Gandhi Bazaar. It had fewer cars but more pedestrians, shoppers drifting slantwise against traffic, drunks lurching out of pubs, clusters of young men in jeans slouching, kicking cans, restlessly looking around. One of the boys picked up a glass bottle out of an overflowing bin, leaning against graffiti painted wall lobbed it lazily towards us. Smashed glass littered the street in front of the car. Boys laughed.

'Bastards,' yelled Babu, tapped the driver's shoulder, 'speed up, and get out of here.'

We turned into a lane full of cars, an army of gleaming metal, roaring, coughing and spitting fumes. A huge truck drove by mounting the pavement, a taste of diesel hit my throat. Sellers of fruits and vegetables were swotting flies with rags. There were leather goods' stalls, vendors of cheap jeans and t-shirts piled in a heap, people were digging deep looking for the perfect pair. Jewellers were desperately trying to catch peoples' attention, pointing at their wares in glass cabinets; a man was repairing watches by the roadside, people leaning on the counters of mobile phone shops.

An hour later the taxi finally stopped in front of a four-storey building.

'Here we are,' Babu said, 'you've had a long day, relax in the apartment and we will go to eat later. Tomorrow we will move you to the house so you can meet the rest of the team.'

Meet the team? It took a while for the words to achieve significance in a mind still reeling from the shock of the long journey.

A man in uniform came out and held the front door open for us. Once inside it felt as if we had entered another world, very quiet and peaceful. The marble floor hallway led to stairs with mahogany handrails. A painting on the wall, splashes of colours and odd shapes, drew my attention. More paintings adorned the stairway and landing. In the first floor apartment Father Petre dropped his case and asked me to do the same. 'We will get something to eat. Do you like hamburgers?'

I wondered what a hamburger was.

'You have never eaten a hamburger?' the priest asked, slapping me on the shoulder, 'now you will.'

The long café with rustic furniture, high ceiling and low lights, was buzzing with young people dressed fashionably in jeans, slacks and t-shirts. Tables were stacked with condiments and pink napkins. English pop music was blaring from invisible speakers. Babu called the waitress over once we were seated. 'For me hamburger and chips, make it medium rare.'

'I will have the same,' I said quickly, relieved I will not have to study the menu she had placed in front of me.

'Make mine rare …quick, quick,' Father Petre said and clicked his fingers, gesturing at her to come closer. 'Where are you from?' he asked eyeing her breasts.

'Nepal, Sir.'

'Thought so,' Father Petre said, dismissed her with a wave of his hand and then swung around to Babu. 'You see,' he said throwing up his arms as if to say he had made his point and there was nothing more to say.

'What … what do I see?' Babu asked and thrust his chin forward.

'Where I come from, European Union, the borders are open for people to come and go as they like. It is good for the economy.'

'Ha, don't you know already they are pouring in from Bangladesh and Nepal.'

'Yes, but not the right kind. We need young able bodied, which is good for business.' The priest tapped the table with his knuckles.

Babu laughed. 'We should let Pakistanis come too?'

'Yes, why not let them come?'

'No, no, no, we can't have that,' Babu said waving a finger like a hyperactive windscreen wiper.

Their conversation, heated at times, was beyond my comprehension. I was falling asleep, having being awake for most of the previous night.

'Good girl,' Father Petre said to the waitress, ogling her breasts again as she leant down to set the plates.

What shameless man, I thought. However, it was minor compared to the things he did in his church. Once I saw the scoundrel take two girls, also Nepali, to his room. There was a lot of screaming and shouting as if they were quarrelling. After the girls left, he appeared from his room with a big grin.

Back in the flat Babu locked himself in his room saying he had calls to make. 'We sleep in the other bedroom,' Father Petre said.

I was horrified. How could I go to sleep with this Romanian priest in the room? Will we have to share a bed?

'Come, come,' he said and led me into the room across the hall. What relief to find two beds in there. Without a word he started taking his shoes and clothes off, grunting like a pig. I stood fumbling with my shirt buttons, too embarrassed to take my clothes off in front of the priest.

'I am going for a shower,' he said.

While he was in the bathroom I undressed quickly and slipped into the bed.

Humming a tune, the priest came out with just a towel round his big belly and picked up a small green bottle from a bag on the table. He unscrewed the bottle top, poured a small amount of liquid on his palm and patted it on his cheeks. While he was doing the patting the towel slipped to the floor, exposing very white round buttocks with a dimple on each side and curly strands of hair jutting down from the middle of the waist. Have you seen a white man completely naked, sir? It is a horrible sight. What woman would want to go near that thing? He jumped into the bed and pulled the sheet over him in one full sweep. 'Aaahhh, this is nice. Good night Kalu.'

The sickly whiff of after-shave reached my nostrils. I held my breath, counted to ten, inhaled, counted to ten again. Babu had said I must take a good night's sleep as they had a busy day tomorrow. Sleep? I was alert as an early morning cockerel. How could I fall asleep in a room with a naked priest wheezing and making strange noises? I started thinking of Durga Bhabi, missing the friends I had left behind and then I thought of the teammates I was going to meet the next day. Did Munna train them too?

Soon the priest's snoring had settled down to a steady rhythm, punctuated by periods of absolute silence as if he had stopped breathing. It terrified me. Oh God, hope he does not die. How will I explain to Babu that I had nothing to do with it?

The door opened with a bang startling me awake. Babu came in wearing black and white striped boxer shorts, a cup of tea in one hand; scratching his crotch with the other. The priest was still snoring. Daylight was creeping in through gaps in the curtains.

'Wake up Kalu, we have to make an early start,' Babu growled, kicked the bed and then pulled a plastic ball from under the table. He began playing with it, hacking it skilfully and catching it in the crook of his foot. 'I used to play football,' he said.

Behind me the priest farted and cleared his throat. The bed shook violently as he jumped out of it completely naked.

'AARRGGHH!' he screamed and ran like a bull towards Babu. Are they going to fight? Perhaps they have had a disagreement, I thought. But the priest was after the ball that flew and bounced off the wall. Pushing and shoving each other they were fighting for the ball. The older man clambered over the sofa, tripped and fell. A chair overturned. Babu began taunting the priest, laughing and juggling the ball expertly in his face. The priest, his testicles draggling between the legs, bolted upright and charged again. Babu pulled the ball back, dribbling, keeping it just out of the big man's reach. Over the shouts, laughter and grunts someone banged the front door. 'Making such racket, have you all gone mad in there?'

They began giggling like little boys, asking each other to be quiet. It seemed to me the two men were good friends. Only later I found out Modiji, that there was a silent rivalry going on between them. Father Petre saw himself as the man in charge. Babu was content to let him believe that while working behind the scene to a different agenda.

Out on the street, Babu was scrutinising every approaching taxi, ready to hail if it was free, complaining, 'whenever you need a taxi you can't find one, when you don't need any they are everywhere.'

'Then you agree with me, hah,' the priest quipped. He was examining a small cast iron statue of dancing God Nataraj, as if searching for a secret marking.

'What I agree with you?' Babu asked, not taking his eyes off the line of speeding cars.

'Open the borders. Let people come in. More people more

taxis, simple, no,' the priest said.

'You are talking *bakwas,* nonsense again, you, Christian sadhu.'

The priest lowered the statue from his face and laughed. 'No ordinary Christian, I am Orthodox Christian sadhu.'

'Orthodox *phorthodox,* it is all *bakwas.* Real sadhus go for fourteen years of *banwas,* solitary meditation in the mountains. When are you going?'

'As soon as Lal Bahadur lets me.'

'I will put in a word for you.'

The priest returned the statue to the flap top leather case and took out another Nataraj. This one was slightly bigger but made of brass metal.

'You like?' he said, seeing me eyeing it with curiosity, 'bought it from a *kutchrawall,* road sweeper in Mysore, very old,' he said gravely as if it was a major discovery, 'I have many more back home.'

I was puzzled why he considered them valuable. I could have got them for a few rupees from market stalls in Haridwar.

Behind us were mud-caked vans parked on the pavement. A boy was peeing on a tyre. Outside a sari shop, a man in short pants was washing the pavement with a broom and bucket of water. The priest glared at him. 'You want to clean the street. Then clean. But I didn't ask you to wet my shoes.'

The man looked up at the priest with an amused smile, a foreigner speaking Hindi. 'Sir, you like to buy sari. Please come inside, please this way,' he started imploring the priest to enter his shop, 'you will be my first customer of the day.'

'No sari. Waiting for taxi.'

'You want taxi? No problem. My brother-in-law has taxi, nice clean, air-conditioned.' He yelled at someone across the road. In no time a taxi came to a screeching halt beside us.

'That's one way to find a taxi,' the priest said with a broad grin.

The house was on Main Road in Indira Nagar. Its view blocked by perimeter wall and trees with heavy foliage. Up close I could see a painted sign, *Romani Orthodox Church,* hanging above the double fronted dark green door. On the left, between the neighbour's wall and the house, a panelled fence and a metal gate with an arbour above blocked the back garden, colonized by flowering creepers.

A thin faced man wearing a vest and loose fitting trouser came hurrying out of the house. '*Namaskar sahib,*' he said to Father Petre and picked up his suitcase.

'*Hanh* Mukund, *chalo*, go in,' the priest said as he followed behind.

'So, what do you think of this place?' Babu asked.

A strange question, I thought, considering I had seen nothing yet. 'It looks nice,' I said.

'Let's have a chat,' he said and pulled out a packet of Goldflake from his trouser pocket. He looked into the distance as if deliberating something important, flipped the packet open, took out a cigarette and placed it between his lips. 'Let me explain the set up before we go in,' he said and looked both ways, making sure there was no one in hearing distance, 'the house is divided in two parts. The front portion is the church where Petre lives. We live at the back. The entrance is through there.' He pointed at the metal gate a few feet to the side and then flicked a lighter to light the cigarette. 'You will have your own keys. About the church, I will tell you we have absolutely nothing to do with it, all that is Petre's business. You are not allowed in or be seen by any of the visitors. If you spot anyone outside, stay away until it is clear. Have you understood?'

I nodded yes.

'You must leave or enter the house with care. We do not want any unwanted attention from the neighbours. There should be no trouble...,' he stopped speaking, waited for two middle-aged men in white trainers to go past. An auto rickshaw loaded with several sacks of produce sped past, narrowly missing a bicyclist. 'Now the team. I have three in the team already as you know, all well settled. I have been observing you for the last twenty-four hours and I am confident you will get on well with them. If there are any problems, you come to me. But do as I say and you will be fine, I'll look after you,' he said solemnly and patted the chest with his right hand, 'anything you want to ask?'

I could hardly breathe through sheer anxiety. There was a lot I wanted to know. However, I dare not ask. What was inside the church? Why the secrecy? Why we had to hide from Christians coming to pray? If I did not get along with the team, would it be back to Haridwar for me. If caught by police will I get help?

'Follow me,' he said and unlocked the gate. Once through he pulled the gate shut with a firm tug. 'Always lock after you.'

The garden stretched from the side to the back of the house, tall bushes edged the property; stop the neighbours from looking in. The concrete path cut in the green turf was wet and muddy from recent rains. Babu's shoe heels clip clopped as we walked to the door on the right. I became aware of people chatting inside the house. The talking stopped abruptly as Babu inserted the key in the lock.

We stepped into a hallway. Several pairs of shoes lying scattered on the floor. Garments were hanging haphazardly on a run of hooks on the left wall. A stale odour of fried eggs hung in the air. A framed picture of Rajasthani girls in traditional costumes was hanging on the left wall. At the top end of the hallway Babu pushed open a door and stood aside for me to enter. I hesitated.

'Go in, go in,' Babu said.

I entered. Sunlight flooding in from a window blinded me briefly. I moved my head sideways and the first thing that caught my eyes was three boys sitting on a sofa. One with arms folded behind his head and the other two were leaning forward. All eyes were set on me. One of the boys sprang to his feet. I stopped in my track, startled. The boy screamed, 'Kalu, Kalu, Kalu.'

I could not understand why he was calling my name. Then I recognised the face. The suitcase slipped from my fingers, landed on the floor with a thud.

We rushed at each other and hugged. When I stepped back and examined his face closely I could see he had aged several years in the short span of time, the skin on his face taut and very pale. He stank of sweat – the kind of sweat from emotional upset, both sour and sharp. Then the memory of the night he had disappeared from the home came flooding back, but in a jumbled order. Was it yesterday or long time ago?

'You alright,' I asked.

'What a surprise Kalu, I knew someone was coming from Haridwar but you, you,' Ramesh said, still panting from excitement.

'I never knew you were here,' I said.

'So, you know Ramesh,' Babu said, a surprised expression on his face.

Ramesh stiffened his neck and I could see Babu was not telling the truth.

'Yes, we were in Durga Bhabi together,' Ramesh replied. His city-folk accent had not left him.

'That's good, you can then show him around,' Babu said, 'let's have some tea now.'

The good memory of the day Ramesh had arrived at Durga Bhabi came back, how I had volunteered to take him on guided tour. Now Ramesh was going to show me around here.

The other two members of the team, Bhushan and Gokul, were both from a village outside Haridwar. Gokul, taller and more athletic reminded me of Munna. At first I took him to be the leader. He turned out to be the quiet type, happy to follow others. His father was a local priest, making a living by hustling the tourists who came to Haridwar for spiritual salvation, to rinse their souls of years of accumulated guilt. The man had a fight with another priest trying to poach his customers and ended up dead from stab wounds. One of Lal Bahadur's scouts picked up Gokul, at the time ten years old and homeless.

Bhushan, short and skinny with a long nose, was the joker. That I could see instantly from his toothy smile. He had a fashionable hairstyle. 'He is a pig-headed stubborn boy,' Ramesh told me later, 'and he is *chhokri-baaz*, eyeing girls all the time.'

Bhushan is stubborn as a donkey, Ramesh had warned me very early on. Here is an example of his doggedness, sir. One day the city of Bangalore had come to a standstill. Trade Union representing BMTC drivers and conductors had called a strike. Auto rickshaws and cab drivers were staying away in sympathy. Schools and colleges forced to shut too. Shopkeepers had decided to stay shut in trouble hot spots. Tourists advised not to venture too far out. To cap it all rain had been falling on and off all night. By daybreak it was falling in strange circular motions, creating a deafening din and flooding the streets.

Babu was insistent we go out to work. 'I am not having you sit idle snapping at mosquitoes.'

We could not defy him. So, we set off on foot to the city centre, dodging rain by sheltering here there under shop awnings. Instead of splitting up into two teams we had decided to work together to create effective distraction, dip and pass. Only the hardened or desperate shoppers were out on the street. After a miserable six hours of hard work we returned to base drenched to the skin. Babu was pacing the room between the sofas and dining table, a lit Goldflake on the ashtray, mobile phone clamped to his ear, talking to someone in whispers. Damp air suffused with cigarette smoke, Ramesh went to open a window wider.

'So how was it?' he asked gesturing with his fingers, while continuing to talk on the phone.

I emptied my pocket on the table: a purse, wallet and some cash which I had just about managed to keep dry. He swept everything off the table and took it to his room.

When he emerged from his room later that evening, coughing and with raised eyebrows, I knew we were in trouble. 'You are short of the target.'

'Conditions were so bad, what could we do?' I said.

'Bad conditions. There is no such thing in our business.'

'Even Commercial Street was deserted.'

'You should have tried harder.'

'But we did,' Bhushan said, a hint of indignation in his voice.

'OK, you will not be paid for today. We will see about

tomorrow. Go away now.' He dismissed us with wave of his hand.

I was ready to stop for the day but Bhushan was having none of it. 'Why will you not pay us?' he said.

'Rules,' Babu replied curtly and began scratching his elbow again, already red and sore from a chronic skin ailment.

'This is not right,' Bhushan said.

'You know the rules Bhushan. How many times I have told you nobody gets paid if the target is not reached.' He picked up a bottle of VAT 69 from the side cabinet, unscrewed the cap, took a slug and then poured a little in the glass. 'And you also know I don't make the rules. They are set by head office.'

'What about the times when we are over our target?'

'That doesn't count.'

'Doesn't count?'

'No, it doesn't.'

'I will go to the police.'

Gokul and Ramesh took sharp intake of breath. Babu stiffened his neck, the glass of whiskey poised inches from his lips. 'What did you say?'

'You heard me,' Bhushan replied brazenly.

Gokul and Ramesh made eyes at Bhushan asking him to shut up. Sensing trouble I intervened quickly, 'Bhushan is only joking, I will put him right. You let him have his share while I will forgo mine,' I said to Babu.

'No,' Babu slammed the glass on the table, liquid sloshing over the rim, 'little mother-fucker you dare to threaten me with police.'

'Apologise to the boss, come on,' I said to Bhushan.

The fool, realising he had gone too far, offered an apology.

But it was too little, too late.

Babu got up from the chair, went over to Bhushan. 'You want to call the police, do you?' He slapped the boy hard across the face.

Bhushan looked up at us stunned and then began crying, 'I want to go home. I want to go home.'

'You want to go home…go,' Babu yelled.

Bhushan ran to the dining table covered with Mukund's plastic tablecloth and crouched under it, cowering like a frightened animal.

'I thought you wanted to go home,' Babu yelled, 'why are you still here?' He strode over to the table and without warning kicked Bhushan on the backside with his size nine boots. The boy's head struck the table leg and his crying turned to howling.

That seemed to enrage Babu even more. 'Shut up, shut up,' he yelled and kicked again. This time the face took the hit, splitting his upper lip.

Blood drawn I thought Babu would stop there. However, I was wrong. He was about to lash out again. In a split second something snapped in my head. I flung myself forward and faced Babu with outstretched arms. 'Enough boss,' I said, 'don't hurt him anymore. I'll make sure he behaves in future.'

Babu appeared surprised by my intervention and then locked his raging eyes on me. I tried to outstare him. It was all bluster for I stood no chance in a straight fight with the big brute.

'You do it or you are next,' he said eventually and waved a clenched fist in my face.

So, there you are sir. We did not get our daily wage. Do you want to know how much it was? It was a mere two hundred and fifty rupees. You are surprised, aren't you Modiji, how little we were paid. But we knew no better. For us it was a lot of money.

Bhushan did not seek pity from any of us, accepting the fault was his for goading the unpredictable beast. We helped him off the floor and sat him down on Ramesh's bed. Gokul fetched a wet towel and wiped his face. We did not try to admonish him. Bhushan had stood up to the brute on our behalf and we were grateful to him.

We sat lost in our thoughts, stunned by what we had just witnessed. For the first time I reflected if this place was right for me. However, where could I go?

Suddenly Gokul spoke. 'I saw a snake eat a dog once, it swallowed the poor thing whole, the head was last to go in.'

All eyes turned to Gokul.

'But snakes can't eat dogs. They don't have big mouths,' Ramesh said after a long pause.

'This snake was big,' Gokul said with open arms, 'huge.'

'Didn't the dog fight back?'

'No. It was crying at first. Then it stopped. Its eyes were open all the time; it was looking around as if searching for its mother.'

'Where did you see this?' I asked.

'Back home.'

'How long did it take?'

'Too long.'

'How long is too long?'

'Dogs don't cry you fool.'

'Yes they do ... it took ten minutes ... I think,' Gokul said.

'And you just watched?

'Yes.'

We were silent again. In the Indra-Lakshmi temple down

the road bells rang out signalling start of evening prayers. Two doors away, in the back yard, some kids had lit a bone fire. Smoke was drifting towards us, an unpleasant odour of burned twigs and wet leaves. Lying on the table was the promotional leaflet of a gymnasium Bhushan had picked up from somewhere. It had picture of a very fit muscular white man with a caption in bold letters: *You too can look like him in thirty days.* I thought Bhushan should take up the offer. A dog barked in the distance. Another dog took up the call. I looked out the open window. The window apparently wanted to take me back to the orphanage, which was fine with me. When I looked into the future, all I could see was a world from which everything I counted important had banished or had willingly fled.

Chapter 11

On the second day in my new home in Bangalore I woke up early. We had planned to spend the day in and around Bangalore's main railway station. Babu emerged from his room bathed, shaved and dressed, having first lit a few incense sticks in front of a small statue of Ganesha, which he kept on a table in his room. Aroma of burning incense was already floating throughout the house.

He came and sat down smartly at the table. A plate of freshly fried omelette was already waiting for him. With a spoon, he sliced the omelette into half, then picked up the ketchup bottle, and held it upside down. The ketchup would not flow. 'Son of an owl,' he swore and slapped the base of the round bottle. Two thick dollops fell on the omelette. Mukund, the house-keeper, came with a cup of tea on a saucer. The cup rattled as he placed it on the table in front of Babu and retreated promptly. Mukund lived in the church with Father Petre.

'Karnataka people are of different class,' Babu said, making eye gestures at Mukund's retreating figure, 'I tell you they are just arse holes, they think they can't be scammed. But it's easy to turn them over, like stealing lollipop from a child. Just keep this in mind, if you are polite to them, they will be polite to you. Don't be greedy and don't be impatient. There are no short cuts to getting rich.'

'First seven days you don't do anything, just watch and learn,' Babu said.

Every day we went out criss-crossing the city. We visited grand palaces, like the Bangalore Palace, Vidhana Soudha. We visited art galleries, temple Dodda Ganesha, Commercial Street shopping centre, Brigade Road. I saw neighbourhoods that were ideal for quick in and out dip, and settings more suited to long term stalking. I saw sites unsuitable for our trade, localities I was never to enter. We walked through local markets. Now and then Babu pointed at someone in the crowd, 'that's a plain clothes policeman.'

'How can you tell?'

'How? Look for men in late twenties or may be early thirties. Study their body language. They always look alert, but never in a hurry. They don't appear to be going anywhere and they never have a shopping bag in their hands. You will soon learn to spot them in the crowd.'

On the eighth day Babu said to me, 'son your apprenticeship is over. Now you must go out and earn your keep.'

It took me three months to settle down with Babu and his team. After that we were sailing, having the time of my life.

I learned soon enough that Babu was a disciplinarian of extreme kind. He was also a control freak. The clothes and shoes we wore needed his approval. One day Ramesh and I, working in a shopping mall, saw a fabulous trainer sitting in the window of a designer shoe shop, displayed prominently with two spotlights trained on it. White with blue and black Nike logo on the sides, it looked like a rock star.

We looked into each other's eyes simultaneously: shall we? That evening we walked into the house proudly displaying the Nikes on our feet. Babu, with feet spread on coffee table, was watching cricket on television. 'What's that?' he growled glaring at them.

'Nike, latest model,' I said.

'I know what they are, you fool. Why are you wearing them?' he said angrily.

'Why shouldn't we?' Ramesh said, hurt at Babu's strange reaction.

'Don't you know in our business we don't attract attention to ourselves on the street? That's rule number one, rule number two and rule number three.' He counted each rule on his fingers.

'But they are only shoes,' Ramesh said.

'Take them back.'

'But why?'

'I said take them back.'

'No.' Ramesh protested.

'You want to keep them, fine,' he said and snapped his fingers, 'first take them off ... take them off.'

'We have paid a lot of money.'

'Off ... off ... off.'

He called Mukund and ordered him to take the trainers to the back yard. 'Roll them in the mud. Make them look old.'

'But why sir?'

'Do as you are told ... make them look worn, just like yours.'

Mukund appeared reluctant, as if it was a crime to spoil something so grand, as he carried the two pairs to the back yard.

'Do it properly,' shouted Babu, 'rub them in the dirt ... jump on them ... go on.'

When Mukund returned with our battered trainers and placed them on the floor Babu kicked them towards us. 'You can wear them now,' he said calmly and went back to watching the test match.

You see what I mean sir. We dare not to appear rich, not even fake rich. While he walked around in expensive silk shirts, smartest of trousers, gold chain and rings. He exuded class and upbringing. Only we knew it was not true.

After that incident I decided to educate myself. Babu was right about undue show of wealth, it was improper and crude. Only his reasons were selfish. I started buying newspapers and began reading them, from the heading to the small print. Mostly I could pick up the gist. But if you asked me the meaning of long words I would struggle. I practised writing too. With a sharpened pencil I started copying sentences onto a clean sheet of paper. After a while I progressed to copying pages from a book I had found somewhere:

The time of my end approaches. I have lately been subject to attacks of angina pectoris and in the ordinary course of things, my physician tells me, I may fairly hope that my life will not be protracted many months. Unless, then, I am cursed with an exceptional physical constitution, as I am cursed with an exceptional mental character, I shall not much longer groan under the wearisome burden of this earthly existence. If it were to be otherwise - if I were to live on to the age most men desire and provide for – I should for once have known whether the miseries of delusive expectation can outweigh the miseries of true provision. For I foresee when I shall die, and everything that will happen in my last moments.

The boys started making fun of me, giving me names such as, *Rabindranath Kalu, masterji Kalu* or they would see a book in my hand and give it a tile: *Kalu Cobra Ki Kahani. Tales of Kalu Cobra.*

One day Gokul brought a leaflet home from the barber's

shop. It was about an ice-skating rink in Mantri Mall, an invitation to sample the newly opened facilities.

Learn to skate today, improve body balance, flexibility, muscle tone and core strength.

He was all excited, waving the leaflet in the air, 'let's go skating.'

'Yes, yes, let's go. I have heard Mantri Mall is full of sexy girls,' Bhushan said grinning.

The skating rink was already busy when we arrived. Families with children on Sunday outing. We hired a skate each, strapped them to our feet and entered the arena holding hands and giggling. None of us had done anything like it before. In no time Bhushan lost his balance and went down screaming. Ramesh tried a long independent glide only to collide with a passing skater, who swore, 'you, stupid people should not be allowed here.' 'We have paid as much as you, you stupid ass,' Gokul retorted, ready for a fight.

'Arre, arre, arre, no quarrelling,' the boy's father called from the sideline.

It took us good half hour to learn how to stay upright. Bhushan attempted an ambitious U-turn, misjudged the requisite depth of arc and crashed at speed into the railings. Undeterred he tried again, this time completing the U-turn without colliding with anyone.

Ramesh had a go. He too managed the U-turn successfully.

It was my turn. I set off, pushing the ice with my left foot, body bent forward at an angle, showing off as if I was an experienced skater. My skate clipped another skater. In desperate attempt to stay upright I over-compensated a left roll by moving my body too far to the right and crashed into the railing.

Limping behind others, at the front gate to our house I happened to look up and spotted a little metal box attached to a batten directly above my head. It was painted matt brown, same colour as the wood. Out of curiosity I raised myself up on a fence rung for a closer look. I nearly fell back realising it was a cleverly concealed closed-circuit television camera sir. A sparrow had built its nest just above the box, making it harder to spot.

So, the bastards have been watching us all this time. I wondered where else were these spying lenses. In no time I found one on the back wall, pointing into the garden. However, the one that horrified me most was staring me right in the face, deftly cloaked in the fabric of the lampshade hanging from the living room ceiling. I stepped out of its range quickly, horrified, as if I had been caught with the pants down. I wanted to smash them to pieces or smear the lenses with flour and water putty.

That night I had a dream. I was standing pushed against a wall, cornered by three angry people, Babu on my right, Father Petre on the left and Panu with her stained lips facing me. 'Don't tell anyone about the cameras?' All three were screaming in my face. Frightened, yet adamant, I was refusing to give in. Panu took a handkerchief and began dabbing at the sweat on my forehead. Then she placed her right hand on my chest and let it slide down to the stomach. I held my breath. Her hand moved further down between my thighs. Then she unzipped my trouser fly. I shut my eyes. Her fingers went creeping in, like a mouse sniffing for food. She cupped my testicles in her hand. I tightened the muscle in my groin fearing she was going to squeeze.

'Not a word to anyone,' she said. I felt the pressure on the balls increasing gradually. 'Not a word to anyone,' she kept repeating and squeezing harder and harder. I remained defiant, ready to absorb any pain. Finally, she gave a hefty tug. I woke up with a scream.

Following day, the nightmare and the cameras paled into insignificance. I had gone to buy some CDs from Krishna Music store half a mile away. As I stepped out of the shop, I happened to see a man crossing the road. Tall and lanky, he was walking with a limp. I stopped for a better look, feeling I had seen him somewhere before. As he picked up walking speed with a pronounced limp I recognised him instantly. I had seen him about four years ago, hand in hand with Ramesh, walking slowly but with purpose towards our orphanage. His gait was ungainly, as if one leg was shorter. That picture had remained fixed in my brain.

How did he know Ramesh was here, in Indira Nagar? Why he had come to rescue his son now, when he had happily abandoned him to the orphanage for so many years? I did consider running up to him, tell him about his son's whereabouts. However, I knew Babu's men were everywhere. Perhaps Babu already knew the father was in town. If so, he would be planning an encounter to scare him away or do something worse. I felt afraid for Ramesh. If the father came too close both could be in danger. I watched helplessly as the tall man wondered off, lost in the crowd. Back home Ramesh was sitting on his favourite chair, eyes half shut, listening to music through earplugs, a keyring wrapped around his finger. The ring belonged to a girl whose handbag he had stolen at the railway station. He said she reminded him of Maria.

'Ramesh.'

Ramesh unplugged his ears and cocked his head. 'What?'

'You alright?'

'Yes, why are you asking?'

'Just asking.'

He gave me a puzzled look.

By next morning I had decided Ramesh should know about his papa. If he wanted to run away, he needed to plan well, not let Babu and the priest suspect anything. Next morning I went to look for him. He was not in his room, though it was still early. My heart began racing. Had he slipped out during the night for a pre-planned rendezvous with his papa? He had given no indication of his intentions. His clothes and belongings were in their usual place. The poster of Amitabh Bachan was still on the wall. He had hung it there to hide obscenities he had scribbled with a permanent marker when his team Kolkata Knight Riders had lost a crucial match. As I was leaving, I found his favourite keyring lying on the floor.

I asked Bhushan if he had seen Babu and Ramesh that morning.

'No, but they may have gone to Cubborn Park to see Baba Ramdev,' he suggested.

There was some truth in it. Babu and Father Petre had discussed conducting a special operation on this occasion. They called it *maha chappa*. It involved bringing in teams from other cities for quick lift-and-go operation. As always Father Petre did the strategy and Babu the legwork. Once I had overheard Father Petre saying to Babu, 'send a box of sweets to the minister; elections are coming in six months.'

A box of sweets. Now you would think that is an innocuous friendly gesture. What is wrong with it? However, let me explain sir. An empty sweet box with picture of Ganesh on the lid came from Ganesh Mithai Bhandar. They wrapped a brick of high value rupee notes in newspaper and secured it with a string. The package placed in the Ganesh Mithai box was gift-wrapped beautifully with a red ribbon. I had overheard Babu give instructions to Mukund, 'take this box of *ladoos* to minister's house. Hand it to him personally or his madam. If she is not there, then give it to his assistant. His name is Krishnamurthy. Don't give it to anyone else. Have you understood?'

'*Hanh* sahib,' Mukund had replied shaking his head dutifully.

'Go, go, quick and tell him Petre sahib is sending his *salam*.

Mukund, having shed his lungi for a brown polyester trouser and white nylon shirt, took off on his bicycle for the ten-minute ride. Poor fool had no idea he was carrying so much money, probably more than a year's salary for him.

As planned, we left later that morning without Ramesh, to work the Garuda shopping mall. I went through the motions, unable to concentrate, thinking all the time, had Ramesh been picked up by his father. I will never see him again. It filled me with gloom.

I hurried home that evening and dashed into Ramesh's room. It had not been disturbed. I looked in the kitchen and all the other rooms before going to the living room. Babu was sitting on the sofa; packet of Goldflake and a lighter were sitting on the coffee table, along with the bottle of Johnny Walker Black Label and the bucket of ice cubes. His eyebrows knotted into V-shape as he puffed on the cigarette furiously. I knew instantly he was worried about something. The television switched to NDTV news. I remember it so well sir, because the news was about Muzaffarpur orphanage scandal. Over twenty-nine minor girls raped over a period of years. The people raping and molesting the girls were none other than a bunch of police and politicians themselves. The very people who should have protected them. My head was spinning for I was thinking of my orphanage back in Haridwar.

Babu gestured with his hand asking us to sit down. 'I have something … to tell you,' he said and paused while absently scratching his elbow. Bhushan and Gokul sat down quietly, sensing something was afoot. Finally, he uttered the words I had been dreading to hear, 'Ramesh is no longer with us.' He said with an air of irrevocability as if it was a done deed, there was no going back.

There was silence for a few moments and then Bhushan said, 'but his CDs and stuff are still here. He never said anything about leaving.'

'Yes Bhushan, he must have left in a hurry. Who knows? Even I don't understand.'

'But why?' asked Gokul.

'We don't know. I thought he was happy here.'

Did Ramesh leave of his own free will or has Babu done something bad to him. It took me back to Durga Bhabi, to the early days. I used to share a bed with eight years old Micu. Micu had a strange illness; he suffered from excessive nosebleed. Almost every other day he bled, sometimes profusely, staining his shirt bright red. However, he never appeared disheartened. They used to take him to the hospital and leave him there for a few days at a time. Once they took him away while I was asleep. When I asked about him next morning, they said he was not coming back. I felt terribly betrayed then. Now I was feeling the same.

'It is not possible Boss, Ramesh will not go anywhere without first telling me,' I said.

Babu stubbed the cigarette under his *chappal* forgetting he was indoors, not out on the street. 'The boy has run away. That's all,' he said with such conviction I almost believed him.

'Why didn't you raise an alarm when you found out he was missing,' I said, 'and you didn't even ask us if we knew anything.' Now I was wondering why was Father Petre not here at such an important moment. What did he know about all this?

'What I am doing now, *heh* Kalu, am I not asking,' Babu said and snatched the packet of Goldflake off the table, took out a cigarette, placed it between his lips, with the right hand crushed the cigarette packet, forgetting it was still half full and dropped it on the table.

'Boss, you are not asking. You are telling us,' I said.

He removed the cigarette from his lips and roared with ferocity I had not seen before, 'Ramesh has left us. What-don't-you-understand-Kalu?'

I shut my mouth remembering the warning Om Prakash had given - don't be fooled by Babu's friendly smile, inside he is a ruthless bastard. I knew he was capable of hurting people if they went against him.

So, that was it, I dared not ask him anything about Ramesh, neither did the boys as if Ramesh had never existed.

In the next few of weeks, Gokul and Bhushan, reassured by seeming rational explanations from the priest and Babu, were starting to settle down. Babu appeared strangely transformed. Gone was the angry snarl and tooth suck at the slightest show of impertinence. He was now taking every opportunity to discuss cricket with them, analysing results, evaluate strengths and weaknesses of players.

I knew all this comradery would last only so long as the boys' memory of Ramesh was fresh. Meanwhile Babu was probably looking for a replacement.

Ramesh was not coming back. To me it did not feel that way. Ramesh's clothes were still lying around. His toothbrush, soap and shampoo were lying on the windowsill in the permanently damp bathroom. All the signs indicated he had stepped out for a while and would return very soon.

After a week, on impulse, I collected Ramesh's belongings, including his clothes and CDs, put them all in his suitcase and slid the case under a bed.

CHAPTER 12

One day Babu instructed me and Bhushan to go to Sangolli Rayana train station. 'People are arriving for the exhibition in thousands. Work hard and come back with good loot,' he said.

Towards the end of the day, satisfied with the day's work, three wallets and cash stuffed in inner pockets in my vest, we headed back home. In an alley behind the station a roadside coffee seller was pouring steaming hot coffee into stainless steel tumblers. We decided to take a coffee break. The street was crowded with office workers. Cars, auto rickshaws and scooters were whizzing past us making an incredible racket. Bhushan squeezed himself in on a bench between talkative office workers. Nearby a man sitting on a stool reading a newspaper held high to his face. I happened to glance at the front page of the Deccan Herald. Halfway down the page was a photograph, bust of a man of about fifty. The face appeared familiar. It held my attention a little longer. Those eyes, the swarthy face, layers of black hair, were reminding me of Ramesh's father. I leaned forward for a closer look. There was no mistaking. It indeed was Mr Banika. Then I read the caption: *Man found battered to death*.

I glanced quickly at Bhushan. He was watching a flock of crows scavenging food from an overflowing bin. Back to the newspaper I read the small print. *Bodies of a man and young boy have been found in the forest beside Premier Golf course ... beaten and stabbed to death ... buried in a shallow grave ... believed to have been dead for about thirty-six hours....*

I sprang to my feet. 'Come on Bhushan we have to go.'

'*Arre* Kalu ... our coffee...' He tried to hold me back.

'Leave it,' I said.

'What has happened to you?'

'Nothing, I am going, you can come later.'

I left Bhushan sitting on the bench bewildered and annoyed.

Back at the house everything was normal. The world was fixed in its usual place, waiting. Gokul was sprawled on the chair listening to music on headphones. Babu, fanatic about cricket, was lounging on the sofa, watching an international on television. He had pulled the light blue *kurta* up to the chest to breeze his hairy belly. He did not look away from the television as I entered the room. However, I sensed the energy, as if someone was watching me. From that position, the angle of light falling on Babu's face made him appear even more sinister. Then his head slumped sideways. He had dozed off. In that moment, it occurred to me how easy it would be to break a sleeping head. A heavy blow with the right object, it would be over in no time.

Where did it come from? This thought of murder surfacing so casually. It disgusted me. Why am I thinking like this? I went to my room and lay down on the bed, still in my casual black trouser and beige shirt. This was our work uniform. We had to dress like office clerks. I looked at my trembling hands and attempted to steady them. Earlier, I had sneaked into a shop for another read of the report. It said..... *the older man of about fifty had his rib cage smashed, nails had been set alight and there were cigarette burns on his body including at the tip of his penis*

... the boy, about fifteen years old, had been stabbed repeatedly ....

I was shocked. What animal would do such a thing? However, in a perverse way I was also relieved, for Ramesh did not have his penis disfigured.

I dare not tell anyone. If Babu found out I knew the father and had seen his photo in the newspaper I too would end up dead in the forest by the Golf course. If they did a little better job of digging and burying, I would be gone for good. And who will miss me sir?

Once a week, on Wednesdays, after sunset, Babu used to get on his Hero Honda motorbike and disappear for an hour or two. He was secretive about it, would not say where he went.

I was waiting for him to fire up his motorbike. As soon as I heard the vroom, vroom of the engine, I ran to the window. Babu was buckling the strap of the helmet under his chin. Once ready he checked the fuel gauge and drove off.

Bhushan and Gokul were watching a movie in the lounge. I sneaked out, went to Babu's room and pushed the door open. A strong whiff of body lotion was hanging in the air. Everything appeared normal; the unmade bed, poster of Aishwarya Rai, his favourite actress, hanging above the drawer units. A small bronze statue of Nataraj, gift from Father Petre, stood in one corner.

Are you wondering why I had sneaked into Babu's room, sir? Let me tell you. I was looking for money, any amount I could lay my hands on. I had a window of an hour or little more. I began the search earnestly, beginning with the wardrobe. It had an untidy run of shirts and trousers in the centre. The shelves were stacked with folded garments, two shoeboxes on the floor. I raised the lids. One had a pair of slippers and the other stacked with papers. I moved on to the drawer units. They contained socks and underwear. Rummaging through them my fingers touched something cold and metallic. I pushed my hand in deeper and found a metal cashbox, about ten by six inches. I pulled it out. It was locked. There must be a key somewhere. The second and the third drawers contained nothing useful. After another rummage through the wardrobe I moved to the bedside units. The top drawer was full of invoices, cigarette boxes, and old cigarette lighters. I pulled out the middle drawer. It was stacked with magazines, Motorbikes and Riders. I picked up the whole lot. My heart kicked into gear as a key, a single key on a circular ring, fell to the floor. The key opened the cashbox with ease, revealing some paper clips, rubber bands, two biros and plenty of dust. I was about to shut it when I spotted another key in the corner. This one was longer, but not on a ring. So now I had to find the box for this key.

I lay down on the floor, scanned the space under the wardrobe, and then sat on the bed to take a broader view of the room, up at the ceiling and down at the floor. On impulse I went to the corner of the room to the mini Ganesh temple, about two feet high, made of wood. It stood on a small table draped with a tablecloth. I lifted a corner of the tablecloth for closer inspection, found nothing useful. I looked at the statue of Lord Ganesh. A pang of guilt touched me, as if caught in an act of something immoral. I did a little bow and was about to walk away when I noticed the solid wooden platform under the statue had a little hole at the front. The platform was the same light pink colour as Lord Ganesh. On impulse I tried the key in the hole. It fitted perfectly. I gave it a pull. To my surprise a drawer slid out. What a cunning donkey you are Babu.

What treasure the drawer revealed, sir! It was beyond imagination. I had never seen so much money in one place. I was open-mouthed when Lal Bahadur had produced a single wad of notes. Now I was staring at nine such bundles, each about three inches thick, held together with rubber bands. Underneath was a large manila envelope. I picked it up and pulled out the contents. A navy blue passport with Ashoka stupa embossed on the cover fell out. I opened it. Babu's picture stared back at me with the name Babu Lal Bajrang. The donkey was forward planning to run away abroad if the police and politicians should become unhappy with him. I wondered where he would go. He could hardly speak English. The other item in the envelope was a 6 x 4 colour photograph. It was the bust of a lady with fair skin and pretty face, about forty years old. Her eyes were focussing squarely at the camera. I recognised the face instantly. On the reverse of the photograph was a handwritten note: *Babu with love*. It was signed, 'Sushmita'. Again, it astounded me. You want to know why sir? Because Sushmita was Lal Bahadur's wife. Clearly Babu and Sushmita had something going on. He must be using her to obtain his boss's secrets and at the same time happily dipping his penis. Two birds with one stone.

Therefore, you see sir, in the world of thieves and gangsters there is no such thing as loyalty. One takes from the other what one can get away with. The stronger buggers the weaker and so on. That is what Babu was doing to us.

I was still looking at Sushmita's photo when I heard the growl of Babu's motorbike outside. I grabbed a few bundles of notes, the photograph and shoved everything in my shirtfront. Then working rapidly, I replaced everything in their original positions. The engine coughed for the final time and went silent. I shoved the second key and the metal cash box where I had found them and ran out. As soon as I entered my room I heard the front door open noisily and then it slammed shut. I remembered suddenly the light in Babu's room was still on. Too late to do anything now. I stood staring at my door, waiting for it to burst open. Instead I heard him go to the bathroom. I dashed across the hallway to his room and slapped the switch to off position. Back in my room I dived into the bed, still fully clothed and covered myself with a sheet.

For three hours I lay very still listening to every sound, creak and knock. Boys chatting, opening and shutting of bathroom door, gurgle of flushed toilet, Babu's cough. Gokul yawning. Slowly the house fell silent. I waited another hour before getting up. Again I stood at the door and listened. Finally, I took off my shoes and walked bare feet to the back door. I opened the door cautiously and slipped out. At the bottom of the garden I put the shoes back on and climbed over the fence into the bushy path between two houses. I crossed over to the neighbour's back garden and into a shed littered with flowerpots, old tea chests. It stank of moist soil. I settled down on an old plastic chair and waited for the day to break. Never, before, had I spent a night out in the open. It felt so strange, every sound magnified tenfold. I could even hear scurry of small animals. Household activities in the neighbourhood, the rattle of pots and pans, someone washing dishes under a tap, a couple arguing, and laughter in another house. Throughout the night I kept a vigil on Babu's bedroom window in case the lights came on.

Finally, at dawn when the birds started chirping, I rose from the chair. I had to be out of Indira Nagar while Babu was still asleep.

Before leaving the hut, I did something very dangerous. I dropped one of my shirts on the floor and walked out with the rucksack on my back. As I waited to catch a bus to the railway station, I could not shake off the fear of apprehension before I boarded a train or the silly misgiving that trains to Kolkata were not running anymore.

Nine months later I killed Babu Lal Bajrang with a knife.

Now, Mr Modiji, I can visualise you holding your head in horror, thinking this Kalu fellow is a murderer. He should be in jail. May be that is where I belong. But I urge you to bear with me, read my story to the end before coming to a judgement.

I want to tell you of a conversation I overheard some days ago sitting at Ramlal's chai stall. A few servants from local households had assembled for an afternoon chat. They were discussing a murder that had taken place nearby. The older man with the moustache was saying to the younger two, '… this accountant sahib was a very demanding man. Always ordering his wife, give me this, give me that. Shout if the food was late on the table or the roti was not to his liking. He beat her if she was not ready on time to go out to a party or something.'

'Were you working in that house-hold?' one of the men asked.

'My misfortune,' he nodded, 'memsahib was very unhappy. What could she do? There were children involved. Once he came home late at night drunk as a *kala bhoot* and demanded from her this.' He made hand gestures, meaning oral sex.

Some of the men began tittering.

'*Arre bhai* this is no laughing matter,' he continued, 'she refused this time. The accountant sahib went mad. He began beating her. The children were so frightened they hid under a

117

bed. Memsahib was running from room to room to get away from him. Finally he cornered her in the kitchen. *Bhai* what to tell you - he was just pulling the hair, kicking, punching – *dham dham dham*. She was crying and begging him to stop. He was not listening. Then she did what we all would have done.'

Now there was complete silence in the chai cafe.

'What did she do?' someone asked in a muted voice.

'She picked up a kitchen knife and pushed it in his stomach.'

The burly chaiwalla dropped the huge kettle on the kerosene stove. 'Did they throw her in jail?' he asked.

'Should they have? You tell me.'

'Yes, most definitely.'

'No, no,' another man said in raised voice, 'think about it *bade bhai,* what could she have done. It was self-defence, no.'

'She could have gone to the police. Killing is *haram?*'

'*Arre baba* which worlds do you live in. You think police would have done anything to stop accountant sahib beating his *bibi.*'

'You are talking correct, *bilkul,*' another man agreed slapping his thigh.

After that an intense argument broke out. There were six men in the cafe excluding me. Three in favour of sending her to jail, the other three were in opposition.

CHAPTER 13

The train arrived at Howrah station four hours late. I stepped into the commotion of the platform, loudspeakers blaring arrivals and departures, competing with the blast and whistles of train engines, everybody on the go. What madness is this? I was being bustled out of the platform by the flow of the commuter traffic. Out in the taxi rank I stood around for a while and went back in having made up my mind to spend the night at the station. The huge waiting room was already full of commuters, bedded down for the night. I ate a meal of *idli, vaada* at the station café, the only one still open. Back in the waiting room I lay down on a clearing on the floor, the rucksack under my head as cushion. Around midnight a uniformed station employee came in and began kicking my legs.

'Sleeping not allowed. This is waiting room only,' he said brusquely.

'But these people are sleeping,' I said, looking around me.

'They have special permission,' he said and jingled some coins in his pocket.

'Alright, I won't sleep then. I will just sit.'

He jingled the coins again. 'The night is long, you sure you will be able to stay awake?'

An old woman lying beside me whispered, 'he won't leave you, better to pay.'

I handed a ten-rupee note. He pocketed the money and stretched his hand out again, rubbing his thumb and middle finger. I gave him another ten-rupee note.

'Alright you can sleep as long as you want,' he said, 'no one will trouble you.'

On the bus next morning I stood pressed against a newspaper-reading passenger and considered my mission. I was going to meet a man by the name of Asutesh at Noapara Metro station. Asutesh was a friend of Timecheck Patel who ran a small grocery stall in Main Road market, back in Bangalore, right by the coffee counter. Ask Patel anything and he will look at his watch before replying. Bhushan and Gokul had nicknamed him Timecheck Patel. I had mentioned to Patel I was going to Kolkata and needed to find cheap accommodation. 'You want accommodation? No problem.' He picked up a piece of paper and scribbled a telephone number on it. 'Call my friend Asutesh in Kolkata, he will help you.' As I was leaving, he gave me a peanut candy. 'This is from me. Come and see me when you are back in Bengaluru.'

What a nice man, sir. I hoped I would meet people like him in Kolkata too. Asutesh answered the phone on the third ring. 'Wait for me by the ticket office I'll be there in half an hour. What colour shirt are you wearing?' he asked.

'Blue shirt and beige trousers,' I replied and waited by the ticket counter, as close as possible, in case Asutesh should miss me. I stood my ground while people around me were jostling for every inch of space. Thirty minutes had elapsed. It felt like fifty. I was getting nervous. Is he coming? Why will he trouble himself for a complete stranger? However, I had no choice but to wait. Now and then, I patted my chest. The money I had managed to save and added to from Babu's cash box was in an inner pocket stitched to my vest.

A man with unkempt long hair, walking briskly, waved from a distance. 'You must be Kalu?' he said aloud. He was dressed simply, an old shirt and fading cotton trousers. About forty years old.

'Mr Patel told me a lot about you and that you will be able to help me,' I said.

'I'll try. I run a charity for the homeless. But I see you are not homeless, nor a charity case. You are looking for somewhere to live and pay rent. Am I correct?'

'Yes, I can pay rent, but I don't have much money.'

'Where do you want to live?'

'Anywhere so long it's cheap,' I replied.

'Ok, let me see,' he said and rocked his head thoughtfully from side to side as if weighing several options. Tapping his chest with two fingers he said, 'alright, listen to me, my wife's cousin-brother is looking for a tenant. He has a nice clean room and very reasonable rent. You go and see him now.'

He scribbled an address on the margin of a newspaper he was carrying. 'His name is Baldev. Tell him Asutesh sent you. Do you know how to get to Chitpur Road? No.' He gave me directions, repeating several times. 'You will be alright. Go now,' he said and gave me a gentle but firm push towards the bus stop.

I walked a few paces and looked back. He smiled and waved as if to say everything will be alright. I felt reassured and relieved he had not asked too many personal questions. Why have you come here? What work you do? Don't you have friends in Kolkata?

On Chitpur Road, I was expecting a nice big house, similar to one in Bangalore or the plush apartment block in Haridwar.

What I was looking at was a *halwai* sweet shop and restaurant at the rear, set in a building with two storeys above it. A bright neon sign straddled the entire width of the shop. It said *Baldev Quality Sweets.* Kids were playing outside, bouncing a ball against the windowpane, dozens of telephone wires crisscrossed the street above my head. Bengali music was blaring from a store. A short distance away flower sellers with their fragrant displays were hogging the pavement. A roadside barber was sharpening a cut throat razor blade. Someone emptied a bucket of water on the pavement and began sweeping with a broom. Odour of burning incense drifted out from a shop selling joss sticks, candles and little statues of Gods and Goddesses.

Inside *Baldev Quality Sweets,* a man behind a glass-fronted counter stacked with trays of sweets was scooping *bhajia* off hot oil. His expression of intense concentration, as if nothing else mattered at that moment other than the frying. Behind him was the seating area. A few tables and chairs arranged in a straight line. On the wall was a cheap poster of Goddess Kali, her ferocious red eyes set on the diners below. Another poster of Rabindranath Tagore adorned the opposite wall. I learned later, Rabindranath Tagore, the great poet, used to live on this street, only a few doors away.

The man looked up as I approached the counter.

'Is there a room to rent here?' I asked meekly, showing him the writing on the newspaper, fearing rebuke or laughed at. Do I look like a property agent or a halwai?

'Yes, Yes. Yes. I was expecting you,' he said to my relief and regarded me from head to toe. I held my breath, fearing he would smell the anxiety that was in my chest. 'Can you afford two thousand rupees a month?' he asked with narrowed eyes.

I nodded yes, though inside my heart sank at having to hand over so much money every month.

He took me to a doorway curtained with thin strips of colourful plastic. 'We make our *mithai* here,' he said ushering me. As soon as I entered, I felt the heat and thick odour of sugar syrup. Gas stoves and huge vats stood against a wall covered in thick soot, splattered milk had congealed into brown jelly. Hessian bags of flours and spices lay on the floor. Two women in dirty saris bent over a large cauldron, stirring milk with long wooden ladles. I saw a tray of syrupy *rosgollas* and my stomach started rumbling, reminding me I had not eaten all day.

'Come, come,' he said crooking his finger. We entered a long, narrow passageway and then stairs going up, wide enough for two abreast. Dark, damp and musty, the walls were dirt stained at shoulder height. Two paces ahead of me, I could see he was a thickset man, but surprisingly agile on his feet. He was wearing shoes covered in grease and the heels had worn at an angle. In the landing, a solitary light bulb dangled from the ceiling. From a jangling bunch of keys attached to his belt, he unlocked the first of two doors. Once inside he went straight to the window and flung it open. The curtain caught the drift of the wind. Turning around on his heels, he swept his hand in a wide circle as if showing me his merchandise. 'Do you like?'

No bigger than the inside of a municipal bus, I walked a few paces left and right to show I was appraising the wares, although my mind was already made up. What options did I have? As for the furniture, it was enough. A bed, an old ward-robe with its doors attached to the frame with odd sized bolts, and a small table pushed against the wall. A small balcony at the back converted into a kitchenette. It had a sink with a water tap and cabinet for pots and pans.

'Make up your mind quickly, there are others waiting,' he said.

After a little more show of fake deliberation, I dropped the rucksack on the floor.

'You will take it then,' he said relieved.

'Yes.'

'Good. So, the rules,' he locked his eyes on mine, 'you pay the rent dot on the first of the month, every month. No fooling around with me. Do you understand?'

I nodded.

Wagging a gloved forefinger in my face, he said sternly, 'you bring no girls to the room. You make no noise. You damage no furniture. Is that also understood?'

I nodded again.

He pulled the greasy latex glove off his right hand, the rubber twanging noisily. The fingers he exposed were stout and rough, a network of fissures covered the leathery skin. He put his palm out at me as if I was a fortune-teller. 'One month's advance rent.'

I took out a bundle of notes from my pocket. As I was counting the money, I noticed his eyes were glued to the notes too and his lips were moving silently as he counted.

'What's your name?' he asked, folding the bank notes, slid them in his shirt pocket and gave the pocket a hefty pat.

'Kalu.'

'What caste are you?'

'That I don't know,' I lied; though I knew by then I was from the lowest of low, *chamar* caste.

'You don't know? What does your father do?'

'He died before I was born.'

'And your mother.'

'She too.'

He laughed. 'How could she have died before you were born?'

'I mean I don't know her,' I said and instantly regretted saying it, fearing he would not give me the room.

'Alright, I don't care about your caste as long as you behave yourself.'

'Most definitely sir, I don't smoke and drink. No bad habits.'

'OK, we talk later,' he said and left.

Alone at last, I inspected the room again, looked in the wardrobe, peered out of the window and then lay down on the bed to size it for comfort. Staring at a spot in the ceiling, I returned to the house in Bangalore. By now, a battle must be raging there, Bhushan and Gokul cowering in fear, denying any knowledge of where I had gone or why I had run away. I felt sorry for the boys and my heart began to burn with guilt. Will I ever see them again? Only God knows. I realised then no one in the world I had left behind knew where I was. No one in the new world of Kolkata knew who I was.

I learned soon enough my landlord, *halwai* Baldev, was a man of many words. His motto: if it can be said in ten why say it in two words. Benson and Hedges was his favourite cigarette brand. He could blow perfect smoke rings. His father, a deeply religious man from Bihar, knew what God knew and told everybody what it was. But I don't have much time for God, Baldev would say to anyone who cared to listen, though I have respect for him. If am in trouble, naturally I will call him, as with lawyers. But as with lawyers, it would have to be bad trouble. Otherwise, it is best not to get too mixed up with him. Certainly, I don't want him in my sweets shop as I have enough on my hands as it is.

He told me the only thing he missed of back home was the *jhijia* dance and the fun of *dal chohhth* festival.

'Why did you come to Kolkata?' I asked.

'Why you think *re*, why?' he threw the question back at me.

I thought, maybe like me he was running away from some serious trouble.

'I came to look for work. Back home I had ten mouths to feed. But job? No. Nobody wanted a *halwai* in my village. People said I should go to Kolkata. There the streets are paved in gold. I took it literally. On day one I was walking down Chowrangee with a friend. My friend saw a five rupee note lying on the pavement. Quick, quick pick it up, he said. I thought, aha its true then, there is gold in the streets of Kolkata. I said to my friend I am too tired today *yaar*, we will start collecting money from tomorrow.' He laughed at his own joke. It was an infectious laugh. People stopped to listen when he laughed like that.

He liked to tell tales of his childhood. Whenever he repeated a story, he added a new dimension to it. The story of super fit chicken, they reared in the yard, best in whole of Bihar. There was one that laid two eggs every night, he said. When he retold the story the eggs had become giant sized and then the quantity had increased from two to three and so on. I discovered he liked to make up stories at the spur of the moment. He had said he was an atheist. It was so untrue for I had seen him going to the temple early in the mornings.

In my room the rear window offered a view of a block of flats, a dreary building with long uncovered balconies on each floor.

The balconies were common walkways for the little apartments. Children were often seen playing there, adults relaxing after sunset. One afternoon I looked out the window. A bearded man was sitting on a plastic chair on the second floor balcony, a cigarette in his left hand and a bottle of beer in the other. The vest rolled up to the chest, allowing the belly to spill out. As if he had all the time in the world, he took a puff, exhaled deeply, waited a few moments and then took a slug from the bottle. Puff, exhale, slug – puff, exhale, slug. When the bottle was empty, he tossed it casually over the banister. He was always there, smoking and drinking, as if he had no care in the world. Who was he? Why did he have so much time on his hand? Why was he always alone? I was so curious.

CHAPTER 14

Modiji, my Sanyo voice recorder did not start this morning. I had to hammer it several times to wake it up. Hope it lasts to the end of my story. In Japan, they would have thrown it away by now. But, we Indians don't discard anything easily; we know how to recycle. Don't we sir? Take for example the space mission, Mangalyaan to the Mars. It cost us less than a quarter of what the Americans had spent on a similar mission. I have a theory how we managed such a feat. We purchased all the discarded junk from Americans and Russians after their space missions were over and used them to build Mangalyaan.

Hah, that was a joke sir.

Let me tell you about my money problems since moving to Kolkata. The cash I had brought with me from Bangalore was running out fast, much of it going to Baldev. My earnings were nothing to boast of. The fact is sir, the training I had received from Lal Bahadur and Munna involved operating in teams of two, three or more. We had a well-rehearsed system of distraction, pick, pass. Working solo in a strange city, among people whose language I did not understand was proving very difficult.

I had started in central Kolkata, believing that is where the big money was. However, big money was deluding me. Frustrated I thought of trying my luck elsewhere. I picked Kalighat, south of the city, best known for the Kali temple and pilgrims from all over the country. It was also the most crowded place I had seen anywhere in Kolkata.

I arrived at Kalighat metro station early one morning, determined not to leave empty pocket. I did a stretch of the platforms and concourse to assess the condition and calibre of punters. Station walls were pasted with posters marketing designer jeans, wedding suits, exotic holidays, none of which I could afford. The station entrance was teaming with people. Bare chested little boys, skinny old men and women bent double, stood with outstretched hands, begging. People were streaming out from under the archway of the platform as if disgorged from the mouth of a giant dragon. On both sides of the station were little shops, pavement stalls, carts on wheels, selling everything from fruits and vegetables, mobile phone accessories, garlands of marigold and jasmine, freshly garnished *murki,* iced drinks, newspapers and magazines.

All this apparent madness and mayhem suited me fine. It was not long before I spotted a punter at the second-hand bookstall. Bent forward, he was going through some publications on a lower shelf. In clear view was a bulge in his hip pocket, thin strip of black leather visible just above the opening. It was a perfect setup for a quick dip. I wiped my hand on a handkerchief, strolled over to the bookstand and pretended to read a magazine cover. Little by little, I slid behind him, waited a few moments and then did with my fingers, in slow movements, what I had done hundreds of times before. The only difference, this time I didn't have the backing of a partner. Babu had warned me, never work under pressure. It can get to you. Force you to make errors, like dipping too early or too late or breathing incorrectly at the crucial moment. But on that day I didn't have a choice.

As I turned to leave, a yell hit the back of my head, paralysing me briefly. 'Oye, give it back. He has stolen my wallet. Stop him, stop him, thief.'

I looked back. The face I saw was of an old man, eyes wide-open, loose skin wrinkled in distress. He was pointing a finger at me.

I took off running. Shouts of 'stop, stop' rang out behind me followed by sound of dozens of running feet. I looked back a second time. Amazing how many people were giving chase, as if the entire population of Kalighat was after me. In Bangalore, this would never happen. People there are so polite, always willing to give you the benefit of doubt. Even when caught, a thief was rarely beaten, but simply handed over to the police. I was told in Kolkata one could be lynched on a mere accusation or suspicion of theft. I put in dummy swerves around pavement stalls, parked cars and rickshaws. When I looked back again, I noticed the number of people chasing me had reduced, but those that remained appeared determined, yelling 'thief, thief, thief'. After a while, the shouts fizzled out completely. Have they grown tired of the chase or are they trying to outflank me from a different route? I kept on running.

At the crossroad, I turned right and dashed into a *bania* grocery store. The shopkeeper at the counter, a balding man with a pencil thin moustache did not raise his head from the newspaper he was reading. I went to the rear of the store, surrounded by drums of cooking oil and sacks of lentils, air pregnant with potent spices. I took deep breaths to calm my nerves, noticed my fingers were still shaking horribly. Last time I had a shake so bad was back in Haridwar. I had selected a lady with an expensive handbag. As I approached her, pushing my way through the crowd, studying her profile from the side, my heart began pounding. She was a beautiful longhaired woman, about forty years of age. The pounding in my heart turned into a riot. I had an uncontrollable urge to grab her hands. Mama, mama - don't you recognise me. For reasons I could not explain, I was convinced she was my mother, a mother I had never met. My heart a beggar – please, please, look at me Mama. She did not stop, walked past me as if I did not exist.

I waited a few minutes and then went to the counter to buy a peanut candy.

'Is everything alright?' The shopkeeper looked me in the eyes and smiled. His pencil thin moustache turned u-shaped. My heart jolted. Does he know?

At Jatin Das Park metro station I caught a train to Mahatma Gandhi Road. Not until the doors slid shut and the train started moving, that I felt the danger was receding. I flopped on a seat at the rear and began replaying the whole episode of the last hour, the botched-up *dip*, the distress on the old man's face, and the run for my life. I could not get it out of my head. The lasting impression was the horror on the old man's face, his pleading eyes. Why did I pick on an old man? I began feeling guilty. Remorse and disgust grew in my heart like a dark seed sprouting.

Back home, I crept into my room, turned on the ceiling fan to maximum, pulled the wallet out and held it to my face. It was old and well worn, made of black leather. A logo embossed on the bottom right hand corner was no longer legible. There was something about its distorted shape; it let you know it had been to places. I unfolded it slowly, savouring the mystery and suspense, wondering what treasures it would reveal.

It had three long compartments for paper money; several

smaller slots tiered along the left for plastic cards and a coin pouch on the right. I peeled open the compartments one at a time. The first one was empty. Second compartment was empty too. The third had a solitary sheet of paper folded to fit the shape of the wallet. A few coins rattled in the pouch. I peeled the folds again, almost tearing it apart, hoping to uncover some inner recesses. There was no money or credit cards. I flung the wallet at the wicker basket dustbin outside the bathroom door. It hit the wall and came to rest by my feet. Dislodged wall plaster fell to the floor. The old man's alarmed face reappeared. This time I wanted to punch it, teach it a lesson. What kind of man walks around the streets with empty wallets?

I went to the balcony and looked out. A gang of boys were playing cricket with a tennis ball and plank of wood shaped into a bat. A cow sat under the shade of a tree on a bed of its own excrement. Two men on bicycles sped past, narrowly missing the wicket. The boys hurled abuse at them. Come back this way and we will make *keema* out of you.

Curious about the piece of folded paper I picked up the wallet and pulled it out. As I unfolded it I noticed it had turned dusty brown with age, disintegrating at the folds. It was a handwritten letter. The writing swung from left to right haphazardly with heavily embellished capitals. The date on top right hand corner was 4th January 1978. That will be over forty years, more than twice my age. Why would anyone hold on to a letter so long? I cleared the table, flattened the paper on the surface and read it several times until I had absorbed it all. It was a love letter, addressed to a Raju and at the bottom was the name Saira.

This, I have to tell you sir, up until then I had had no

exposure to matters of romantic affairs, no understanding of affected breakups, heartaches and unwanted pregnancies, but I was moved immensely by what I read. I felt very unclean, like a voyeur peeping into someone else's intimate affairs.

That night I lay on the bed in silence, but not in peace. The old man's face kept reappearing. I was so curious. What did he do for a living? Why was he carrying the letter in the wallet? It must have been there for almost forty years. Now he is probably pining for the disintegrating piece of paper.

Who is Saira? Is she dead or alive?

It was impossible to set aside the thoughts of Saira, Raju and the letter, even though I tried very hard. I told myself, Kalu this has nothing to do with you, forget about it and move on, look after number one first. I am not lying to you, sir, I tried and tried, but it was not any good. I kept picking up the letter and reading all over again.

It was the month of July. As you know, Kolkata bakes at this time of the year. Unlike Haridwar or Bangalore, here you sweat all the time, even when sitting under a fan. The rich have their air-conditioners and coolers; the poor have three blade fans, which spin only when electricity is available. No standby generators for us. I had been in the city only a few weeks, still struggling to make a living.

I was in my room getting ready to leave when I heard a knock on the door. Who could it be? I did not know anyone in Kolkata, except Baldev and his wife, Pratibha. They were busy with customers downstairs. I thought of Babu and felt a jolt in the stomach. How did he find me here? I dashed to the kitchen and picked up a knife. Back at the door, I opened it a few inches. A young man I had never seen before was standing pressed against the wall in the dark corridor. About twenty five-years old, wearing a black shirt, jeans and very scruffy trainers, long hair tied at the back with a rubber band, a shiny black guitar in his arms.

He smiled and said, 'I'm your neighbour,' and then gestured with his head at the other door in the corridor. 'What's your name?'

'Kalu.'

'I am Roby. Just on my way out ... to give blood,' he said nodding, but seemed in no hurry to go.

I invited him in, relieved he was not a threat.

'I will come in for one minute,' he said. Once in my room he swung around on his heels, did a three hundred and sixty degrees turn, taking in the layout, sat down on my bed and placed the guitar on his lap, as if to play a tune. 'Are you happy here?'

'Yes,' I replied and then remembered Baldev's stern warnings about not making noise or bringing guests to the room. 'But what all is allowed here?' I asked.

Roby seemed amused by the question. 'Smoking, drinking, dancing, music, sexy business - no problem here,' he said with a brisk shake of the hand and then added gravely, 'but dying is not allowed. Baldev doesn't like people dying here.'

I felt terrified. Death! Blood! What kind of place is this?

Roby laughed. 'Hey, hey, it's alright. Khokan babu lived in this room before you. Three months ago, he went away, just like that,' he said pointing solemnly at the ceiling, 'Bihari went mad. Not pleased at all.'

I was horrified, visualising a corpse lying on the bed with its head on my pillow.

'Don't worry little brother; you are not jumping into a dead man's bed. Khokan babu died in hospital. Heart attack.' He ran his fingers across the guitar strings, creating a riot of metallic twangs.

'I hate capitalist bastards,' Roby said, scanning the front page of a newspaper I had purchased yesterday.

'I also don't like them,' I shot back just to agree with him while making tea.

'Poor people in this country work their guts out for a few *paisas,* while the rich sit in big, big houses with their fat wives, their fat bank accounts and their fat children going to fat fee paying schools. It is outrageous. We are not going to take it lying down. We will crush them.' He punched the newspaper as if it indeed was the face of a capitalist.

I placed the teacups on the table. My head was buzzing now, reminding me of Munna back home and the bloody fight he had with his stepfather. 'You said you were going to give blood – yes?' I asked.

'Yes, I did.'

'What did you mean?'

'Oh, that,' Roby said, 'once a month I go to the hospital to donate some of my blood. It goes to the blood bank.'

'What do they do with it?'

'Well they use it in emergency. It is for comrades who may have fallen very ill or had accident or something and need emergency blood transfusion. It's not for fat capitalists who can afford to pay. What blood group are you? I am O positive.'

'I don't know.'

Phew! I was relieved there was no fighting or bloodletting involved.

I was impressed by Roby's eagerness to help the poor and by his bravery, assuming giving blood required courage. A good man, anyone would say. But was he one of us? I had learned a long time ago not to accept anything at face value. Later when I questioned him more, I discovered Roby was not one of us in the strict sense. He was from a family of capitalists - capitalists he had said he despised so much. It is just that he was an idealist and a rebel. He had quarrelled with his father who wanted him to join the family business. 'My passion is music. Father wanted me to be businessman like him. When I refused, he said flatly no *band-walla* would live in his house. So, I left.'

Next day, in the *maidan*, across Victoria Memorial, I came across a Manipuri dance troupe giving a free performance. An audience of several hundred tourists and office workers were watching and relaxing on the green. I mingled with the crowd and managed two *dips*, both from American tourists, netting more than two thousand rupees and a few dollars. The feeling of elation that came with it somehow got associated with Roby. I felt meeting Roby was a good omen and from that day on developed a fondness for my long-haired neighbour.

CHAPTER 15

Now I must tell you about my friend Sanju. Exactly three weeks after I met Roby, I was downstairs with a drink of sweet *lassi,* watching a Bollywood movie on television. The restaurant was full to capacity with rickshaw pullers and taxi drivers, smoking cheap cigarettes and reeking of sweat and poverty, enjoying a simple meal of dal-roti or fish stew and rice. The rickshaws and taxis were standing in a row on the pavement. The neighbourhood dogs were looking in expectantly, a safe distance from the reach of Baldev's long *lathi,* stick. They sat waiting for someone to throw out a piece of half-eaten roti or meat bone. I was sucking the dreg of the *lassi* with a straw, determined to get my money's worth. Yes, I had to pay for everything, even for a glass of water if chilled with ice cubes. That is how tight fisted Baldev was.

'*Re*, I came to Kolkata without a single paisa. Who gave me anything for nothing? No one. I had to sweat for every rupee and paisa,' he would say aloud to anyone who cared to listen, especially if the person looked as if he might ask for credit.

The movie progressed to a scene of action-packed fight between the hero, Amithabh Bacchan, and a bald-headed villain. A man two tables away jumped up yelling, '*khatam kar do saale ko*. Finish off the bastards.' More shouts followed, everybody rooting for the good person.

In the midst of the mayhem, I saw a boy entering the shop. Skinny and tall, dressed simply in clean clothes, a brown suitcase in his hand. He scanned the shop nervously, the gaze travelling from the rowdy diners at the back to the counter where Baldev was sitting cross-legged on a chair, three fountain pens tucked in his white kurta chest pocket. Baldev saw the boy and called him over. I could not hear what they were discussing but Baldev was rocking his head energetically with excessive hand gestures, the boy inert and expressionless, only his mouth moving. Shortly Baldev got up and led the boy to the side door.

Next day Baldev said, his eyebrows jumping in excitement, a hand caressing the fountain pen tops, 'my establishment is moving up in class.'

'What do you mean?'

'The new tenant is no lowly domestic or road building labourer. He is a student at Presidency College. He is renting a room for three months until he finds somewhere permanent.'

'What shame,' I said, 'in three months your establishment will come down again to where it belongs.'

'Get lost *re*. You keep away from him. I don't want him getting any wrong impressions.'

I did not have to keep away from him for it seemed he was keeping away from us. He left the room early each morning and returned late in the evening.

Then one day I bumped into him on the stairs. 'Do you live here?' he asked. His accent was of a village boy. It threw me into confusion, for I had assumed he was a city fellow from a middle class family.

'Yes, first room, first floor.'

'*Bhai*, do you know where is Dhakuria lake?' he asked.

I wanted to laugh. Who in Kolkata does not know Dhakuria

Lake? I told him it was a well-known landmark. Any taxi driver will take you there.

'How to get there by bus?' he asked.

I was surprised, only the poor travel by buses in Kolkata. 'Sahib, for you it will be difficult. You better take a taxi or Metro.'

Next time we met, he told me the lake was beautiful. 'There is nothing like it in Bangalore.'

'You are from Bangalore? I have lived there too. Indira Nagar,' I said.

'Me too, Indira Nagar,' he said. He seemed thrilled to meet someone from the city. 'But my real home is in Maharashtra. I had to leave home when my father died.'

At the age of twelve Sanju had gone to Bangalore and worked as a servant boy for a rich lady. The rest you already know about him, sir.

'Madam sends me money every month. It's only enough to pay my college fee and the rent. Nothing left after that,' he was complaining. We were sitting in his room surrounded by textbooks and note pads. A small laptop computer was sitting on the table. He said he had bought it second hand. It was an essential tool for the coursework.

We chatted for a long time. I liked him and he appeared happy with my company. Slowly, over the days I told him everything about myself, about the orphanage, about Lal Bahardur, Om Prakash, and Harshna, and about Babu in Bangalore. He was shocked at first and then he said he understood my problems. I made him promise not to tell anyone.

Believe me, sir; to this day, he has not betrayed me. I trust him as a brother.

I liked Roby too, but with him, my relationship was slightly different. We laughed and joked often, but at superficial level. I never let him see inside me.

'Yo, man you want to go to Pine Tree?' Roby had asked once. We were in the market sharing a bag of *bhujia* sprinkled with pepper and lime.

'What's Pine Tree?' I asked.

'It's a night club you fool, on Camac Street. I can get you in free.'

'Free … let's go. I will take anything going free.'

Two days later, we were at the club. What a shock it was sir, for I had no idea I would be leaving my world of beggars, thieves and village idiots behind and stepping into the sphere of the rich and sophisticated, young and trendy, employees of international banks and high-tech companies.

The security staff at the gate welcomed us with salutes. The concierge whisked us through, no need to sign the guest book sir. In the central hall, a rotating crystal ball was scattering light like mini fireworks. Glass and glitter, like a Bollywood film set. The DJ was hammering music so loud it felt like the floor was vibrating. Roby and his band had a nightly spot. He described his music as Indo-jazz fusion. A strange kind of composition, no pizzazz or glamour, I thought. However, when he performed on stage I shook my head, tapped the floor with my foot and cheered enthusiastically. I did not want anyone to know I was an unsophisticated country mouse.

You should have seen the applause Roby and his drummer and saxophonist were receiving. They had a two-hour slot with thirty minutes break in-between. When he came offstage at the break time, there was a girl by his side.

'This is Tanya,' Roby said to me, 'she loves our music.'

Tanya smiled at me and my heart began thumping. She was a stunning beauty sir, in blue *churidar* designer dress, wrists wrapped in silver bangles, necklace with a blue stone. Maybe I am exaggerating a bit sir. The thing is she was my dream girl.

'What instrument do you play?' she asked me.

'Ah, I don't play anything, I am here to listen,' I said. How I wished I were a musician like Roby.

'Me too,' she said, 'I love jazz.'

Roby left me with Tanya, saying he had to ready his guitar for the next session. I began panicking, as I did not know what to say to her.

After a long silence, I picked up courage and asked if she would like a drink.

'Yes, yes, why not,' she said.

We took a table with a rose in flute vase, a blue spotlight above our head.

'What would you like?' I asked.

'Lemonade with ice for me,' she said.

I ordered a glass of lemonade and a coke for myself.

'You don't like alcohol?' I asked.

'No.'

I liked the demure determination with which she said no.

'Why not?'

She thought for a moment and said, 'I have seen what it does to people. My father was an alcoholic. He tore the family apart by his drinking. But he is no more.'

'Your mother is alright?'

'She went three years ago.'

'Oh, sorry. You must miss them.'

'Of course, I miss them both. He was such a jolly man when sober.'

'In a way you were lucky,' I said, 'you had ma and papa.'

'Don't you?'

'No, I have never had a family.' Unable to meet her gaze, I looked into the glass of coke, at the tiny bubbles rising to the surface, disintegrating with silent plops.

She went quiet too. All around us people were chatting and laughing. How I wished I could be like them; tell jokes so she would not stop laughing. I just did not know how.

She must have sensed my discomfort. 'Kalu, relax it's alright,' she said and leaned towards me over the table. I caught a whiff of her sweet perfume again.

'I am fine,' I said, 'what do you do during the day?'

'I work. I am a secretary in a bank.'

'What does a secretary do?'

'I guard my boss's dirty secrets. That's why we are called secret-*ary*.'

She asked where I lived. 'In the same building as Roby,' I replied.

'Oh, do you?' she said impressed. I guessed she did not know what kind of a dump place Roby lived in.

In the main hall, the crowd burst into applause. Roby and his band had walked onto the stage. All three bowed in acknowledgement and began their first number. We turned our chairs to the stage to watch the performance.

Around ten o'clock Tanya announced she had to be home soon. 'My grandmother is not well and refuses to sleep until I am home.'

'How are you getting home?' I asked.

'I will take a taxi, Kalu,' she said.

'Aren't your friends going with you?'

'They will not leave so early,' she said.

'Shall I come with you to see you get home safe,' I said, expecting a polite refusal. After all she hardly knew me. But she took me by surprise when she said, 'ah, will you, Kalu? I live in Salt Lake. Is that far from where you live?'

'Not very far,' I said without elaborating. How could I say I live in Chitpur, a neighbourhood of hand potters, artisan perfumers and tunic makers, weavers of wigs, flower sellers and hotels that rent out rooms by the hour?

The door attendant hailed a taxi for us and held the door open.

'Good we got a taxi so quickly,' she said relaxing beside me.

'Yes, that was lucky,' I said, and again I caught a whiff of her sweet smelling perfume and the warmth of her presence. I wanted to snuggle in closer and place an arm around her shoulders. But I dare not.

As the taxi slipped into the flow of traffic I felt instantly elevated to a higher social status, as if I no longer belonged to the wretched people waiting at bus stops or trudging home on foot, bent double as if carrying a weight on their shoulders.

At the top end of Camac Street we turned left heading for Chowrangee the main thoroughfare linking north Kolkata with the south. Further, along we saw a drunken fool under a lamppost, singing a Bengali romantic song to a non-existent audience. His voice rising and falling as if in pain, a jilted lover threatening suicide, come back my darling, come back to me.

'He reminds me of my dad,' Tanya said laughing, 'when he was drunk, he used to sing just like that and insist we listen to him.'

'Interesting character,' I said, 'what kind of work did he do?'

'A sailor, he used to go away for weeks or months and tell us fascinating stories of his travels. One time he told me a story of a night spent lost in Zanzibar city.'

'Lost in Zanzibar, very interesting,' I said.

'You want to hear it?'

'Yes, I do.'

'No, you may not like it. It's too long.'

'But I want to hear it.'

'Alright then,' she said and began relating her father's story with such conviction as if she herself had experienced it. The ship had docked in Zanzibar after six weeks on sea. A group of sailors had gone into the town to eat, drink, and enjoy themselves. At some stage during the night, her father split from the crowd found himself wondering lost in some back alleys. He decided to look for somewhere to sleep for the night. After a long search, he found a guesthouse and knocked on the door, half expecting not be answered. However, a woman did come out, a Muslim, looking haggard and starved. She led him inside the house, to a room at the back. Tired after the long day he lay down on the bed and fell asleep in no time. At some stage during the night he woke up feeling someone had settled down beside him. He switched on the lamp, to see what was going on and immediately noticed a dip on the mattress beside him, as if someone invisible was lying there. Terrified he jumped off the bed and ran to the door. He could not get out for she had locked the door from outside. The lady came down demanding to know why he was making so much noise. Someone is in the room, he said, I don't want to stay here. She refused to let him leave. You are hungry, you are hungry, she kept repeating. It was true. He was feeling hungry although he had eaten only a few hours earlier. He said that had nothing to do with it. She insisted he was hallucinating. It happens when one is hungry; she brought him a piece of Arab bread and goat cheese. He ate the bread and went back to sleep.

An hour later, the bed shook again. This time he heard a noise, someone sighing as if in pain. He jumped out of the bed and began banging on the door again. But this time the lady did not come. After ten minutes of banging and shouting, he gave up and decided to stay awake for the rest of the night with all the lights turned on. As soon as the day broke, he got up to leave. To his amazement, the door opened without an effort. He ran from the room and as he reached the main part of the house, he had to slow down because there were gaping holes in the floor and then he noticed there were no windows, half the roof was missing, rubble and spider webs everywhere. The house appeared unlived in, completely deserted. There was no sign of the Muslim lady.

Back on the ship, he could not wait to tell his mates. They laughed at him. Ha, ha it must be the rum. But he was convinced what he had experienced was real, it wasn't hallucination.

Later he spoke to another sailor who was a native of Zanzibar. This man gasped in surprise and touched her father all over the body as if making sure he was real. Then he said gravely, I do not know how you came out alive my friend. The house definitely exists. It belonged to a rich Arab couple. For some reason the woman had locked her husband in the basement and starved him to death. Some years later, she died too. Since then the house has been empty, many people have gone in there to lay claim to it but no one has come out alive.

Tanya took my arm and pulled me closer. 'My dad swore by it. He said only he knew what he had experienced that night and it was all true. No one could convince him otherwise.'

I felt goose bumps all over. 'It's not real, is it?' I said.

'I trusted my father,' she said.

Finally, the taxi stopped in front of her house in an ordinary middle-class street. It was not a lavish neighbourhood I was expecting. Her apartment was on the ground floor of a two-storey building, the entrance shared with a traditional laundry and dry-cleaning business. Two men in white kurtas were exchanging pleasantries and shaking hands.

'Kalu you are a gem. Thank you for seeing me home,' she said and opened her handbag to share the cost of the taxi ride. I stopped her instantly, 'don't worry I will take care of it.'

'I will be at the club on Friday,' she said, gave me that smile again, making me weak at the knees and then she opened the door and climbed out of the taxi. I watched her cross the road, past the men in kurtas, into the brightly lit porch where she turned right and disappeared from view.

The driver whipped around on his seat. 'Who is going to pay me?' he said sharply.

'I will pay. First take me to Chitpur Road,' I said.

'You have money?' he asked, 'it is night-time, I charge double.'

'I will pay according to the meter. Now move,' I said.

He started driving. I sensed he was watching me, suspicious that I might jump out without paying. I realised, though I was wearing my best clothes and acting like a rich kid, this fellow had seen through me. He knew who I really was.

'Who was that girl,' he asked suddenly, eyeing me through

the mirror, 'what classy lady.'

I ignored him, annoyed at his impertinence.

'You have done well, little brother. What is the secret, tell us also,' he said in a friendly manner as if I was one of his types.

'Just drive and be quiet,' I said abruptly.

'Don't get angry little brother. I was just asking.' He coughed loudly, rolled down the window and spat. 'So where are you from brother?'

'Uttarakhand.'

'Cigarette,' he said, took out a packet from his shirt pocket and offered it to me above his shoulder while steering with one hand.

'I don't want it,' I said.

'Take, take,' he said, 'I have matches here.'

'I don't smoke.'

'So, tell me brother, girls in Uttarakhand won't be seen out this late at night, will they? Unless they are … you understand me?'

'No, I don't understand you.'

He cackled a mixture of laugh and cough. 'You are not that naïve little brother. You have been giving it to her – haven't you – *hanh*.' He did a rude hand gesture.

'*Bakwas bandh karo*, stop this nonsense,' I said.

He kept on smirking and shaking his head, which annoyed me even more. As he slowed approaching a traffic light I opened the door and jumped out.

'Mother-fucker, come back,' he yelled looking over his shoulder, helplessly, for he could not stop in the middle of a junction with cars approaching from all directions.

That will teach you a lesson, you son of a pig. I ran and

turned into a side street. Up front was an indoor market. I dashed in. It was shutting down for the night. Shops had their produce covered with hessian sheets while the traders were preparing to leave. Some were bedding down for the night in the narrow aisles. Stepping over them, I made my way to the back exit and came out into a very narrow unlit lane. This was where the market traders dumped their perishing fruit, vegetables, unwanted packaging. An overwhelming stench of decay hung in the night air as I picked my way carefully, past a cow chewing corn husk and scavenging dogs. One bared its teeth and growled, taking me for a competitor.

Now I hear you say, Kalu that was a dastardly thing to do, not pay for the taxi ride. Not at all sir. You see I taught him a lesson. He should behave properly with his customers. In any case, it was a matter of four hundred rupees or five at the max considering it was late. He would probably have blown that money on prostitutes and caught disease in return. Don't you think I did him a favour?

I left the alleyway and turned into a main road. I was still a mile and half from home. From Central Avenue I entered Zakaria Street. This would lead me onto Rabindra Sarai, the home stretch. Here and there, under shop awnings or house porches I could see huddled bodies, asleep, covered from head to toe in thin sheets. They were the migrants from villages, hoping to make it big in the city one day, God willing. For now, they must share the streets with dogs and holy cows. I walked past windows with metals bars. The lights were still on in some of the houses. A dog barked in the distance, another took up the call. I kept a steady pace thinking of Tanya, wondering what she must be doing right now, perhaps putting her grandmother to bed. I had just passed a shuttered car repair workshop when I saw a man in a clearing on the pavement, squatting on the flats of his feet, arms folded across the knees and his head sunk into the shoulders, an emaciated figure, no flesh under the dark olive skin. A dirty sweat stained shirt on his back. He was very still. A rat, inches from his feet, sniffing around for food. A cycle rickshaw stood nearby.

I called out, 'oye, bhaiya.' The rat dashed into the gutter. But the man did not respond. Again, I called, 'bhaiya, are you alright.' He did not move. Clearly, he was very ill and could not be left there alone. I saw a pharmacy nearby and knocked on its door, rattling hard to wake up whoever lived in the apartment above. A bare chested man in thin *lungi* came out flapping the *chappals* on his feet.

'You can't see the pharmacy is closed?' he said angrily.

I pointed at the squatting figure on the pavement. 'I think he is very ill.'

'So what can I do? Take him to hospital.'

He saw the helpless expression on my face, rolled his eyes and walked around the squatting figure, observing him from all sides. Finally, he stooped down and took the man's wrist in his hand to check the pulse.

'Dead,' he said moments later, 'do you know him?'

'No. I was just passing and saw him sitting there.'

'He is probably from the Bankur basti,' he said dismissively.

'We can't leave him here,' I said.

Lights came on in some of the windows. A man leaned over a first floor balcony. 'I have already called the police,' he yelled, 'two hours the wretched fellow has been sitting like this, hasn't moved an inch.'

More people came out, crowding around the unmoving rickshaw puller, arguing if he was from Bankur or Barrabazar. 'All day long these fellows are here with their rickshaws, congesting our street.'

'Shouldn't be allowed unless they have permit.'

There was laughter. 'Brother, what are you saying? Just give 100 rupees to the policeman. That's your permit.'

'If I have my way, I will ban them all.'

'Yes, they are a nuisance.'

What a bloody state of affair sir. A poor man, probably from a village in Bihar, was lying dead on the pavement, while these people were arguing, whether or not, he had permit to enter their neighbourhood. What's more pathetic, when the yellow Tata Indica of Kolkata police arrived on the scene, these upright citizens scuttled back to their homes as sharply as the rat had dived into the gutter. Once again, I found myself alone with the dead rickshaw puller. Two policemen in tight fitting white uniform lumbered towards me as if annoyed at being disturbed so late in the night.

'You are Roy Chowdhury?' one said sternly, 'you telephoned?'

'No, I am Kalu.'

'Is he your father?' he asked pointing a baton at the rickshaw puller.

'No, I have no connection with him,' I replied.

'Then what are you doing here? Tell me,' he said sternly.

'I was only passing this way and saw him sitting like this. I think he may be dead,' I said.

'Dead?' the taller one with thick black moustache scowled in disbelief, 'this is a serious business. Are you sure?'

'I think so.'

'Let me see.' He prodded the rickshaw puller's chest with the baton, first tentatively, then harder. The poor fellow toppled over, legs still folded and arms over the knees, as if determined not to give up that pose even in death.

'*Orre baba,* you are correct,' Moustache said looking impressed, 'you want to join Kolkata police. We will make you a detective, Detective Sherlock Holmes with a pipe, *hanh.*' He laughed and slapped me on the back. 'How old are you son?'

'Twenty.' I lied.

The smile disappeared. 'You look sixteen to me,' he said.

I said nothing.

'Did you kill him?' he asked and put on a stern expression again.

'Me?' I laughed, as if it was a ridiculous suggestion and my heart began pounding at the same time.

'Where do you live?

'Nearby.' I did not want to give him the address.

'What is your father's name?'

'I don't have a father.'

'Any family?' he asked stepping closer, as if suspecting I was about to run.

'Now that I have told you everything I will go,' I said.

He appeared unimpressed. 'You come with us to the station. Give a statement. We will have tea and biscuit. You can tell us everything. Who you are, why you are out at this time of the night and that you didn't kill this man.'

I started panicking. I understood then why others had run away so promptly. They knew the police would harass them for statements.

'But I haven't done anything,' I said.

'If you haven't done anything then what have you to worry about. Come get in the car.'

The second policeman, younger, with a baby face, intervened, 'let this boy go sir. I think he is innocent, just a mixed-up kid.' Then he said to me, 'you want to go home boy?'

'Yes please,' I said.

'Come with me.' He took me aside under a tree and whispered in my ear, 'are you sure you didn't do it?' His breath was full of alcohol.

'I didn't do anything, I promise.'

'I believe you. But it's not up to me. You have to convince my boss.'

'How?'

'Have you got any money?'

'About five hundred.'

'Show me.'

I took out the bundle of rupees kept aside for the taxi driver.

'Anymore, this is not enough,' he said pocketing the money and making a face as if it hurt him to ask for more.

I said no. He made me raise my arms and patted my body, searched my trouser pockets. Luckily, he did not look further down inside the socks on my feet or he would have found another three hundred. 'Go see my boss. He will let you go.'

I fell on my knees and touched Moustache's dirty boots. As I was rising up I felt a sharp smack to the side of my head.

'Go straight home now. If I see you out this late again I am going to put you in jail, you understand,' he said.

'Yes sir.'

That is all for now Modiji. Even now thinking about that evening, I get goose bumps all over. First, the taxi driver who had taken Tanya for a whore and I knew what he wanted. Then the two policemen, who were meant to uphold the law, turned out to be rogues. What a clever good cop, bad cop, double act. Moreover, the good residents of the street, they had seen everything from their windows with lights switched off. They didn't lift a finger to help me. What a bloody joke sir.

CHAPTER 16

Sanju was nibbling his thumbnail as I told him about my extraordinary find, a love letter in a wallet belonging to an old man. His textbooks and note pads neatly arranged on the table, even the biros were in their rightful place in the glass jar.

'Why is a letter so special? You must have found many *ajab gajab*, stranger things.'

'No ordinary thing, *yaar*,' I said, 'forty years – forty - the old man has been carrying it around in his pocket.' I unfolded the piece of paper carefully and showed it to him. Every night before going to sleep, I had been reading and re-reading it, its image permanently stamped in my head. I had tried to decipher some hidden meanings or messages. Who were these two people? Where did they live? Did they meet up again?

> ... *Ammi and Abbu know everything. They know you are from a pundit family. They have made life hell for me. To make matters worse my uncle and cousin are coming over from Lucknow. I fear for your life and for mine. Please believe me. It's true..... I just don't know if I can take any more of this...*

Were the uncle and cousin coming over to beat up Raju?

> ... *you were pleading with me to tell you the truth. You wanted nothing but the truth. On your face was so much pain. Please forgive me, my love Raju, I could not bring*

myself to do it at first. I just couldn't coax it out of me.
It was chocking me. But I know I must be brave and tell
you. So here it is. I want you to be brave too and accept
what I am going to say ... Raju, there has been something
growing inside me, slowly, slowly it has been taking shape.
It sucks air from my lungs, fills me with fear, and makes
me dizzy. I saw the doctor last week. We talked for a very
long time. She said it is usually pain free. I could be home
the same day. Now that I have revealed the truth, do you
hate me? Please don't...

'I want to return this letter to Raju,' I said, 'poor old man -
must be pining for it.'

'You go looking for this man you will be looking for trouble,'
Sanju said once he had finished reading.

He was of course right sir, for who knew how the old man
would react, go mad and call the police or set his neighbours
on me. It was a risk I had to take.

'How will you find him anyway?'

'That I don't know yet.'

'Let me get this straight. You say he was browsing magazines
at the station and did not appear in a hurry,' he asked.

'Yes.'

'In that case he is almost certainly a local man? If you want
to find him, I suggest you go back to Kalighat, to the spot
where he was reading the magazines and ask the shopkeeper.'

'How will the shopkeeper know who he is?'

'If he goes there regularly then the shopkeeper is bound to
know him.'

A few days later, on an unbearably hot day, I had gone to

155

work on Park Street, hoping to make one or two quick dips and leave. It was a hard slog; three hours had passed without a single dip. I was thinking of giving up when I spotted an Arab lady in a long black cloak, a large designer handbag on her arm. She was ambling along in a free and careless manner. I started following her from shop to shop, trying to get into position. I did not see the blind beggar standing outside Flurys bakery. We collided accidently. The beggar, who I had assumed was actually blind, tapped his stick on the floor and let out a flurry of swear words. 'Are you blind or something, can't you see where you are going?'

Now this is the problem with our people Modiji. Had I been a rich businessman with a big belly this fellow would not have behaved in such shameless manner. He would have lowered his head humbly, grovelled for forgiveness for not being fast enough to move out of his way. He would have said something like I am much ashamed I have inconvenienced you *bada seth*.

However, he had seen I was someone of similar status as him, so decided there was no mileage in being civil to me.

I was debating whether to respond to this fake blind beggar in kind, show I was his match at hurling abuse when I saw a familiar face in the crowd. The long nose, youthful crop of hair on upper lip, sun soaked complexion. It was my friend Bhushan from Bangalore. He crossed the road casually and turned west towards Park Circus. I thought of Babu and dived in panic behind a street hoarding. Have they shifted their operation to Kolkata? My heart sank at the thought.

In the Maidan, a short distance away, some kind of demonstration was taking place. I rushed into the crowd without much thought. It did not take long to realise I had joined a protest rally organised by CPM Communist party of West Bengal. All around me people were waving banners, shouting slogans; a TV reporter was waving a microphone, interviewing a few agitated men in red headbands. As if from nowhere a group of musicians appeared, carrying musical instruments and broadcasting paraphernalia, cheered on by hoots, whistles and claps. Instruments hooked up, the band of five burst into life with an almighty bang and an echo of the loudspeakers. At the southern fringe, a long line of policemen had taken up position with helmets and long *lathis,* staves.

In no time I found myself taken in by the self-righteous passion and energy of the protestors. I headed north to explore what was going on at Victoria Memorial. A bunch of stragglers who had managed to evade a police barricade near Esplanade were boasting of their exploits. 'It was a good one,' one of them said describing a fight with the police, 'I grabbed his baton. He could not do nothing, shit scared he was.' The boy flashed a baton tucked in the waistband of his trouser.

'That's nothing. I crushed his head with a brick,' his friend boasted and raised the flap of his bulging rucksack, exposing a policeman's helmet, 'see I have the fucking trophy.' They laughed, snorted like pigs and moved on.

Behind me I heard a commotion. Three men were raining blows on a TV cameraman. The poor man was running around in circles, clutching the camera like it was a baby, refusing to fall over. The crowd was in a state of frenzy, screaming *maro, maro, maro*, kill, kill, kill. Another man in clean white shirt was shouting a commentary into a microphone. Someone snatched the microphone. A punch landed on his stomach followed by a flying kick to the head. He disappeared from view like a sinking ship.

Rally organisers had come prepared with loud hailers. 'Don't be intimidated by the police. This is people's square. It belongs to us. We have the right of peaceful assembly, everybody sit down. Do not leave the square. Sit down.'

Those closest to the police line went down first, squatting on the ground in tight knit formation. Taking cue from the front the next batch followed, soon there was a rush of bodies falling like dominoes. In no time, the entire green was a sea of heads. Only those at the periphery were still standing.

A line of police moved north towards a ditch. From the right, a batch of newly arrived university students rushed in to confront the police. A half-eaten guava landed on my shoulder, someone had lobbed it like a cricket ball. I was walking around in a daze thinking of Bhushan, beset with a feeling Babu's men were following me. Ahead some men armed with sticks, poles, iron bars charged a police line. Another group had attacked a police car, setting it on fire. A mushroom of black smoke spiralled upwards. The crowd cheered.

A lone, exhausted policeman took off his helmet and began wiping sweat on his face. A mob of about fifteen in red head-band started closing in like a pack of hyenas, screaming slogans. The policeman saw what was happening, dropped the helmet, switched the baton to his right hand and raised it above his head. 'Get back, get back.' But for all the show of bravado he couldn't disguise the fear in his eyes. The crowd smelled blood and moved in for the kill. Somebody brought down a long pole on his bald head. Then there was free for all, punching and kicking, screaming, '*saale ko maro*. Kill the bastard, kill the bastard.' A boy rammed the sharp end of a pole in his neck.

Blood spurted like a mini fountain.

I did not go home from the *maidan*, fearing Babu's men may be waiting for me. Instead I went to the Pine Tree club on Canning Street, hoping Roby would be there. As I stepped inside, into the reverberation of bellowing saxophone and slow beat of drums, my senses relaxed. Roby and his band were performing their favourite numbers. Gibson strapped to his shoulder, head bowed, his fingers were plucking the strings with awe-inspiring dexterity. The drummer on his right was bobbing his head up and down, as if attached to the shoulder by a spring. The cheeks of the saxophonist were like two balloons, impossibly large. At short intervals people burst into appreciative clap, reserving the loudest for the end of a number. Seeing Roby on stage, centre of attraction, filled me with pride. Hey that man playing the guitar is my friend; I wanted to shout at top of my voice.

I took a stool by the bar and sat facing the stage. A big man nearby, in white jacket and black trouser, clicked his fingers at me. 'You, cum ere,' he said.

I did not move.

'Where are you from?' he asked.

'Uttarakhand,' I replied.

'Siddown,' he said, 'Siddown.'

I pointed at the legs of the stool under me, 'see I am already sitting,'

'Siddown anyway,' he said moving closer, reeking of stale ale, 'let me tell you something country boy. I do not give a shit about your people, too many of you in Kolkata. You may be nice. My friend who is a fock'n liberal says you lot are nice hard-working people. But I say right under the skin you're nothing but shit.'

I was in no mood for a fight. Moreover, I had Babu to worry about. I ignored the fool. 'What, don't you have tongue in your mouth?' he screamed, getting enraged at my refusal to respond to his insults.

His friends tried to pull him back. He was intent on fighting. 'I want to teach this shit a lesson, who does he think he is.'

I slipped away as security guards arrived.

It was midnight when Roby and I left the club. Out on the street two girls were coming towards us, dressed provocatively in low cut dresses and giggling, leaning into each other, boobs wobbling like jelly.

'Roby,' one screamed, 'loved the music.'

'Right,' Roby waved as if he was a famous pop star.

The girls whispered into each other's ears, stopped and came over. 'Who is your friend?' one asked.

'His name is Kalu.'

The younger one came towards me, clicking heels, whores swinging hips. 'I am Preety,' she said and giggled like a school girl. I could see, under the makeup she really was young enough to be at school.

'Where do you live?' I asked, thinking of hiring a taxi and giving them a lift. Before she could reply a shout came from behind me, 'oi you, leave her alone.' The man in white jacket with his mates was running towards us.

'Oh, hell, let's go, run,' Roby said, pulling me by the arm.

I stayed put, did not want to show Preeti I was a coward. Someone pushed me from behind, knocking me flat on the street; my right arm missed the wheels of a passing car by mere two feet. I rolled back on to the pavement narrowly avoiding another approaching car. Up on my feet I looked back. The white jacket and his friends were laughing and jeering, goading me to take them on. 'Let's see what you are made of you little shit.'

I caught a glimpse of Preety swinging her handbag. 'Let him go, let him go you cowards.' For a brief moment, I considered facing the bastards; show them what a country boy was capable of doing.

Roby, who had run on ahead, came back for me. 'Come on Kalu,' he whispered in my ear, 'he is Bannerjee's nephew, don't mess with him.'

We began running, did not stop until we were well clear of the club.

'Who is Bannerjee?' I asked Roby who was now panting heavily and leaning against a lamppost.

'Mamta Bannerjee, the Chief Minister.'

'And the girl.'

'Preety? Ah, she is a local tart,' he said.

I refused to accept Preety could be a tart. She was reminding me of Ramesh's Maria from back home. Ramesh wanted to take her with him when we were planning our escape from the orphanage. He would not have it any other way. So, we had gone to look for her. Found her sitting on the floor. Ramesh had sat down beside her and told her of our secret plan to run away from Durga Bhabi. 'Do you want to come with me?'

She did not reply but began pleating Ramesh's long hair.

'I want you to come with me,' he had said.

'What will I be doing out there, I don't have anyone. You don't know about that, do you?'

'No, tell me.'

'I used to clean up after the animals had been skinned, wash away the blood, and pull the hide out to dry in the sun. That was my job. Every day, morning till night, not allowed to rest. Once when Bhagwandas was not looking I sneaked away and went to sleep in a wagon under the shade of a tree. It was so, so peaceful. But that sly old Bhagwandas found me. He beat me so hard. For three days I couldn't even stand on my feet.'

I could see Ramesh's eyes moistening. 'You were beaten.'

She continued, 'I had a mother though. She was given to Bhagwandas as his wife. Someone said Bhagwandas was my papa, but I do not believe that. Do you?'

Ramesh said he did not believe Bhagwandas was her papa.

'You know your papa?'

'Yes,' Ramesh said feeling guilty.

She stopped pleating, wrapped her arms around the knees, hands cupping her elbows. She peered into the dirt by her feet. 'Do you still want to take me with you?'

'Yes, yes,' Ramesh said impatiently.

'Then do.'

Sadly, she never made it out. As you know, Ramesh was kidnapped that very night.

Chapter 17

Modiji, let me ask you a question. What are the chances of lightning striking the same spot twice? Exactly. The probability is so remote that one might say it will never happen. Like you, I was of the same opinion until something happened that made me change my mind. On Park Street again, I was working the cash loaded shoppers. I was about to relieve a lady of her purse when the sighting of a face in the crowd shook me to the bones. It was Bhushan. He was walking towards me in his distinct lopsided gait. As before, I dived for cover. It occurred to me that the last time I had seen Bhushan was exactly at the same spot outside Flurys bakery and the time was almost the same. Bhushan had already seen me and was gesturing with his head, asking me to go into the bakery. I hesitated. Is it a trap? Bhushan tut, tutted and rolled his eyes, go in, it is safe.

We went in, as if each was alone. At the rear of the restaurant, we took a table facing away from the street, odour of freshly baked bread and pastries in the air.

Bhushan shook his head but did not speak. I continued to look around me, fearing a trap.

'Calm down,' Bhushan said. His distinctive voice instantly transported me back to Bangalore.

'How are you?' he asked.

'Fine, fine, are you alone?'

'*Are bhai* I am alone. Now relax.'

'Tell me why you are here.'

'I am here to help the Kolkata team, just for a few weeks.'

'I didn't know they were operating in Kolkata?' I said.

'They are everywhere,' Bhushan said dismissively, 'who cares.'

'Are you still in the same house?' I asked; visualising the interior, the sagging sofa, the dining table with permanent tea stains, posters on walls. I saw Ramesh's face and the past came rushing back, crowding me from all side.

'Yes, we are in the same bloody house. *Saala* Petre went away for few weeks, but he is back now.'

'Why are you wearing those?' I asked, pointing at the black glove on his left hand.

Instead of an explanation, he started pulling the glove off, slowly, one finger at a time while grimacing in pain. Once off, he raised the free hand to reveal a white bandage wrapped all the way from the wrist to the fingers. Only his thumb was free. He wiggled the thumb to show it had movement.

'Babu did it.'

'Did what?'

'He accused me of stealing money.'

'So did you?' I knew to steal from Babu took exceptional courage. If Bhushan had done something like this, it had to be desperation or pure stubbornness.

'You know how much money we have been making for him?'

'Yes, I know.'

'We work so hard for him.'

'Don't I know?'

'I asked for a raise, just a little bit. But no, the mother fucker went mad and started threatening us, saying he will send us to work for the Mitra gang.'

'What did he do?'

'They held me down and gave me a knife. Cut off your thumb as punishment, they said.'

'Cut your own thumb?' I screamed. I found it hard to believe Babu would do such a thing.

'Shush, keep your voice down *yaar*. Yes, Petre said if I don't do it myself, he would take the knife. But he would have to cut off the whole hand. It was up to me to decide, lose the thumb or the hand.'

'Are you saying you tried to chop off your own thumb?'

'I had to do something to stop them. I thought the sight of blood would satisfy them. I stabbed my hand, just to show them some blood. But *saala* knife was too sharp, it went in deep.'

'How deep?'

'Came out the other end,' he said and his eyes opened wide, as if he could not believe he had actually done it.

'*Bap re bap*. And then.'

'Then they pretended to be sorry, bandaged my hand and later took me to a doctor.'

I felt so sad for Bhushan. 'What do you want to do now?' I asked, ready to help if I could.

'I want to leave Babu and Petre. But I have nowhere to go.'

I saw the fear, hopelessness, resignation under those drooping eyelids. 'You could go back home?'

'Home? I have no home.'

'The village – where you were born.'

'Who is there for me?' he said and his eyes drooped further in sadness, 'I want to come to Kolkata.'

'What will you do here?'

'Work with you.'

'Work with me? Do you understand what that means? It's dangerous.'

He looked thoughtful for a moment and then his shoulders sagged. 'I better go then.'

'Wait,' I pulled him back down. 'You want to come to Kolkata. I'll help you. You will have to do as I say.'

'Yes Kalu, I will.'

'Don't talk about this with anyone, even Gokul. I will speak to Baldev. Find you a place to stay. How much time do you need?'

Bhushan shrugged his shoulders.

'You will need some time. Meet me at Howrah station in the main hall, next month, Monday twenty-third at two thirty. Meanwhile save as much money as you can. Steal if you have to.'

He raised the bandaged hand, 'with this?'

'I know, I know, do what you can.' Then I told him where Babu hid the money. He looked so shocked, I thought he was going to get up and run.

'Alright, if Babu even smells what you are planning, you are finished. You understand?'

'I know, I know.'

'He will give you the knife and insist you cut off both your hands,' I said.

Bhushan looked at his hands with grave seriousness and then smiled realising it was a joke.

I went home that day feeling very disturbed. Had I done the right thing encouraging Bhushan to run away? This feeling of guilt that I was pushing Bhushan towards a certain catastrophe, persisted for several weeks until one day I became a victim.

I want to tell you about a burglary. It took place, not somewhere far away, in a stranger's house, but my own. A thief had become victim of theft. You might think it is funny but I did not feel that way. I arrived home late one afternoon. Even before I unlocked my room, I sensed something was wrong. A draft was filtering through the crevices around the door. I opened the door and froze as I stepped in. The room was in complete disarray. My bed badly dishevelled, it looked as if a dog had been rooting through it. Of the two pillows, one was lying on the floor ripped apart as if split open with a knife and the other with the inner pink sponge pulled out like innards of a small animal lay at the foot of the bed.

The thing is sir; those pillows were like safe deposit boxes to me. I had carefully unstitched the fabric around them, cut a slot in the sponge with a sharp blade and inserted an A-four size envelope. I was using this pocket to store all my money. Fluffed and patted into shape they looked ordinary pillows complete with a patch of grease stain from my hair.

Robbed of every single rupee I had saved since arriving in Kolkata. It was no small amount, 134,000 rupees. My target was 300,000 within a year. I wanted to cry at the thought of having to start all over again.

Even the wardrobe and the drawers turned inside out. I stood at the centre of the room and listened for any unusual noises.

Downstairs Baldev was slouching on a chair, smoking and blowing rings.

I told him of the burglary.

He sprang to his feet, dropped the half-smoked cigarette on the floor, scrunched it furiously under his greasy shoe and bounded upstairs to the room. He leaned over the balcony, inspected the exterior wall, the flat roof, the back alley where kids often played cricket.

'They must have climbed up that drain pipe,' he said straightening and caressed the fountain pens in the breast pocket, checking they had not fallen out, 'we will put barbed wires around all the pipes. Then we will see how they come up here, *saale chor?*'

'It is too late, damage has already been done. You should have thought of that a long time ago,' I said and wondered if he would make some reparations.

'Did I know this would happen? Why did you leave the window open?'

'Uncle, I always close the window before going out. You can see the latch has been broken,' I said.

'I will send someone to fix it,' he said, but did not ask what or how much was my damage. Perhaps he thought asking questions about money would amount to admission of guilt.

Now let me tell you why I was putting aside the money. I was planning to go back to Uttarakhand and mount a search for my mother. It was my sincere belief that the woman was still alive.

This burning desire to find her was lit long time ago. I was eleven then. I remember the day well. It had rained heavily for two whole days. Water leaking through cracks in the roof was flooding the building in many places. I was helping Sushila *didi* sponge water off dining room floor. In passing, I asked *didi* if she knew anything about my mother. No one seems to know, I complained.

'Has no one ever told you about her?' she appeared genuinely surprised.

'No one tells me anything.'

'Kalu I don't know much but I will tell you what I know.'

She made me sit down on a bench. 'Now listen to me Kalu, what you are going to hear may be painful, but I want you to be brave.'

There was sincerity in her voice. I knew instantly she was going to tell me the truth.

'Outside Champawat, in a stretch of open drain which carried the town's sewage waste, a man was at work, trapping frogs to sell to schools and colleges in nearby Dehradun. He heard a muffled noise in bushes nearby. At first, he took it for an injured animal or bird. When he searched the undergrowth, instead of an animal he found a baby boy, naked, with several scratches on its arms and face. Rats had been gnawing the soft skin and it was a miracle the boy was still alive. The man rushed the child to a nearby hospital were nurses took charge. For five whole days, no one came to claim the child. On the sixth day, they spotted a very frightened looking young girl pacing the yard outside. She was about sixteen or seventeen, scruffy with tattered clothes. On her face and arms were bruises of severe beating. Nurses came out and coxed the poor girl in. As soon as she entered, she ran to the child, picked him up and held him tight to her chest, weeping all the time. Finally, she returned the child to the cot and turned her back on it. No one knows what had happened to the mother after that.'

'Who was she? What was her name?' I said, 'tell me why she didn't think of my feelings? Didn't I deserve a family - mother, father, brothers and sisters? Why was she so selfish?'

'Son, she said very little. She gave no address or name, only that she belonged to the chamar tribe. She had left a memento for you, requesting the nurse to keep it safe and to give it to you when you were older. When the nurses asked her what name she would like to give her child. She shrugged her shoulders. So they settled on the name Kalu, after the man who had rescued the child.'

'Didn't anyone try to find her?' I felt an urgent need to do something. Perhaps I should be out searching for her. Knock on every door; examine every woman's face over the age of twenty, confident if we come face to face, we will recognise each other. The invisible magnetic force between mother and son will bring us together.

That is how I acquired the name Kalu sir. You already know why Cobra was appended to my name – Kalu Cobra. As for the memento, I had kept it hidden in a crevice in the bed frame and took it out from time to time. I used to feel it in my fingers, sniffed it in the belief if I tried hard enough, I will be able to smell her. It was a silver pendant, three little rings about half inch in diameter, welded together in a triangle and attached to a chain.

A few days later, I met Tanya at Pine Tree and things went from bad to worst.

Tanya appeared pleased to see me. 'Oh, Kalu, you have come. Come and join us.' She was sitting at a table with three friends, two girls and a boy with a black shirt unbuttoned half-way down the chest, flaunting a thick gold chain nestling in his chest hair. She introduced the group, Sonu, Sujata and Ashoke. The flashy hero in black shirt was Sonu's boyfriend. Showing off his wealth, he talked nonstop of the housing complex his father was building near the airport. 'Daddy has gone into partnership with an Omani investment company. *Yaar* you should have seen the lavish reception they gave us in seven-star

Intercontinental hotel. What luxury. I told daddy he should build a hotel just like that one.'

'Build a hotel in Kolkata?' Sonu said sarcastically, as if mocking him for such poor taste.

'No *yaar*, Kol is a dump place. I told him we should build in London.'

'My daddy is taking me to London next month *yaa*,' Sujata interrupted, 'I am sooo excited. He has promised to take me to Ascot racecourse too. Love races, don't you?' She stirred her gin and tonic with a straw, making the ice-cubes tinkle.

'Me too,' Ashok said springing up in the chair, 'we are life members of Royal Calcutta Turf Club. The other day I won two thousand on Tofaan baby. *Ooof* what race that was. He was losing, losing, losing all the way and then *phataak* he put his head in front at the last minute.'

While they were boasting unashamedly about their wealth and high class connections I was thinking of how to make up the loss I had suffered as a result of the theft. It occurred to me these people were not my type. What am I doing here? If they even sniff I am a chamar and a *phoketmaar*, they will have me thrown out of Pine Tree and order the club fumigated.

Tanya leaned over, out of her friends' earshot. 'I can't stand him, he is such bore,' she said.

'Why do you put up with it then?' I said.

'What to do, he is my good friend's boyfriend.'

'So tell us Kalu, what do you do for living?' Ashok asked suddenly. My blood pressure soared. Sujata and Sonu too looked at me with their synthetic smiles and shining teeth.

'Oh, is this the time,' I said tapping the watch on my wrist, 'sorry I have to go.' I got up and without another word walked away.

'Kalu, Kalu, stop,' I heard Tanya calling. I ignored her.

'Stop Kalu.' She caught up with me at the exit.

'Before you touch me, you should know something,' I said.

'What?' she said, looking surprised and hurt.

'I am a *chamar* boy, that's what.'

The two door attendants suddenly stopped talking to each other and looked in our direction.

She hesitated for a moment. 'Kalu, I don't care if you are *chamar* or whatever. I do not judge people by their caste. Look at me. What do you see? Do I look like I am from *khan-dhami*, aristocratic family?'

I beheld her; looked into her eyes and realised I was in love. It is not right, I thought, she is a respectable, educated girl with a career. I am just a village boy who has never seen the inside of a school. As for a job – I am a thief, a pickpocket. How could I ever tell her that? I felt a fraud, like a shoeshine boy in love with a famous film star. My heart ached so badly.

'Sorry Tanya, I must go,' I said and brushed past her, not looking back.

On the way to the Metro station, it started raining. I quickened my pace, passed the double fronted sari shop where I had stalked a young couple only two days earlier. The rain turned to full-fledged downpour. I started running. By the time I reached the station I was thoroughly soaked. As I was jostling my way to the platform, my MOTO C Plus mobile phone started buzzing. I thought Bhushan was ringing to update me on the progress.

'Listen to me Kalu.' I heard a stern voice. It sent me into panic. 'Are you listening?'

'Yes,' I said. My brain was whizzing now, how did Babu get my number?

'You are a very stupid boy,' Babu said with exaggerated calmness. I recognised the preamble, calm before the storm. I thought he was going to scream abuse, threaten to break my legs for stealing his money and for encouraging Bhushan to defect.

'Where is the photo?' he said, still in a calm voice.

'Photo? What photo?' I said confused. Babu was not one to talk in riddles.

'Don't play games with me. You know what I am talking about.'

I had to think fast. Though Ramesh and I often took useless photos with our mobiles, we never had any printed. Babu was talking about a photograph, a physical object one could touch and feel.

'I don't know what you are talking about,' I said.

It took a while, but it came eventually. He was referring to Sushmita's photo I had found in the cash box. It had a message scribbled on the back for Babu, personal, kind of thing secret lovers say to each other.

'I don't have it,' I said. That really was the truth. Somewhere in the move from Bangalore to Kolkata I had discarded it. It was of no use to me.

'Listen to me carefully. I am giving you one chance, that's all. Put the photograph in an envelope and seal it carefully. My men will come to collect it. You decide where you want to meet them?'

I blurted out without thinking, 'Metro station, Noapara. Next Tuesday.'

'If you disobey me, you know very well what will happen to you?'

'Yes.'

Blackmail is the operative word, sir, blackmail. The thought had never come to me or I may have kept the photo and guarded it with my life. But as far as Babu was concerned I still had it and that was alright by me. It gave me the upper hand. I knew how Babu's mind worked. If he were in my position, he would have given the photo to a friend for safekeeping, with instruction to send it to Lal Bahadur in case something happened to him.

I realised I had the upper hand for once, the tables had been turned, master – slave to slave – master. I could screw the bastard until he begged forgiveness. I could almost hear him grovelling, 'please, please don't do it Kalu. Lal Bahadur will kill me. Just name your price, I will give you anything.'

I will laugh in his face, 'oh, you want me to name my price. Absolutely alright by me, so, first I want you to lick my arse after I have done the shitting ...'

Sir, my Sanyo is playing up again. It screeches horribly when I press the ON or OFF button. I will have to take it to Ali. He runs a gadgets repair business from his front room. How clever the little fellow is at repairing things. He has a thirty-five years old Toshiba VHS video recorder that still works. Sanju and I were with him the other day watching an old, old movie called Bombay Talkie, on his Toshiba hooked to a television. Shashi Kapoor and Jennifer Kendal, music by Shankar Jaikishan. What dialogue! Have you seen it sir? Even Sanju liked it and that is saying something. He is usually very critical of Bollywood movies, calls them 'lugubrious crap'. Strange English words he comes up with these days. One day, after seeing another film, My Name Is Khan, he announced he had received an 'anaphylactic shock' and did a fainting gesture. I think he does it to annoy me, because he knows I will not understand.

Chapter 18

I decided to ignore Babu's ultimatum. Let him think I have the photograph and was not going to relinquish it easily.

I went to Kalighat metro station and stood at the very spot where I had first seen Raju. Over on the roof beams pigeons were cooing and fluttering noisily. Not far away a boy was lying on the floor, fast asleep. His shabby clothes and bony face suggested he was a workhand at the market stalls, augmenting his income by opportunistic shoplifting. As before, the bookseller was standing behind a spread of second-hand books and magazines on a wooden platform. Occasionally someone would stop to gaze at the titles, pick up a book or two and flick pages. If anyone lingered too long with an open book in hand, he would say sarcastically, '*dada* are you going to buy or read for free', or, '*boro babu* this is a book shop, *hanh*, book shop, not a library.'

I started foraging at random; some of the books were in Bengali language. The bookseller pointed at the book in my hand and asked in a flat voice, '*moshai* can you read Bengali?'

'Oh yes, absolutely,' I said.

'Then why are you holding it upside down?'

I grinned and raised my hands acknowledging he had caught me. 'Brother can you help me?' I asked.

He cackled with frustration and threw a hand up in the air. I could see he had very few teeth in the mouth. 'Moshai if you are looking for credit the answer is no,' he said.

'No, no, I am enquiring about a *bhodrolok* who comes to buy books and magazines from you, tall, about seventy-year old, very little hair. Have you seen him today?'

'Old man?'

'Yes, old,' I said.

'O, *choto babu*, people come to my stall all day long, some are tall others are short, old and also schoolboys, rich and poor, I am very famous, *hanh*, all over Kalighat.'

'I know, but do you know this old man?'

'*Choto babu*, how big the crowd is. You look. Tell me how I can remember any face.'

'Alright,' I said, 'do you remember last month a man got pickpocketed standing there, just there,' I pointed at the exact spot, 'do you remember the incidence?'

Again, he said, '*O, babu*, people get pickpocketed here all the time. This is Kolkata, do you understand, Kolkata.' He made a rolling hand gesture to make his point, laughed and then turned to a man standing beside him, 'no money in this business brother, no one buys books, they want to read free or ask stupid questions.'

I started to walk away, into a rush of oncoming metro passengers. I had gone a few paces when he called me back, '*Oi, choto babu*, come here, come here.'

I went back to him.

'What do you want? Speak to me, speak,' he said turning his left ear towards me.

I described Raju's physical appearance again, the day and the time when he was pickpocketed. 'I need to speak to him about an urgent matter,' I said.

'Oh, you want Rajbabu, masterji, oh,' he cried, 'yes, yes

someone stole his wallet here.'

'Yes, that's him, Raj, Raju,' I said, 'he was a schoolteacher? I didn't know.'

'*Hanh, hanh*, all his life, masterji. Very respectable.'

'Where can I find him?'

'That, I don't know,' he said shaking his head, 'now you will buy a book?'

I picked up a book at random. 'Yes, this one. But I must find him, can't you help?'

'Hundred and ten *taka*,' he said.

I did not haggle, gave him hundred and ten rupees. He folded the money, shoved it in a pocket sewn on his dirty shirt and said with a toothless grin, 'he lives behind Kali Bari, on Debidarshan Street.'

Rascal, I thought, knew all along what I wanted, just strung me along to sell a book.

Back at base Baldev was drinking tea out of his favourite long glass. 'Kalu, come here *re*. I want to talk with you,' he said and puffed air on the liquid, took a sip, grunted, 'ahhh.'

I waited for him to speak.

'Two men were here this afternoon. I think they were looking for you.'

My heart missed a beat.

'They asked for *chana puri* and ate sitting there, gawking at everybody like monkeys. Two hours they sat. Then they asked Pratibha, where is the boy from Uttarakhand.'

'What did she tell them?'

'She thought they were income tax people, snooping. So she asked them to go away, told them she knew nothing about any boy.' He gestured with his thumb at their apartment door

178

behind him. 'She is a sharp lady.'

'Yes, yes, she is,' I agreed readily.

He took another sip of the tea, raised his head and eyed me gravely, 'Kalu I don't want no trouble here. Do you understand?'

I went to my room, switched on the news on television. They were discussing a crime; murder of a boy at Sealdah station. The mother had confessed to the crime, though at first police had recorded it as suicide. Wasn't the boy found with hands tied behind him? Yes. How could it be suicide? The panel laughed.

Suicide, suicide, suicide – I could not get it out of mind as I placed the kettle on the stove. While the water was boiling, I scanned the front page of The Statesman I had picked up earlier. It carried a story of a man who had committed suicide by jumping off a tall building. Someone had unwittingly taken a picture of the man hurtling down. The building was remarkably similar to one I had passed early that day.

The man who fell, what was he thinking as he went down? Was he terrified? Did he jump voluntarily? Did he feel weightless on the way down? He must have jumped with a smile. A running jump perhaps, as kids do diving into a swimming pool, legs and arms spread out, shouting *wheeeee* all the way down. What fun.

Next day I barged into Sanju's room, slumped down on a chair. 'I am going to kill myself,' I announced solemnly.

Sanju stopped typing on his HP250, took a bite of a raw green mango, looked at my face briefly as if he had spotted a fly at the tip of my nose and went back to typing.

'I mean it,' I said louder.

'You want to kill yourself? Then hurry up so I can finish your book with – and Kalu killed himself. The End.'

'Don't laugh. I will kill myself.'

'Don't do it in my room. I can't stand sight of blood.'

'Don't worry, you won't have to. I will jump from top of Tata Centre.'

'Tata Centre,' he paused as if assessing what I had said then continued calmly, 'it may not work. Listen to me, that building has only eighteen floors. You stand better chance from Everest House. Or for a hundred percent clean kill South City Tower is best. It has thirty-six floors. You will be dead even before you hit the ground.'

That annoyed me even more, why does he not take me seriously? 'I will kill you. I will kill you,' I screamed at him.

'*Orff-o*, now make your mind up. Is it me or yourself, you want dead?' he said.

'Me.'

'Then do as I have suggested,' he said, 'but first take this.' He offered me his half-eaten raw mango.

I took it from him and bit into the uneaten half. The tangy acidic flavour made me wince.

'Hmm, tasty, no,' he said, 'take another bite.'

'Shut up and listen.' I threw the mango back at him. I told him about the phone call from Babu, about the photo that I do not have any more.

'He thinks you have the photo. Good.'

'What's so damn good about it?'

'He will not dare kill you.'

'Not kill me? *Yaar*, you should have heard him on the phone.'

'Yes, yes, that he will do. He is trying to frighten you.'

I understood the logic. Later we went for a walk to the *ghat*, taking the back streets, past the *Murgihat* indoor market reeking of dead and dying chicken, a thousand birds clucking in disharmony. In the slum behind us, smoke drifted upwards from cooking fires. Narrow lanes, cars and bikes competing for space with man and cows, we walked on in silence. At the end of the lane, some men were clearing a drain. Black sewer sludge lay piled by the side of the open manhole. Men standing around the hole were hauling a rope attached to a pulley, which disappeared into the ground. The head of a small boy emerged out of the earth and then the rest of the body, clinging to the end of the rope. Covered in slippery sewer sludge, his hair was stiff by the muck. On closer inspection, he looked no more than ten or twelve years old. His small body, thin arms and legs were ideal for exploring the dark narrow arteries of Kolkata's drainage system. The men were using him as sewer rat, without regard for his safety. I felt sorry for the boy, probably another abandoned child, picked up from a railway station or from one of the many slums by the river.

This was happening in open view of hundreds of grownups going about their business. Yet no one seemed to notice. Not my child, so why should I care?

Sanju saw me starring. 'Come on, let's talk to them,' he said.

I tried to stop him. 'It's pointless.'

'Come on *yaar*, let's see what they say.' He walked up to the men and addressed the tall one with a *gamacha* tied around his head. 'How old is this boy?' he asked pointing at the little figure now emptying a bucket of sludge.

'Who are you?' the man asked brusquely while continuing to shovel muck into a little mountain, beads of sweat on his face rolling down to the neck.

'This boy is underage. You are breaking the law by employing him. Do you understand?'

He stopped shovelling, looked at Sanju as if he was an interfering nuisance. 'I have contract with the *sarkar* government to clear these drains. It is my business who I employ. Why are you meddling?'

'It is illegal to employ children to do this kind of work. You could get two years in prison.' Sanju said with such authority one would think he was the law himself.

The man unrolled the dirty cloth from his head, wiped his face and forehead, rolled it back on the head and then placed a finger on his right nostril, exhaled forcefully through the other. A thick blob of mucus shot out and landed inches from Sanju's feet.

'*Sahib*, please send the person who will put me in prison, I am waiting,' he said and then scowled at his four employees who had stopped work and were looking on amused. 'Back to work,' he ordered and clipped the little boy on the head, 'you, little fucker, get back in and take the bucket with you. We haven't got all day.'

You see, there was nothing we could do. Whom could we complain to then? Call the police? Hah, that is a joke. Sanju said our police are so poorly trained they would not even have heard of the Prohibition and Regulation Act of 1986. It states no child under the age of fourteen shall be employed to work in any factory, mine or engaged in any other hazardous employment.

CHAPTER 19

I put on the new shirt purchased from a shop in Burrabazar, adjusted the sleeve and the collar.

'You look like an office *babu*,' Sanju said smirking.

'I have to look respectable. After all I am going to meet Raju.'

On the train to Kalighat station, I sat next to a young couple with two bulky holdalls on the floor. At Park Street metro station two Arab men came on board, reeking of after shave lotion, reminding me of Father Petre and his lavish use of Park Avenue. I started rehearsing my speech to Raju. I will offer him an apology and receive his anger. Beyond that I trusted my instincts to right what I had done wrong. If Raju insisted on calling the police, I would not run but take my chances.

Out of the station, I turned left and walked along Kali Temple Road and then turned into Kali Lane. It was packed. Lined with little shops, people were selling everything from hot tea and fried *pakoras*, garlands and bouquets of flowers, coconut pieces and bananas wrapped in green leaves. Long lines of visitors were buying the fruit wrapped in leaf, to place at the feet of Kali Mata. The crowd was flowing in one direction, towards the temple. I was cutting through the crowd, against the flow. Every now and then, someone would yell, 'Kali Mata *ki*.' A chorus of, '*jai, jai, jai*' would ring out in response. Houses on both sides of the road were old and mossy grey, some with washing on balcony railings, saris, shirts and pyjamas. I took a wrong turn somewhere and found myself on Ishwar Ganguli

Lane. I asked a man standing outside a South Indian restaurant for directions.

'Do like this,' he said, 'go to Kattick Ghat Road by Tolly Canal and ask again.

Ten minutes later I was by Tolly canal, shallow and muddy, stinking of rotting vegetation. I asked a group of shirtless boys playing cricket on an opening.

'Dada, Debidarshan is that way. Take a short cut between those two houses. My friend also lives there,' one of the boys volunteered the information, eager to help a stranger.

'I am looking for Rajudada... masterji,' I said.

'Yes, yes masterji lives there,' all six boys shouted in unison, 'number 18.'

To my surprise Debidarshan Street was nothing but a long dirt track with small rundown houses on either side, similar to ones I had seen earlier on Kali Lane. Discarded household rubbish lay scattered by boundary fences. A hoarding for Amul butter used as a wall for a *jhopatty*. Behind it, several goats, tethered to a post with exceptionally long ropes, were grazing on clumps of grass. So quiet, it seemed the entire neighbourhood was still asleep. Number 18 was a mid-terrace house. A small paved path lined with *tulsi*, marigolds and other plants led to the green door. A pair of leather sandals sat on the top step. It seemed strange, a schoolteacher, a learned man, should be living in such squalid conditions. As I took a step closer I was gripped by a sudden irrational fear, imagining the policeman with moustache and his baby faced companion waiting for me inside.

I knocked on the front door with pounding heart and stood back.

The door opened with a slight creek. A face appeared and then the whole body. He was tall and lean, receding grey hair, clean-shaven face, and sagging skin under the chin, a check shirt, undone at the sleeves. 'What do you want?' he said. His voice was soft with a slight crackle.

'Are you Raju….,' I said. I must have mumbled my words for he asked, opening the door a little wider and leaning forward, 'what did you say?'

'Are you Raju?'

'Yes, I am. What do you want?'

'I have something that belongs to you.' I took out the folded letter from my pocket. Trying not to appear nervous but still my fingers shook as I held it up to him

He looked surprised as he studied the letter still in my hand and then stepped back in horror. His gaze darted between the letter and my face several times.

'Is it yours, sir?' I asked.

'Yes, yes, it is. How did you get it?' he said and then snatched it from me, taking care not to touch my fingers, as if I was contaminated.

'Dada it is like this. I found a wallet lying on the pavement with this letter inside. I was going to throw it away, but my friend read it and he said whoever owns this letter must want it back. So here I am.'

He stared at me and then his eyes narrowed. 'You are the pickpocket, aren't you?' He pointed a finger at me, much the same way he had done at the station.

I thought he was going to shout - thief, thief, thief.

'I didn't steal,' I said quickly, 'I am here only to give this back to you. That's all.'

'If you didn't steal, then who did, who?'

'I don't know.'

'Yes, you did,' he screamed, 'you dirty thief. Get out, get out, get out.' He went red in face and bent down as if he was going to pick up his slipper to hit me with. 'Go or I will call the police.'

I decided to come clean. 'What can I do *dada*, I have to eat too.' I rubbed a hand on my stomach and then joined them together begging for forgiveness.

If you are wondering Modiji, why did I not just shove the letter in his hands and run like hell, why risk being set upon by his neighbours, I can explain. The fact is, having read and reread the letter so many times, I was bursting with curiosity. I wanted to know who this man was, why he was carrying the letter in his wallet. Even more important, I wanted to know who Saira was. Why did they split up? My curiosity was so great I was prepared to take all risks.

'You have to eat, so you steal from the poor. You have no shame, you immoral rascal. And did you find anything to eat in the *batua*, did you?'

'Forgive me dada, I have done wrong,' I said, still with hands joined together.

'Done wrong? I should hand you to the police,' he said but made no move to get to a phone.

'Forgive me dada.'

'*Acha, acha*, you go now,' he said and then slammed the door shut.

I was not expecting this to happen, the abrupt closure. A heavy weight of disappointment settled on my shoulders. It's all lost. What will I tell Sanju? He will smirk, did not I tell you.

I was still contemplating what to do next when the door opened again. Raju's face reappeared. My heart stopped. I thought he had called the police.

'Wait,' he said, 'how did you find me?'

'*Dada* I went to the station and asked a few people. It took a while, but I got lucky. Someone there told me where you lived,' I also added, hoping it would please him, 'Raju *dada*, it seems you are famous around here.'

His lips cracked in a smile. 'I used to teach at Sri Jagadamba. That's why they all know me in the *para*.'

'You read a lot *dada*? The bookseller at the station said so.'

'Yes, we should all read more; it's the only way to gain knowledge. If we don't read, then what will be the difference between us and animals?'

I kept quiet.

'Do you want to learn to read?' he said after a long pause.

Yes, I nodded without hesitation.

'I will teach you, but first you must tell me about yourself.'

'What to tell *dada*. I don't have ma, don't have baba. They put me in an orphanage when I was very little and that's where I have lived most of my life.'

'What is your name?'

'Kalu.'

'Kalu … Kalu what?' he said, 'what is the caste?'

'They just called me Kalu. No one knew who my father was so I have no surname.'

I began crying. Not howling or anything like that, just made sad eyes and let some tears roll down my cheeks. Remember sir, I told you earlier, in my days in Durga Bhabi, I had become adept at turning out tears at will.

It had the desired effect. I saw him panic as he raised a hand to appease me, as if I was going to start whining and be a nuisance. 'Don't cry, don't cry. You better come in,' he said and opened the door wider.

I followed him into the back room. It had two bay windows, furnished with a small sofa, a coffee table and a sideboard. On the right was a small dining table covered with a patterned plastic sheet. Two small jars of pickles and chopped onions and a stainless steel plate with a half-eaten cutlet sat on the table. A few newspapers and books lay at the other end. More books were crammed in a cabinet with glass doors. On top sat some crystal figurines of animals. Compared to the drab exterior the ambiance here was pleasant, though the air smelled strongly of burned mustard oil. I guessed he must have been frying something.

'Wait here,' he said and went to the kitchen. I stood by the table, astonished at the dramatic turn of events. Only a few days ago I had no hope of finding him. Now I was inside his house, at his invitation.

He came out with two potato cutlets on a plate and a glass of water. 'Champa made these earlier. Come, eat,' he said.

'Oh, Raju *dada*, what are you doing. I have already eaten,' I protested.

'Don't you like these?' he said.

'Yes, yes, I do but ...'

'Then eat.'

I took the plate from him. They were delicious. I assumed Champa was the maid, not his wife, for there was no feminine touch to the house; everything belonged to him, like the men's brown shoes by the entrance. Shirts, socks and vests hanging on the washing line in the back yard, a bath towel slung on the back of a chair along with a khaki cotton trouser.

'How much can you read?' he asked.

'Just little, little,' I said.

'Did you ever go to school?'

'No sir.'

'I see,' he said and then went quiet. I could tell he wanted to do good; teach a poor country boy to read and write but was nervous about inviting a stranger to his house. Somehow, I had to find a way of reassuring him that I was harmless.

'*Dada,* I am very ashamed I stole your wallet. Will you forgive me,' I said and lowered my head to let him think I really was remorseful, 'when I read the letter I felt so guilty.'

'Yes, yes, it's alright,' he said as the wrinkles on his face intensified, made him appear older and frailer.

A week later, as promised, I went back to Debidarshan Street. Masterji was waiting for me.

'Come, come Kalu.' He made me sit at the dining table and gave me a notebook and pencil. 'Make notes whenever you want to,' he said and started the lesson by asking me to name everyday objects, like cats, dogs, chair and table, cars, buses, trains and others. I had to name them in English. That was easy. I knew the English equivalents for most of the objects. The ones I didn't he pronounced and wrote down the word in the note book and sketched a rough outline of the object.

After half an hour of this exercise he sat back, placed both palms flat on the table and said, '*baas,* that's all for today.'

'How did I do, Raju *dada?*' I was feeling pleased with myself even though I had not learned anything new.

'This was just the start. I was trying to work out how deep

in the water you are. Next week we will start properly,' he said and then called the maid, '*ki ranna hoi geche, Champa.*' Smell of cooked food was already drifting out of the kitchen.

Champa, a short lady in white cotton sari, came out with a plate of rice and fish stew and placed it roughly on the table. I caught her eyeing me with disapproval, as if saying you are of lower status and therefore have no business sitting at the table with my master.

Raju appeared not to notice. 'Come eat,' he said, 'there is *sandesh* after this.'

This time I ate without protesting. Raju sat at the top of the table sifting through books, as if selecting which one to read next. The heat was unbearable, even with the pedestal fan spinning away at full speed. I undid the top two buttons of my shirt.

'Are you hot?' He called Champa from the kitchen. 'Move the fan towards Kalu, he is sweating.'

Champa came and repositioned the fan, directing the breeze in my face while rebuking me with her eyes: couldn't you have done it yourself, you stupid boy?

I decided to play her up. 'No, no move it six inches this way .... more ... ah that's so good.' I watched her burn with anger at having to pander to my needs. She did not know I was a *chamar* boy or she would have gone fully berserk and demanded I sit on the floor and not touch anything.

'Raju *dada*, how long have you been a teacher?' I asked.

'Twenty years. Before that, I was in the army. Subedar Major, Assam Rifles,' he said puffing up his skinny chest, 'I have had posting in many places, Kashmir, Ladakh, Nagaland, Assam. Twice I was selected for the Republic Day parade in

New Delhi.'

'So why did you leave the army?'

'Why I left the army? This is why.' He brought his right leg forward and pulled the trouser leg up, revealing a straight metal rod with a carved wooden foot at the bottom end. A shoe laced to the dummy foot, identical to the one on his real left foot. 'We were fighting Naxalites in the jungle.'

It took a few moments to register, the realisation that not only had I robbed an old man, I had done it to an old cripple, a war veteran. I was genuinely horrified. He must have seen the distress on my face. 'It's alright son. I can walk,' he said with a wave of his hand, 'it's true I can't run. But then who wants to run at my age anyway.'

'*Dada*, you live alone?' I asked, 'how do you manage.'

'When you have no choice, you learn to manage, son. I have Champa,' he said gesturing at the kitchen, 'she comes every day, cooks for me and little bit of dusting, mopping...time passes.'

He must be a lonely man, living alone with just books for company. Maybe that is why he was so pleased to see me. He was evidently a bachelor. Then who was Saira. All evening I had been itching to ask him about her. 'Raju *dada* ... can I ask you a question?'

'Question? Yes,' he said lowering the book.

'The lady in the letter, Saira ... who was she?' I asked softly so Champa would not hear.

Raju sat up abruptly. I thought he was going to order me to leave. He surprised me once again by the reply. 'I wanted to marry her. But it didn't happen.'

'Oh, Raju *dada* ... did you never get married then?'

'No.'

'But *dada*, there are thousands of beautiful girls everywhere begging for husbands.'

'No Kalu, it's not like that. If I couldn't marry the person I loved, I wasn't going to marry at all. I wasn't interested in the second best,' he said and then stood up and retrieved a key from a flower vase. With unsteady fingers he unlocked the top drawer of the sideboard and pulled out a little jewellery box.

'See this,' he said and opened the box, exposing a gold ring sitting on a cushion of fading black velvet, a pink stone at the top and intricate designs etched on the shiny metal. 'I bought this engagement ring for her. But ... never got a chance to put it on her fingers.'

I realised then how much he must have loved her, forty years on, still cherishing the memory by holding on to the ring in its original box.

'Have you not been in touch?'

'No ... never,' he said with a sigh.

'Why couldn't you marry?'

'It's a long story son ... she was Muslim.'

I understood. An upper class Bengali Brahmin marrying a Muslim would be a major family scandal.

'Do you ever wonder where she is now, did she ever get married?'

'What will be the point? What was to happen has happened. It can't be changed.'

'Would you like to meet her ... perhaps once,' I asked tentatively, ready to apologise if he took offence. I was visualising two lovers who had lost touch with each other, unexpectedly coming face to face. What dramatic scene that would be, full of emotion and tears.

He did not say 'yes', but did not say 'no' either. He just stared at a book cover.

'It's possible she feels the same about you,' I said.

'But it will not be right. She is probably married, has a family and children. She has to look after them, a big responsibility.'

'Suppose we find her, and she says yes to meeting you, what then.'

'If she agrees I will meet her, just once before I die. But son I don't know where she lives. She could be living in America, Australia, Dubai, who knows where? People are travelling everywhere these days,' he said and shut his eyes with his head up slightly, exposing an unruly spray of hair in his nostrils.

'Where was her family living in those days?'

'Rajabazar. But that was a long time ago.'

On the way home, I was thinking of nothing but Saira and Raju. How wonderful it would be to see them together. By the time I got off the bus at Chitpur Road I was fully convinced Raju and Saira would want to meet and I should do everything in my power to make it happen.

CHAPTER 20

Modiji, bad news today. The Sanyo has finally died. This morning, as usual I pressed the ON button to start recording. It made a loud purring noise and then went quiet. I did everything to make it work, even changed the batteries. Sanju tried it too. 'Good it has stopped working,' he said beaming with a smile, 'now I won't have to do any more typing for you.'

'We can't stop now, the real juicy bit is about to come.'

'*Yaar*, my exams are coming soon. If I fail, you know what will happen. Madam will stop sending me money.'

I had to convince him that the project I had started was important. It was of national interest. However, I did promise to hurry it up, finish as quickly as possible. So from now on sir, I am going to cut out casual chitchat and stick to the central issue. I hope that is all right with you.

I took my Sanyo to Ali, implored him to bring it to life. He opened it up, part by part, put it together again and then handed it back to me. 'Kalu, get yourself a box of matches and kerosene oil. Your Sanyo needs a good funeral.'

I had become so used to its purring sounds and clicks and clanks, their absence disturbed me. I asked Ali to find me an identical replacement.

'Is that a problem? You ask Ali and it will be done. Come let's go.' He pulled out his motorcycle from the corrugated shed. 'It may not be the same model but the make will be same,' and then he added, 'my friend is a collector of electronic equipment, Sanyo, Grundy, Decca and what not. A real *pagal*, madman he is.'

He pushed his Hero Splendor Plus motorcycle onto the road, rocked it from side to side a few times, raised his left leg and straddled the bike. 'Come on, sit,' he said. I sat down on the back cushion, placed my hands on his shoulders and we took off for Durgapur. In no time we were on Radha Nath Mulick Lane heading north.

Wind was hitting my face, a pleasant experience. 'Ali, what speed is it now?' I asked.

'Forty-five.'

'Now Ali, what speed?'

'Fifty-five,' Ali yelled over the roar of the engine, 'it can do hundred and fifty-five.'

On Barrackpore Trunk Road Ali speeded up even more.

'What speed?'

'Almost sixty. Hold tight we are going to lift off.' He gave the engine another boost.

'How old are you Ali?'

'I am twenty-five. Why are you asking?'

'Are you afraid of dying?'

'No, why would we die anyway? I have been driving for years.'

'You are Muslim, aren't you?'

'Yes.'

'If you do have an accident and are killed, will you go to heaven?'

'Yes, all good Muslims go to heaven after death,' he said, slowing down approaching a busy junction.

'What about me? I am not Muslim.'

'You should become Muslim,' he said, as if suggesting a short cut to heaven.

I thought of Father John, the priest I had met in Park Circus. He had also talked of heaven. Christ loves you as you are. Your soul is as precious to him as anyone's is. Take him to your heart, and you will definitely go to heaven. I thought of Babu's philosophy on life and death. I hated to agree with him, but his was the only sensible view on this subject. '*Re* I don't believe in God, full stop,' he would say and clap his hand as if dislodging dirt, 'religion is a bad thing. This idea of going to heaven is *bakwas,* nonsense, just an invention. It was thought up by rich Brahmins to keep the poor lower castes from rebelling.'

It seemed to me that the main reason for having a religion was to cheat death and live again, here or in heaven. Well, I did not want another life, thanks, not if it was going to be anything like the current one.

'What if someone renounces Islam?' I asked

'Renouncing Islam is insulting Allah. They will definitely go to hell.'

In Durgapur I discovered Ali's friend was not another Muslim but a Sikh whose family was originally from Lahore. I wondered what his philosophy on life and death was. He seemed more interested in talking business. 'As it happens, I do have a Sanyo,' he said and placed a highly polished portable model with push buttons and indicator lights on a table. It was a later model with on/off/recording indicator lights. I was delighted to find the operation of recording and playback was much simpler than my previous model.

So now, we are back in business Modiji though Sanju is not very happy.

By the time I returned to Chitpur Road it was already dark. An overcast cloudy night, it appeared rain was imminent. Fearing a trap by Babu's men, I had started taking a back alley route to the shop. With the new Sanyo wrapped in a carrier bag, I entered the side lane, turned right and right again into the unlit alleyway. Barely able to see I picked my way carefully, sidestepping cow dungs and household waste. I was seven doors away when I saw the red glow of a lit cigarette and a man standing under a bougainvillea bush. He saw me, took a puff, but did not move. I kept walking. To turn back would be show of cowardice. I could sense his gaze on me. He tossed the cigarette, the glowing ember an arc of light in the gloom. I looked behind me and my heart missed a beat. Another man in black shirt was coming towards me. Only three of us were in the alley. The man with cigarette stepped out from under the bougainvillea, revealing a scar on his forehead, thick bulbous lips and no neck. His head appeared attached directly to the chest. Behind me, I could sense the man with black shirt had caught up with me.

I was trapped alright and my only hope was to talk my way out.

'*Bhaiya*, what are you looking for? I may be able to help,' I said to the man in front, trying to sound casual but friendly.

He did not reply nor move out of my way or take his gaze off me. It sent shivers down my body. What do they want? Maybe they want to rob me.

'You want money,' I said, 'here take everything I have.' I put a hand in my trouser pocket.

'We don't want money,' he said in a polite manner. His voice was incredibly effeminate, in spite of the burly appearance.

'What do you want then?'

'The photo,' he said and instantly my stomach felt as if it had received a blow. I wanted to empty my bowels.

So Babu has caught up with me at long last. Now he is going to carry out the threat he has been promising. The reality hit home like a hammer to the head. Sanju's words came to mind: he is going to frighten you, but not kill you. The words were of no consolation, looking at the big man with no neck.

'I don't have any photos,' I said.

'Oh, you don't have it,' he said courteously, as if it was a rhetorical question.

'No.'

'Excuse us for troubling you,' he said looking down at the ground momentarily, as if pondering, 'you do one thing for us then, I will call my boss so you can tell him you don't have the photo. We will be on our way.' He dipped a hand in his back pocket as if to retrieve a phone.

'No, I am not speaking to anyone,' I said.

'Then you do have the photo.'

'No, no, no, tell Babu I don't have it any more.'

'You don't understand brother. My saying won't do. It has to come from you,' he said and rocked his broad shoulders from left to right without moving his head.

'I don't know anything. Just go away,' I said.

'*Are baba*, we will go once you give us what we have come for. Come on lets go in,' he said and pointed at the back entrance to Baldev's shop which was lit by a small bulb under an arch.

'Get lost,' I said.

'That is not possible,' he said, still very polite, 'our instruction is to bring back a photo.'

I started to move away from them.

Black shirt, who had not spoken so far, came forward and grabbed a fistful of my shirt. 'Where are you going?'

'Leave me alone,' I said, 'you are not getting anything from me.'

I did not see it coming but felt the punch on the face. It blinded me momentarily.

'*Saala gandu*, I gave him a chance,' the man with no neck growled and aimed a kick at my legs. I tried to step back, hit a rock and fell. They were now kicking me all over the body, taking turns. The Sanyo in the carrier bag rolled to one side.

No neck walked around me, working out where to kick next. I followed the dirty black boots, so I could see the trajectory. It was coming for my face. I tried to move out of its way, ended up with face in a muddy pool. A metallic taste in my mouth, I realised I was bleeding.

I put my hands up. 'Stop, for God's sake why don't you believe me? I really don't have it.'

Black shirt knelt down and said softly in my ear. 'Actually we don't like doing this to you. Why don't you give us the photo? Then you will save yourself all this pain, no.'

'It's lost,' I said, 'please believe me.'

'You telling the truth?' he asked, as if he wanted to believe me.

'Yes, yes.' I felt hopeful for once. Perhaps they do believe me.

'No, he is lying,' no neck said roughly and resumed the kicking.

I started crawling, head low, squelching in mud and cow dung. If I could reach the end of the alley, even halfway there, someone might see us and intervene.

'*Haramzada* thinks his friend is coming to save him,' no neck said, gave a hollow laugh and then jumped on my head with both feet. Bells started ringing in my ears. I felt my stomach heave and then I vomited.

'Get up. Get up, you son of a swine, on your feet. See what you have done,' he said.

I raised my head. A light came on in a window. I could not tell how far it was. I heard some voices. The ringing in my ears died down. Both my eyes closed. There was silence, as if I was floating in a dark tunnel.

'Kalu, is that you?' Pratibha screamed as I staggered in through the back door, '*O baba*, look at you.' She placed both hands on her head.

'It's nothing,' I said and tried to smile. I did not want to show I was hurting.

She took my arm and helped me to a chair. 'Sit down, don't talk.' She ran to the kitchen and returned with a bucket of cold water and a towel. 'Purohit, call Baldev sahib, quick, quick,' she yelled at the kitchen porter and began wiping my face with the wet towel, dabbing at the cuts on my face and arms, refreshing the towel by dipping it in the water. The water was rapidly turning pink. I could hear her heavy breathing as if feeling my pain too. I wanted to hug her, push my face in her white sari with blue border, like Mother Teresa.

'Who has done this to you? You need to go to hospital,' she said raising my face with fingers under the chin.

'No hospital.' I shook my head. Droplets of blood fell on my trouser. She pushed my head back and pinched the nose with the towel. 'Hold it there and don't move.'

'Where are you, *re*?' she screamed again for Baldev, 'Purohit bring me the first aid box.'

Baldev came in and stopped dead. '*Hari Ram*, what is going on here?'

I did not reply. I had to come up with a believable explanation or he would insist on calling the police.

'Was it that *gunda* Partho?' Baldev said with hands on his hips and feet wide apart, 'this time they have gone too far.' He was referring to a gang of layabouts who had been intimidating the neighbourhood with their anti-social behaviour. 'I better call the police.'

'No need,' I said and winced in pain as I tried to raise my arm, 'I gave them a beating too, they won't come back.'

'You beat them?' Baldev said in disbelief.

'Yes, I did.'

'Don't stress him,' Pratibha scolded Baldev, 'can't you see he is in pain.'

The nosebleed had slowed to occasional drip. Pratibha wiped my face again and started bandaging.

'Go now, change your clothes,' she said once she had finished and stood back with hands on hips, as if she had done what she could. 'You need to take care of yourself.'

'Yes, auntie,' I said. I was going up the stairs, I heard him whisper to Pratibha, 'I don't know what trouble that boy is in. I want him out of here.'

I did not leave my room for three days. Pratibha was sending food up to me twice a day. I ate very little, had no appetite. The visions of the big fellow with no neck and girlish voice and his black shirted companion started haunting me. They know where I live. What is to stop them from coming back? Maybe next time they will kill me. Sanju tried to console me, 'he is only trying to frighten you. That's about the furthest he will go, as long as he believes you have the photo.'

On the fourth day, there was a knock on the door. It was Purohit. 'Baldev sahib wants to talk to you,' he said in his thick Oriya accent.

Suddenly I wanted to weep. Baldev is going to ask me to vacate the room. Where will I go in this condition? I will be at the mercy of Babu's men. They will drag me back to Bangalore.

'Are you alright?' Purohit asked sympathetically. As far as he was concerned, I was a brave man, a hero, for standing up to the neighbourhood *gundas*.

'I am alright. You can go,' I said to Purohit and hobbled down the stairs, slowly lifting one foot and then the other, exaggerating the discomfort. Baldev was standing at the bottom of the stairs, a hand on the banister, a dour expression on his face and a blob of saffron *tilak* freshly applied on his forehead. He must have just returned from the temple.

I was ready to plead for leniency: look at me, how can I go anywhere in this condition? Have a heart. He waited for me to reach the last step and then said in a low voice, 'who is the girl?'

He is going to accuse me of smuggling girls to my room to justify eviction. 'There is no girl here,' I protested, 'come have a look.'

'Says her name is Tanya,' he said with a nod of the head to indicate she was outside the door.

'Tanya ...?' My head began reeling. All this was too much – first Babu's beating, then Baldev threatening to evict me and now Tanya. What does she want?

'Oh Tanya, she is my friend's older sister,' I offered a believable lie. There was some truth to it; she was certainly older, about twenty-five years old, though I could not be certain. 'She has come to check if I am alright.'

'Uh, check if he is alright.' He jeered as if it was a joke. 'I will send her up, but remember, none of that type of business or you will sleep on the pavement with the servants and rickshaw pullers.'

I hobbled back up and began straightening the bed hurriedly, pushing clutter under it, under the chair, shoving used food containers inside the bin. What will she think of this hole? I was still hobbling around when she opened the door and breezed in. Her cute smile, pink top and black slacks, sweet-smelling perfume, instantly brightened the room.

'Kalu, what has happened?' she said scanning the bandages.

I shrugged my shoulders. It is nothing.

'Roby told me you were attacked by some *gundas*.'

I shrugged my shoulders again; unaware I was still holding on to a corner of the bed sheet. She came over, took the sheet from me and set it down, expertly sweeping out wrinkles and creases, totally in control.

'Why didn't you run instead of fighting? You are a stubborn fool.'

I did not reply.

'You look a mess, have you bathed or not?' she said, like scolding a child, 'go and get changed while I make tea.'

I rushed to the bathroom so she would not see the tears in my eyes. I could hear her pushing furniture around and rattle of pots in the kitchen. When I came out, washed and in a clean shirt, she was tidying up the table, giving it a wipe with a kitchen cloth.

'Tanya, you don't have to do all this?' I said.

'What am I doing, nothing. Sit down I am bringing the

tea,' she said, 'just tell me where the sugar is.' I noticed she had already placed water to boil on the stove.

'In the jar on upper shelf, sorry I don't have much,' I said, feeling mortified at what she would find.

She came in with two steaming hot mugs, the only mugs I owned, and placed them on the table. 'Drink while it's hot,' she said and sat down on the chair.

'Tanya, why are you here?' I really could not understand why she was here, after the way I had insulted her at the club.

'I had to come and see you,' she said softly. Her voice was comforting. Better than any of the ointments Pratibha had applied on my bruises.

'I was attacked. I had to defend myself.'

'Poor Kalu,' she said, 'you should be more careful.'

'I will be alright,' I said, 'how is your grandmother?'

'She is becoming a nuisance. Worries when I leave home. Something may happen to me. I tell her, Dadi I am twenty-five, I can look after myself. But she doesn't accept it. And she worries when I am home too.'

'Why does she worry when you are home?'

'Get married she says. At your age you should already have children. Look at me she says. I was eighteen when your father was born.'

'Maybe she is right, you should consider it,' I said.

'When I am ready.'

'When will that be?'

'I don't know. But now I must be back to work or my boss will be mad,' she said consulting her watch, 'I only came by to see you are alright.'

'I am alright Tanya. The bandages will be out within a week,'

I said while trying to subdue my emotions but failing miserably.

'Oh, Kalu, come here,' she said and took me in her arms. I felt her warm cheeks against mine and it was the most wonderful thing I had ever experienced.

After she shut the door and left, I wanted to howl like a baby, throw myself out of the window. This life is not worth living.

That night I lay in bed for several hours, trying desperately to fall asleep. My hand touched something soft and plump. I sat up screaming and jumped out of the bed. I was still screaming when Roby burst into the room. '*Uloo ka patha*. Why are you creating such racket?'

'Cockroach, cockroach, cockroach.'

'Where, show me.'

I pointed at the bed sheet, 'kill it for me.'

He went to the bed and lifted the sheet slowly. 'Ah, got it,' he said cupping something in his hand.

'Kill it; throw it out of the window, quickly.'

Instead of going to the window, he turned around and threw it at me. I ducked in terror.

'It's that thing, girls wear in their hair, a clip, you fool,' he said snorting with laughter.

I sat down on the chair, my heart still pumping like mad.

'Aha, so how did a girl's hair clip get on your bed,' he said and made a face as if he had caught me in the act, 'you dirty swine, does Baldev know about this?'

'It's not like that,' I explained, 'Tanya had come to see me this morning. The clip must have slipped off her hair.'

He looked surprised that Tanya was here. 'What did she want?'

'Nothing just came to check if I was alright.'

'Have you been fucking her, you swine.'
'Don't talk rubbish. She is not that type of girl.'
'I know, I know,' he said, 'but do you know she likes you.'

Chapter 21

The address Raju had given me was 49 Sealdah Road near Hari Para Masjid. Her family name was Banu, Saira Banu.

I picked Sunday for the mission. On the bus, surrounded by a crowd of rowdy cricket fans going to a Sunday match, I considered the task ahead. There were at least forty nine homes on Sealdah Road. If I knocked on every door, the possibility of coming across at least one person who knew Saira or her family was reasonably high. As I neared the destination, self-doubt began creeping in. Was it wise to knock on strangers' doors, enquire about people who may or may not have lived there? What if they laugh and slam the door on my face.

Sealdah Road was a typical inner-city street of small houses and tenement buildings built before the British left India. Rust stains from leaking drainpipes, washing fluttering on railings, crumbling masonry, wrought iron grilles on windows. The front rooms of many of the houses had been turned into shops or eating places, some spilling out onto the pavements with tables, chairs and shopping carts. None of the houses was numbered. I asked a mango seller about number forty-nine. He looked at me in anger, as if I had insulted him. 'These are top class mangoes *babu*, *kasuri*, *hanh*, top class. For forty nine *rupiah* you only get this,' he did a hand gesture of masturbation and asked me to get lost. He had obviously misunderstood me.

I moved on and stopped an old man walking with a stoop, a rolled up carrier bag in his hand.

'Uncle I am looking for number forty-nine.'

'Just there,' he said pointing, 'what, Biswas babu you are looking for?' He honked and spat a blob of phlegm in the gutter.

'No, not Biswas, I am looking for Banu.'

The old man shook his head. 'Banu, I don't know.'

'Banu family used to live at forty-nine many years ago uncle, around ninety sixty or ninety seventy.'

'Wohhh, that long?' he sang in a rickety voice, coughed, brought out more phlegm and spat. 'You do like this. First speak to Biswas babu, *henh*, no harm in that. Then go to Salem *moshai* at thirty-seven. He was born in that house. What to tell you, he knows everybody on the street, even dogs and cats. He is bound to know your man.'

I thought number forty- nine was the tiny guesthouse. A board above said Ali Shah Hotel. Inside a boy behind a counter in dirty white uniform was staring at pictures in a Filmfare. A sign above said Rs 500 per night. I asked the boy if this was forty-nine. 'Next door,' he said insolently and went back to his magazine. A Maruti stood outside number forty-nine. A nameplate attached to the door read, Mr M B S Biswas, Chief Engineer (Retd). Panic set in even before I had knocked on the door. Has Saira married Mr M B S Biswas and still lives here? If she opens the door, how will I talk to her about Raju in front of Mr Biswas? Will her children open the door?

A young girl in ponytail appeared.

'I am looking for Mr Biswas,' I said.

She asked me to wait and went back in. I could hear the familiar voice of an NDTV newsreader. A big man in white shirt appeared at the door, blocking out view of the hall behind him.

'Uncle, sorry to inconvenience you, I am looking for Banu family.' I explained everything in detail, that it was important to find them.

'No, not heard of them. We moved here ten years ago,' he said.

'Do you know of anyone else on the street who may have known the family?'

He gave the question due consideration. 'As a matter of fact, I do,' he said, 'Salem ... Salem has been here a long time. That house with green door.' He pointed into the distance. 'Number thirty-seven. Tell him I sent you. My name is Subendhu. Tell him also I am waiting for the beer he promised.' He laughed *Ho, Ho, Ho*, exposing remarkably white teeth.

Number thirty-seven indeed had a green door. On the concrete porch, a boy was roasting *bhutta* corn on a small brazier, fanning the charcoal feverishly with a square piece of cardboard. Five customers were waiting patiently at the steps. One took out a handkerchief and wiped his forehead. 'I am melting here, hurry up,' he said to the boy.

A man standing at the back said, 'you come here every day and every day you say the same thing.' He was about sixty years old with greying hair, blue shirt and shining black shoes. The shoe caught my eye, I had never seen footwear polished to such perfection.

'Babu I am saying to the boy, not you,' the customer replied irritably.

The boy speeded up the fanning. His spindly arms moving at an astonishing speed, spreading puffs of dry ash in the air.

After the last customer had departed, the man said to the boy, 'fifty rupees from now on.'

'Sahib have some pity, fifty is too much. All day the smoke fills my lungs. Look at my fingers – charred like the coal itself and my papa beats me if I don't bring home enough money,' he said bowing at sahib's feet, 'and Shaikh babu has to be fed too.'

'Stop this acting *shakting* business. I know how much you earn. You give me fifty tomorrow or find another pitch.'

Sahib saw me standing. 'What do you want?' he said roughly.

'I am looking for Mr Salem. Does he live in this house?'

'Yes, what do you want, first tell me?'

'Are you Mr Salem?'

'Am I Mr Salem? What do I look like – Shahrukh Khan or something?' He chuckled. 'Speak.'

I explained about the Banu family at number forty-nine.

Salem looked intrigued at first and then suspicious. 'Are you sure you are not selling anything?'

'I am not selling, just asking a few questions.'

'You better come in then.'

Once in the dark hallway he said, 'looking for Banu *dada*, eh.'

'Yes.'

'*Hmm*, he has gone,' he said with a nod of the head upward.

'Do you know where?' I asked.

'*Are bhai* don't you understand, gone, gone,' he said pointing a finger at the sky, 'passed away.'

It was not surprising Banu senior had died, considering Saira would now be in her late sixties or seventies. 'What about the rest of the family?'

'They moved out after his death.'

'Which year did they leave?'

He said he could not remember.

'Do you know where they have gone?'

'*Nahin bhai* I don't know. But my mother might.'

'Thank you.' I stood back, expecting Mr Salem to go in and speak to his mother.

'Yes, but not now. She is in hospital. I'll speak to her later. OK. You come back later, in a week.'

I pressed for more information. 'Do you remember a girl living there? Her name was Saira.'

'Yes, yes, I remember her. She was older of two sisters. Both were older than me. I had nothing to do with them.'

'Did Saira have many friends?'

'How do you expect me to know all that?' He scribbled a telephone number on a piece of paper. 'Call me in a few days.'

'Thank you,' I said taking the paper from him.

On the way out, I bought a roasted corn-on-the-cob from the boy with charcoal grey fingers.

I handed him all the money in my pocket, about three hundred rupees. He looked at the bundle of creased notes in amazement and then at me, as if saying this is too much.

'Give it to Papa,' I said. It was a small gesture. Probably it will please his papa for a few days, but nothing would change in the long term.

What I have already figured out Modiji is this. Handing out small amount of money here and there does nothing to help the poor. I have my own theories about how to bring about workable social change. But no one is interested in listening to me. Roby starts yawning whenever I bring up the subject. Sanju asks me to shut the fuck up about my half-baked theories. 'Who is at university studying political science – you or me?'

Halwai Baldev starts scratching his crotch anxiously. 'Will your theories lower the cost of my chapattis?'

'No …'

'Then leave me alone. Go talk to that dog. He has all the time in the world.'

That afternoon I went to work in New Market. Shoppers were still out in force. I spotted a well-dressed woman with a heavy shopping bag and a Louis Vitton handbag slung casually on her shoulder. She looked fatigued and hot. This will be easy picking. At a sari shop counter, she dropped the bags on a chair and demanded attention, 'Show me Chanderi silk and georgette crepe saris.' I stood at a respectable distance, letting the staff believe I was her servant, the bag carrier. While the assistants were running around attending to her whims, I lifted the purse from her handbag.

On the way home, I jumped off the bus a stop short of my destination and walked the rest of the way. I had been doing this for a few days. The theory being, if there were any suspicious characters hanging outside Baldev's shop, I would spot them first.

It was seven in the evening. Naked yellow bulbs or white fluorescent tubes had started coming on here and there. A man was belting out a Bengali song. A gang of boys were pelting stones at a dog and bitch joined in copulation. Someone emptied a bucket of water over the animals in an attempt to separate them. The dog dashed across the road narrowly missing an approaching motorcyclist. A short way ahead, a crowd had gathered around a yellow and black taxi. People were rocking the vehicle from side to side, screaming at the driver to come out. 'Open the door you son of a bitch.'

'What happened?' I asked a man watching the drama from a distance.

'The bastard drove the taxi into the poor fellow's auto rickshaw, right in the back, *thaak*, like that.' He demonstrated with his hands how it happened.

Someone else said, 'these fellows don't pass their driving test. They just buy the licence by offering their backside for buggery.'

The mob was on the verge of overturning the taxi when the driver opened the door, shivering like a frightened puppy, and hands joined together pleaded for mercy. However, mercy was in short supply that day. They beat him to the ground. Two policemen arrived at the scene. The crowd shifted, created a path for them to reach the driver. The poor man was lying on the pavement unconscious, bleeding, probably with broken limbs. Someone had found the key to the taxi and was driving it away while a section of the crowd was giving chase: how dare he not share the loot.

I was watching from a distance, careful not to get involved, while munching freshly roasted peanuts. A hand came to rest on my shoulder. I swung around. Who do I see grinning like a cat? It was the policeman with big moustache I had met the other night.

'Aha, it's our Sherlock Holmes,' he said jovially and gestured smoking a pipe. 'So tell me have you thought about it? *Hanh*. You want to join Kolkata police. We will make you a top detective, secret agent 007.'

The baby-faced assistant, this time in a surprisingly clean uniform, appeared.

'Look who we have found,' moustache said to his companion, 'our Sherlock Holmes.'

'This is very fortunate. We have been looking for you,' baby face said.

'Looking for me?'

'Ah, ha, ha, nothing to worry about,' he said adjusting my shirt collar and flicking imaginary fluff from it, 'you are alright. We just wanted to let you know you didn't do the murder of the *rickshawallah*. You were hundred percent innocent. *Shahbash.*' He patted me on the shoulder.

'Of course, I am innocent. I told you that night,' I said.

'You see my boss has twenty years of experience. Solving murders is his mission in life. He works selflessly, day and night, to catch bad people and put them in prison. After thorough investigation, he concluded that poor fellow wasn't murdered after all. He died because his time had come. God came to take him away.' He lowered his head like a pious religious man and did a *namaste* to God. The boss nodded with approval, looking suitably sombre.

So, give me my money back you rascals, I wanted to say.

'There is something else we wanted to talk to you about. You see my boss has received a report that you might be involved in some dishonest business. Not that we believe any of it. But, we have to ask anyway. It is our duty you see.'

I looked on nervously. Are they cooking some other money making scheme?

'The report we have received is that you have been doing a little bit of that trick of the fingers, picking pockets of rich people ... no, no, no we don't believe it. I told my boss it's not possible, how that simple honest boy can be doing something so criminal. But we have to ask. You understand, don't you?'

My heart started pounding. How did they find out? How much do they know? I wanted to believe they knew nothing.

'I don't know what you are saying. Maybe you are confusing

me for someone else. It's possible. Isn't it?' I said.

Moustache put on a stern expression. 'Boy, tell us the truth. Are you a *phoketmar*?'

'No *sahab*, absolutely not.'

'You are lying.'

'No, I am not lying. Why are you doing this to me?'

'Yes, you are lying. Do you think you can fool me? Twenty years in the police force.'

'No, I am not fooling you.'

'Then why do you look so frightened, eh?'

'You're shouting and all. It's frightening me.' I said.

'I am frightening you. Wait till you go to jail and meet the dogs there,' he made a face, caricaturing the face of ferocious *Ravana*, 'then you will understand the meaning of fear. Take him to the station, make him talk,' he said to the assistant, striking my leg with the baton.

'Yes boss.' Baby face took my arm. 'Come on.'

I began protesting, 'how can you do this to me.'

'Come quietly, you will be alright,' he said and dragged me to an alleyway between two shops. We walked along an open drain. Crossed to the other side using a footbridge constructed with planks of wood. An old lady with a bag full of vegetables eyed us with suspicion. Five minutes later he stopped in front of a warehouse constructed with timber and corrugated sheets. The door opened, as if by itself. Whoever had opened it had retreated further back without showing the face. A light came on. It revealed another, smaller warehouse. This one was brick built with a single steel door. He turned the long handle and pulled. The door opened with a painful groan. A blast of cold air hit my face. Under the white glow of a single tube light, I could see pink flesh of skinned animals hanging by hooks from the ceiling. No heads, just carcasses slit open at the chest. Floor littered with blobs of jellied blood. On one side several machetes, knives and handsaws lay scattered on two, heavily serrated and blood stained, wooden worktops. The air smelled of dead flesh, the sort you get from butchers stalls, in the market, only magnified several folds. The only noise I could hear was a faint crackle coming from the tube light.

'Let me go, *sahab*,' I said now in full panic.

'How can I let you go after what you have done? Pickpocketing is a serious crime.'

'*Sahab*, take two hundred rupees,' I said and quickly retrieved the folded bank notes from my pocket, 'here it is, take it. This is all I have'

'You want me to disobey my boss?' he said sternly.

'No *sahib*.'

'My boss is a very strict and honest man of twenty year service.'

'Yes, *sahab* very honest, just like you. But if you talk to him he will listen.'

He stopped beside a carcass and patted it, as if checking for freshness and quality. 'I will try for you,' he said while still examining the dead animal.

'Yes, *sahab*. Please try.'

'Have you got two thousand rupees?' he said, moving on to the next carcass, which was somewhat smaller, still discharging a slow dribble of blood, 'hah, this one is fresh.' He gave the flesh two or three hefty smacks.

'Two thousand,' I yelped, 'where will I find so much money, *sahab*. Have pity.'

'I know how much money you people make. Two thousand or jail. Make up your mind.'

'Alright *sahab*. I will borrow the money from friends. Shall I bring it to the station?'

'No. Take it to Kumar at the *paan* shop. You know where it is?'

I knew Kumar's *paan* shop. 'I will deliver the money to Kumar. You can rely on me.'

'*Accha*, good. From then it is five hundred rupees a month,' he said.

'Every month,' I cried, 'it is not fair, *sahab*.'

He scanned the cold storage room, at the grey ceiling and the concrete walls; a calendar was hanging on one side, Jai Ma Kali Meat Company, printed in bold. Below it was a picture of Kali Mata, complete with garland of human skulls and bloodied daggers.

'How do you like the jail?' he said and grinned broadly, 'good, eh, no *kheech peech* noises from outside, no disturbance, no heat of the sun, cool and peaceful.'

My legs turned to jelly. What could I do sir? I had to agree to his demands. 'Alright, I will give you five hundred a month.'

'*Shabash beta*,' he said, 'just do as I say you will have nothing to worry about. We will look after you. No one will ever bother you.'

'Can I go now?'

'You can go.'

As I turned to run he stopped me again and pushed his hand in my trouser pocket. The bastard took everything I had, including the change.

I ran out of the freezing warehouse, turned left instead of

right; unaware I was heading in the wrong direction. I wished the time would roll back and take me back to my first home. I yearned for Ramesh's company, wanted to get back to the old ways. I remembered his singing, the practical jokes and his Maria. I wondered if she was still there, aloof from everyone, on the bed rocking back and forth, back and forth, back and forth. For once, I wished I was with her, both rocking back and forth in unison, in silence.

In the restaurant, Shanta the new cook came hurrying. 'Kalu, why are you crying?'

I was not even aware I had been weeping. I blamed the tears to putrid smoke. Someone was burning rubbish in the back alley.

I saw Pratibha leaning over the double basin. It was full of bloated shirts and underwear. Suds were bubbling over the rim. 'Kalu*uuu*, come here,' she yelled when she saw me. She lifted the bulk up out of the water and let it fall again. She believed in washing clothes in the evening. I like to get the work done before going to sleep, they will be half-dry by sun rise, and then fully dry two hours later, ready for ironing, she explained.

'You know I come from a good, respectable family,' she said.

'Yes, Pratibha aunty, you told me before.'

'I am educated too. I went to school and all.'

'Yes, yes you told me that too.' I was wondering where we were going with this. I was in no mood for idle chitchat.

'But he, he is illiterate, nothing in that brain, it is hollow, like a dried out coconut shell.'

'What has he done Pratibha aunty?'

'He wants to keep chickens in the back yard. You see. I told you he has nothing there.' She tapped her head with soaking wet knuckles.

'Chickens? Here? I don't believe it,' I said. I knew though anything was possible from Baldev. He didn't care what anyone thought of him; in fact he enjoyed shocking people.

'You don't believe me?' She plunged the ball back in the basin; bubbles erupted as if from an active volcano and slid over the side. 'Come with me.'

In the yard Baldev was rummaging in the shed, like a squirrel foraging in the undergrowth, shifting things around, making a lot of noise. He came out with a square cage-like structure made of wire. 'Where did we get this from?' he asked all excited, holding up the cage as if it was a stroke of luck he had found it, 'perfect for raising the chicks.'

'What do I know where it has come from?' she cried and turned to me, 'you have a word with him, put some sense in there.'

I fell in love with the birds instantly. Poor things were cowering in a makeshift cardboard box cage. Already I had a favourite, the youngest of the three with white feathers.

'Now chicks have a comfortable home, all we do is feed them daily. When they grow big in a few weeks they will be ready to lay eggs.'

'What's wrong with eggs from the market?' she yelled, throwing wet garments on the clothesline.

'*Arey bibi*, these eggs will be brilliantly tasty to eat. Trust me,' he said, smacked his lips and sneaked a glance at me, rolled his eyes as if to say, see what I have to put up with all the time.

'Don't *bibi, bibi* me. Take them back where they have come from or I will.' As she draped another garment on the clothesline, the pole holding the line taut lost its bearing and hovered dangerously over the cage.

'Hoh, hoh, hoh,' he ran to save his little birds, 'you trying to kill them already, stupid woman.'

I did a double back and went to my room. Strange couple, I thought, dragging others in their comical squabbles.

Another time I had seen her in a furiously angry state, refilling chiller cabinets, banging the door as she worked, bangles on her wrists jingling noisily. 'I have been married to this man fourteen years and still I have not gone mad. You believe it Kalu?' she said to me, gesturing at her husband as if he was a lowly creature. Baldev was lounging on a chair, picking his nose.

Baldev rolled his eyes and slapped the forehead forcefully, 'she hasn't gone mad, but I have.'

Pratibha retorted, '*Re*, you are lucky my mother didn't let me see you before marriage. I would have rejected you if I had.'

'Ha, ha, ha,' Baldev laughed and turned to me, 'says she would have rejected a handsome man like me, a Mumbai film star.'

'Handsome film star, my foot. Would you marry him Kalu?' she asked, taking it for granted I would side with her. Then realising the absurdity of that question both the wife and husband burst out laughing.

Chapter 22

I was at Subhash Chandra Bose International airport, stalking a Punjabi family: husband, wife and four small children, lugging bags stuffed to the brim. We were under the noisily purring electronic keyboard when I heard someone call my name. I turned around sharply.

'Oh, Nandu-*da*,' I cried, 'fancy meeting you here.'

Nandu-*da* was our neighbour from six doors away. He and his friends regularly congregated in Baldev's restaurant, wearing kurtas and sandals, they lazed for hours, often discussing politics and solving world's problems over cigarettes and endless cups of tea. I had heard them discuss ancient caste system and of the many ethnic and tribal groupings that existed in India. I did not understand much but felt as if they were talking about me. Once I asked him who are *chamars* and where did they come from. He was quick to explain: The *chamar* tribe were a nomadic people based mainly in central and northern India. Their trade was collecting dead animal carcasses and turning the skin into useful objects. Hence, the name *chamar*, which loosely means hide or skin. Years ago many of these nomads had migrated to central Asia and then on to southern and eastern Europe where they are now known as gypsies. I was fascinated by these stories and of the fact that I may have very distant cousins living in Europe.

'I am on my way to Delhi, to a writers' conference, a gathering of authors, poets from all over India. We discuss books we have read, tell stories,' he explained.

'That sounds very interesting,' I said.

'Yes, it's a two day conference, a big *adda* over chai and cigarettes and then we go home. I have an hour to kill, come let's have a milkshake.'

He took me to a restaurant and sat facing the giant electronic timetable. 'I must keep an eye out for the flight,' he said. He drank the milkshake like a thirsty hyena while I sipped tea served in bone-china cup and saucer. I do not mind admitting, sir; this was the first time I had held such delicate crockery in my fingers.

'Nandu-*da* I want to ask you something.'

'Go on ask.'

'Nandu-*da* it's like this. I grew up in an orphanage. My ma had abandoned me when I was a baby. She must have her reasons but now I want to find her. Can you help me?'

'Your father?'

'Don't know nothing about him.'

He called the waiter over. 'Bring another,' he said pointing at his empty glass, which still had a ring of foam on the inner surface, drifting slowly downwards.

'You're not to blame, you understand,' he said, 'it's your mother who abandoned an infant. Why did she do it?'

'Don't know Nandu-*da*. People have told me different things. What to believe?'

He was quiet for a few moment, looked anxiously at the timetable above. The waiter arrived with the milkshake. Nandu-*da* snatched it off his hand, took a swig and asked for the bill, 'I have a plane to catch,' he said showing him his hairy wrist, although he had no watch there.

'Now the thing is how to find your family when you know nothing about them, not even a name. Chamars, like other tribes are difficult to trace because they are nomadic *adivasis*. Let me tell you something little brother, you and I are both the same, children of *adivasis*.' The expression on his face took on a serious aspect. 'Like you I was also born to a tribal family, Nayak tribe of Marvad in Rajasthan. They are not heard of much these days. But, in olden days they were famous for artistic singing and dancing. Have you heard of them?'

'No. Even about *chamars* I know only what you have told me.'

'I have done some research. Around the fourteenth century, Nayaks used to travel from village to village, performing Bhavai, a kind of folk dance, theatre. They were always welcome to put on a show and in return received a little alimony or food and shelter from the villagers. This was a long time tradition. In the nineteen and twentieth century it started to die out. Now there are only a handful of dedicated performers left.'

Now I understood why he was so knowledgeable of gypsy history, the traditions and values.

'Will you help me?' I asked again.

'Why? What will it do?'

'I want to meet her, just once.'

'Wish I could be with my mother too.' He slammed the table with the flat of his hand, startling two ladies at the next table. 'But it's not possible.'

'What are you saying Nandu-*da*? But your mother lives with you. I often see her sitting on the balcony meditating.'

Wrinkles appeared on his face suddenly and he looked intensely at the back of his hand. 'Kalu I will tell you a secret.

223

The woman you see on the balcony is not my real mother. My real mother is dead.'

'Oh Nandu-*da*, that's very sad. How did it happen?'

He leaned forward, wiped his spectacles with a handkerchief, took a sip of milkshake and said, 'Kalu you know I am a storyteller, it's in me, in my blood and genes. So, I will tell you this story which I have not narrated to anyone before.' Again, he went through the motions of wiping the spectacles thoughtfully and then began.

'Many years ago there was a family of *Nayaks* living in Rajasthan, father, mother a nine-year old son and seven-year old daughter. They were keeping alive the *Bhavai* tradition of storytelling, living a nomadic lifestyle, moving from village to village, and never accumulating possessions. The father played a crudely fashioned string instrument, which he had made using dried out gourds, goat's skin and its entrails for strings. The children accompanied him with a hand held *damroo*. Life was getting tougher for them. They were now feared as potential thieves and conjurers. There was never a certainty their performance would generate enough income to feed them all.

'One day they arrived at a village near Alwar. An invitation came from a rich merchant's house, where a wedding was taking place. After the performance when the guests were feasting, someone discovered an article of the bride's jewellery had gone missing. Suspicion instantly fell on the visiting singers. They were accused of theft, beaten and had their musical instruments smashed, and then thrown out of the village. The family took shelter in a disused shepherds hut. For two days they stayed indoors, too frightened to come out. On the third night, the mother got up quietly and shook the boy awake. 'Shush, don't disturb anyone. Come with me.' She took the boy to a *ber* fruit farm a quarter of a mile away. Selecting the nearest fruit laden tree, she asked the boy to climb and throw *bers* down in her *choli*. They had been picking for only a few minutes when a man appeared from nowhere. He said nothing to them, just stood watching. The woman quickly joined her hands together. Please big master we are just taking a few, enough to fill our stomach. We have not eaten for two days.

'Take whatever you need, I won't tell anyone, he reassured her with a sympathetic smile. Having collected what they could carry, the pair prepared to leave. *Are*, that is not enough, the man said, take more if you want. She thanked him saying it was enough to feed the family. As they were leaving, he asked the woman if she had something for him. I have no money to give you big master. But, you do have something, he said, you can't leave so soon. She realised what he wanted. Let me go, I am begging you, big master, think of the poor boy.

'The man disregarded her pleas, dragged her to a nearby charpoy, made her lie down, pulled the sari above her waist, undid his pyjama and lay down on top. The boy watched in fear. He did not know what was going on, but sensed it was not right. On the way back to the hut, weeping tears, the woman made the boy promise not to tell anyone what he had seen.

'The family left the village, having mended the musical instrument, ready to put on a show again, earn a little money to eat. In the next village they were not allowed to perform. Apparently, word had spread that a travelling family of singers were going around stealing fruit from trees. The next village, near Neemrana, greeted them with same hostility. They tried to persuade the elders, we are not criminals, please give us a chance. They received no sympathetic hearing. For two months, the family drifted from village to village, getting more and more desperate, begging or stealing bits of food here and there.

'One day they were passing through a town which was on the outskirts of Thar Desert. It was mid-afternoon, sun beating down mercilessly on their heads. So intense even the tar on the roads had started bubbling. Suddenly the father dropped the heavy shoulder bag in the middle of the road and started screaming incoherently. The family stood by helplessly, waiting for him to calm down. This went on for a several minutes and then suddenly his expression changed. He took off running towards a three-storey building, shouting in excitement, as if he had seen the door, which would lead them to salvation. Mother asked the children to stay right there, not to move until she returned. She ran after the father who had now entered the building. Several minutes passed, children did not know what was going on. They heard screams coming from the top of building. Their father was sitting astride the roof top banister as if riding a camel. He appeared to be enjoying himself, as he raised his arms above the head, performing a dance routine. Moments later, he started tumbling down the front of the building. Flapping his arms and legs, as if attempting to reverse the fall, he landed on the parched earth with a loud thud. Almost simultaneously, they heard another scream. The mother was tumbling down this time, her sari flowing majestically in the wind like a boat's sail. As soon as she landed on the ground, cracking her spine and bleeding from the ears, she started crawling towards her husband. She was clearly in pain but in her eyes was determination. When level with her husband she pulled out a sagging breast from her blouse and pushed the nipple in his bleeding mouth. She kept it there until life drifted out of her body.

'Before she took the last breath someone in the crowd had asked her why she was doing this. She had replied, he was screaming like a little child before he jumped, ma I am hungry, give me milk, give me milk.'

Nandu stopped speaking and his eyes glazed over. I touched his knee to see he was alright.

He started again softly. 'From the first floor flat a young lady had seen the drama unfold. She was a doctor, sent by the government to work with the rural community. The lady came out and took charge. She dispersed the crowd, called an ambulance and ushered the children into her flat.' At this point Nandu-*da*'s voice faltered.

'It's alright Nandu-da,' I said.

He took two sips of the now very flat milkshake and said, 'Kalu she is the lady you see sitting on the balcony meditating.'

I studied Nandu's face, remembered the first time I had seen him. He was tearing into a fish *pakora* like a savage. I noticed the strands of grey hair in the curls over his ears, his prying intelligent eyes, educated hands and awful human power. His story was bearable because it was in a way my story too – to refine and retell. So much in common, we could be brothers. I wanted to find my mother more than ever. And I wanted to forgive her for abandoning me. Whatever made you do it, does not matter now. Ma, come back to me. I will look after you, just as Nandu-*da* does for his mother.

He looked at the watch that was not on his wrist, took out a business card from his pocket, threw it on the table and ran towards the exit, collided with a chair, a waiter, another chair.

Moments later, he was back. 'The suitcase,' he said grinning sheepishly, lifted the black case up in his arms as if cradling a baby and dashed out again.

I picked up the card. It said *Jayanand Sengupta, Author, Historian, Visiting lecturer of modern history.*

I telephoned Mr Salem the next day.

'Yes, it's most fortunate my mother remembers Yasmina Banu. As you know the family had lived in that house for many years. But after her husband died, they moved to Ballygunge. My mother even went to see her. She said the house number was eleven. When I asked her why she remembered something so unimportant, she said, *beta* you were born on the eleventh day of the eleventh month,' Mr Salem laughed, 'strange how old peoples' minds work.'

I pressed the phone tight to my ear to block out all external noises.

'Now the difficulty is this, when I asked her to name the street, she could only remember the word Lake. It could be Lake Street, Lake Road or Lake something else. You will have to work it out yourself,' he said.

'Is she sure about Lake?'

'Yes, yes very sure. She says the house was near a lake, lake Dhakuria. That's why she remembers the word Lake in the street name.' Again, Mr Salem chuckled.

'Does she know what happened to Saira? Where she is now?'

'Well, she knows Saira was sent to live with some relatives in Dubai. She believes that girl was the cause of all the troubles in that family. She had boyfriends and everything. She was a bad girl. It's because of her the father died. She killed him.'

'I have another question. Does your mother know who the

boyfriend was? I mean what was his name.'

'What are you talking? How will she know his name?' Salem sounded annoyed and disconnected the phone.

I went to Sanju's room later that day. He was sitting on the floor, leaning against the bed, surrounded with books and an open notepads. I told him about my conversation with Mr Salem. He listened without passing a comment, which was quite unusual. I guessed he was under a lot of pressure, worrying about the exams. At the same time he was always short of money, going without food to pay college fee and the rent. I felt sorry for him, reading and writing, reading and writing, all day long, just for a certificate.

'Isn't there an easier way to get a certificate?' I asked.

'Not possible.'

'Everything is possible *yaar*, everything has a price. You only have to know how much and who to pay.'

'Don't talk nonsense. You better hurry up, go look for your old lady. Or it may be too late.'

'What do you mean – too late?'

'If she is still alive, you don't know how long she has to live. On the other hand, Babu wants to make *keema* out of you. Do you know which will happen first?'

He was right again. I must hurry up my search for Saira.

'Are you sure you want to get the certificate the hard way. I can make life easy for you,' I said.

'Fuck off now.' He chucked a pencil at me.

'Look *yaar*, you have done so much reading and attending lectures. You know all that there is to know by now. Why not be smart and save some time and money, eh. Consider it.' I was thinking of moustache and his companion. They were bound to know some good forgers.

'No,' he said most emphatically, 'I am going to finish my course the proper way and then go into politics.'

'Hah, are you going to be politician? *Arre yaar* have you ever heard of an honest politician. They all pay for their big degrees and diplomas. They will say anything people want to hear. Make promises they can't keep. Sell the grandmother for a few extra votes. Can you do all that?'

'Not me. I am going to be different. I am going to start a revolution, stop all corruption in politics. You just wait and see.'

'That's if somebody doesn't make keema of you first for being honest.'

'We will see about that,' he said defiantly.

So, there you are Modiji. As Premier and politician, you have seen everything there is to see. Do you think my friend Sanju has a chance? No, no, no do not answer that just yet.

The following evening, I returned to Sanju's room. This time I brought him one of his favourite snacks, *jhal muri* flavoured with lime and chillies. He stopped working on his laptop, accepted the paper bag and started eating, pouring fluffed rice straight into his open mouth.

'Here, I have shortlisted streets which have names starting with Lake, all in Ballygunge,' he said mumbling from a full mouth and threw a piece of paper at me, 'I have found five streets with very similar names: Lake Road, Lake View Road, Lake Terrace, Lake Avenue and Lake Place. Just pick a street and work your way down.'

It was a daunting task. I will have to knock on every door in lower Ballygunge. I took the Metro to Jatin Das Park and then a bus to Southern Avenue. On the way I studied the map

Sanju had drawn. All five streets were within a radius of three miles. Lake Road was first on the list.

'*Dada* can you tell me which way to Lake Road,' I asked a watches salesman.

'Yes, yes, it's there, round the corner,' he said, 'what number?'

'Number eleven.'

'Eleven? I don't know where that is. The houses are not in sequence. Some have been knocked down and rebuilt into apartment blocks. Good luck,' he said sarcastically as if I had no chance of finding it.

I walked the three-quarter mile stretch of the mainly residential street three times up and down. Another resident explained why the numbering system was so illogical. 'They are all monkeys working in Kolkata Corporation. As they only have five fingers on each hand, they have difficulty counting beyond ten. That is why eleven was missed out when allocating numbers to the houses.'

Someone else said, 'see that house, number D34 and the next one S34. Both number 34. When the owners complained, the corporation said it is too late to rectify, in any case, it is a minor issue. If the mail got delivered to the wrong house, the owners could easily swop with each other.' There was a cackle of laughter all round.

'So why D34 then?' I asked.

'Ah, that I can explain. That's Mr Dasgupta's house. He made it D34. D for Dasgupta and Mr Suri did the same, made it S34. Makes sense, *hanh*. The postmen are happy, and visitors don't get confused.'

'Which house belongs to Banu family?' I asked, feeling cautiously optimistic. These people appeared to know so much about who lived where.

'Banu, no Banu here. But there is Basu. If you want Basu I can tell you which house.'

I gave up and went to Lake Avenue next. Fortunately, it was a little shorter and numbered methodically. Outside an office building a bunch of drivers in uniform were sitting under a tree, smoking and playing cards.

'*Bhaiya*, where is number eleven?' I asked

They ignored me at first and when I asked again, one of the drivers gestured at me to come and join them. 'Want to play cards, only one-rupee boot,' he said.

'Don't play cards. I am looking for number eleven only, I have urgent business.'

Another driver with belly spilling out of his shirt, said winking at me, 'what kind of business you are doing little brother? Tell us we will like to do some too.'

I glared at him. 'Do you know number eleven?'

'Oh, don't get angry little brother. I was only joking.' He did this gesture with his hands, like a magician doing a vanishing trick. 'Whoosh, it went,' he said and asked his mate, 'did you see it go?'

'Yes, yes we saw,' another driver said,' one minute it was there, standing tall and next minute – gone, *phatak*.'

'What are you talking about gone, how can a house go away?' I said

'Fire, fire, *chote bhai*, the house caught fire. *Baas* in no time it was ashes.' He pointed at a piece of land between two houses, cordoned off with corrugated sheet fencing. 'They say it was insurance job.'

'When did it happen?' My heart sank. If this was Banu

family residence, I might as well go home now.

'Three years ago,' the driver with greasy hair said, 'still want to do business?'

'Get lost. Go lick your master's arse. Look he is coming,' I said pointing at a *sahib* in business clothes coming down the steps.

'You little rascal.' He picked up a pebble and chucked it at me.

I asked a few more people. No one had heard of a Banu family. When I asked a maid at the gate of a house she replied promptly, 'yes I know Banu,' and rearranged her sari tighter around the waist with a suggestive hip movement.

'Which house?'

'Oh no, not here, Banu lives in my village back home, in UP,' she said. She started twirling her ponytail.

'What good is that to me?'

'Are you looking for work? I can help you,' she said changing the subject.

'Not looking for work, but if I have need in the future I know where to come.' I said.

'What is your name?' she asked.

'Kalu.'

'I am Sarita. If you need a job let me know.'

'How will I find you?'

'Just come and ask. I am always here.'

'Madam may not like it,' I said.

'Nooo ... she is very nice, treats me like family.'

'Give me your mobile number, it will be easier.'

'*Naheen to,*' she giggled coyly, 'I have to go now,' she said. Her hips swinging as she turned to open the gate.

I resumed the search. I had gone a short distance when it started raining, as if God was tipping buckets of water on our heads. I ran into a little roadside cafe, Ganesh Grand Hotel (veg and non-veg), a busy little place, full of customers from the market and builders from a nearby construction site. A beggar boy, about twelve-years old, was sitting on a flat rock under the canopy, waiting for the rain to subside and humming a song under his breath. He was a grotesque figure with bloated stomach and big hips, but he had no legs from knees down or fingers on his hands. Under his armpit was a wooden platform with attached casters, a crudely constructed mobility platform.

A customer sitting nearby asked the boy if he would like some tea.

'Thankyou *barra sahab*, I don't eat or drink all day, only at night, strict policy,' the boy said proudly.

The man chuckled at his reply and asked where he got the nice *gaadi* cart.

'My Beggarmaster gave it to me. Gift. He is such a kind man,' the boy said and gave the casters a spin with the stump of his hand, 'see brand new, he gave it to me recently only.'

'Have you mother, father?'

'No *sahab*.'

'Then tell me boy, who ate up your hands and legs?'

I was disgusted, what insensitive thing to ask a cripple.

'Don't know *sahab*. I am not complaining. I get enough to eat, a reserved place on the pavement. Beggarmaster looks after everything for me, pays the police on time.'

Some of the other customers laughed. The boy, encouraged by their interest, continued. 'When I was little, too small to beg on my own, the Beggarmaster used to rent me out to ladies, to

234

be carried in arms. I was in great demand. A suckling cripple is a very good earner. What sympathy it generates. I drank milk from many different breasts.' He smiled mischievously. 'I wish I could still be carried around in women's arms, their nipples in my mouth, better than bumping along all day long on this platform, busting my balls.'

The men in the cafe burst out laughing. 'This boy is no fool. He will go far.'

So far so good Modiji, but what happened next made my heart weep.

A man in paint-splattered shirt finished his tea, got up and paid the woman behind the counter. As he was leaving, pocketing the change, the boy put his fingerless hand out, eyeing the loose change, '*Sahab*, please can I have a few *paisas, sahab*.'

'*Hut, hut, hut*, out of the way. Why should I give you the money? *Saala*, what do you think, is this your father's inheritance?' the man shouted and kicked the cart as he went.

The boy in his eagerness to hold on to his precious transport toppled over. The tea lady, a fiery looking white-haired woman, shouted at the boy, 'Oye, *haramzada*, go beg somewhere else. Why are you pestering my customers?' She picked up a half-eaten bun left by a customer and chucked it at him. 'Here take this and don't come back.'

Strangely, the boy appeared unfazed by the insults, as if it was an everyday thing. He hauled himself on the platform and set off in the rain, pushing the rain-soaked pavement with his fingerless hands, like a skier on snow, weaving a path through hundreds of legs.

Back home Baldev was sitting on a wide chair with his legs folded under him, chewing a *paan* loaded with beetle nuts and lime powder. I told him about the legless beggar in the market, what tragedy and injustice. He pivoted on his side, raised a buttock, passed wind and sighed with relief. 'It is boy's kismet that he was born like that,' he said and threw both hands up as if to say there is nothing anyone can do about it, 'Gods wish.'

'Bullshit,' Sanju interrupted, 'the boy could have been crippled on purpose by gangsters. There is big money in begging. Don't you know?'

'*Hanh, hanh*, I agree with you,' Baldev said, 'I have heard of criminals doing this kind of thing. But it is still the boy's kismet that he got trapped by these men.'

'So, you are saying uncle everything is kismet. Whatever happens in this world we should accept as it is? Is this what you are saying uncle?'

Baldev coughed. Phlegm rose from his chest to the mouth. Instead of spitting, he swallowed. 'This is God's wish, we can't do anything.'

'Yes we can. If that boy was born in a rich country like *Amrika*, do you think he would be rolling in the gutters and begging? No. They would send him to hospital; give him new legs, hands, whatever is needed. He would be in school, learning. Do you know there are people with artificial legs running marathons, competing in Olympics, doing high jumps?'

Baldev was speechless. I could tell he was struggling to comprehend the point Sanju was making. Just then Pratibha yelled from the back, 'your chickens are making a racket. You better go and quieten them, or I will throttle their necks with my bare hands. *Hai Ram* can't get a moments peace in this house.'

Baldev slapped his forehead and rose from the chair. 'It is

my kismet I got trapped by that woman.'

Next day I went back to Ballygunge. From Deshapriya Park I walked south towards the lake. Fourth turning on the right was Lake Terrace, a short lane mostly of apartment blocks. The very first house on the ground floor was number eleven. In fact, it was P 11. Why it had the prefix, P was not clear. At the end of the entrance stood a dhobi workshop set in a garage. Men in vests were ironing shirts, singing and whistling Bollywood songs, odour of freshly laundered garments in the air. The nameplate on the door said Dewan AK Kocchar.

'Anybody in?' I asked one of the dhobis.

'The house is empty. Kocchar sahib has moved out.'

'Oh, I see. Who lived here before Kocchar?' I asked.

'Kocchar sahib and his family only,' he said, 'many, many years.'

'Did Banu family ever live here?' I asked, hoping for a positive response.

An older man with white moustache shouted from the rear, 'no Banu *fanu* here. Before Kocchar sahib his father-in-law used to live here.'

Across the road was a gymnasium building with the sign Bajrang Vyamaghar. On impulse, I went in to investigate. A statue of Lord Hanuman, the God of strength stood under a canopy on the left. Visitors to the gymnasium, before going in, were bowing or touching Lord Hanuman's feet. I went and touched his feet too.

Yes, I know, I know, sir, you are thinking this fellow Kalu is such a Godless person, what is he doing praying to this deity. He is a two-faced hypocritical fool. You are absolutely, right, sir. I do not usually go in for this kind of thing, kissing Gods' feet.

After all, how many can you kiss; there are hundreds of Gods in India. Now I make one exception. Let me explain. One day Sanju had dragged me into a temple near Kidderpore. Unlike most temples in Kolkata which are dedicated to a single God, this one had many deities lined up in a straight line, deities like Kalimata, Durgamata, Parvati, Saraswati, Lakshmi and others whose names I don't know. I assumed this temple was devoted only to female Gods until I saw the statue of Hanuman with the distinctive monkey face and long tail. It was sitting neglected in a dark corner, covered in dust and soot deposits from oil *diyas*, which burned day and night. Around us people were chanting prayers, burning incenses, throwing offerings of flowers and coins on the mat and priests in flimsy dhotis were ringing brass bells.

'Look at him,' Sanju whispered, 'how composed and powerful he looks.'

'Yes, yes, I have seen Hanuman before, let's go,' I said, wondering why he had dragged me to this depressing place.

Sanju was insistent. 'Go chant this prayer three times: *har har mahadev ki jai*, and touch his feet,' he said and pointed at Lord Ganesh's the right foot.

'What is it?' I said, seeing nothing special.

'Look carefully.' He pushed me forward. It was then I saw, a small area of the right foot, three or four inches in diameter, shining bright, as if someone had used furniture polish to buff it up. Then I realised the bright sheen was due to years of touching and stroking of the foot by thousands of his devotees. So vivid, it was visible even in the dark.

'Alright, I will do it,' I said just to appease Sanju. I stepped forward, feeling a fool, mumbled *har har mahadev ki jai* three times and put my hand out aiming for the polished spot. As soon as my finger touched the foot I recoiled in shock as if I had been electrocuted. For a split second I went blank, did not know what had happened to me. Just as quickly, my whole body relaxed into a state of extreme peace. I stood like that for several minutes.

'How do you feel?' Sanju asked on the way out.

'I feel good.'

I cannot explain why this happened, Modiji, but I have been back several times since and am now a devotee of Lord Hanuman.

On Lake View Road, the very first building was a nursery school. Children in identical uniform were playing in the open ground, throwing balls, skipping, chasing, fighting, and screaming. What fascinating sight it was. I felt jealous and angry and deprived all at the same time. How I wished I could have gone to school too.

Number eleven on Lake View Road was a corner house, shaded by a mature *peepul* tree, its foliage taller than the house itself. Windows on the first floor were wide open. I could see a ceiling fan spinning at speed. A child was screaming in the house next door. Someone was sawing wood in steady rhythmic pattern, bang, bang, bang, of hammer on nails. An old Ambassador with dented bodywork stood on the drive. Does Saira live here? I stared at the entrance door, imagining a white haired old lady coming out, leaning on a walking stick. As if I was seeing an apparition, the door flew open at that very moment and a lady appeared. I panicked believing it was Saira. However, this lady was much younger, of about fifty. Dressed in orange and white salwar kameez, designer sunglasses, she walked briskly to the driver side of the car. Fearing she was going to drive away I stepped forward. 'Please, madam. I am looking for Saira Banu. Does she live here?'

The lady removed her sunglasses, set them into the hair. 'I don't know anyone by that name. Have you got the right address?'

'Madam the address is correct. You see her family definitely lived here about thirty or forty years ago. It's important I make contact with them.'

'But I told you I don't know any Saira Banu.'

'*Accha*, I understand madam. Would anyone else in the street know about them?'

'You could try seventy-six,' she pointed the car key at a door to her left, 'they have been here a long time. Maybe they will remember your lady.'

I thanked her and moved on. There was no Ambassador at seventy-six, only an old rusting bicycle chained to a post. A warning sign at the gate said, *beware of the dog*. I waited for the dog to come out barking. Nothing happened. I walked up the path cautiously. The man who opened the door was about seventy years old, his silvery white hair contrasting sharply with the dark skin. Behind him a dog appeared. An ugly looking creature with drooping eyes, wads of loose flesh on its cheeks, nails like cheetah's claws clicked the floor as it walked.

'Spotty...*sit*.' the man shook a finger. Spotty sat down obediently, dribbling saliva, reminding me of Basha, Lal Bahadur's fat bitch.

'He is harmless, soft as a *gudia* doll, if you ask me.'

I explained the purpose of my visit, as best as I could, keeping a wary eye on Spotty.

'Son, let's get this straight. You are trying to trace a family that used to live at number eleven. And you want to know if I can help.'

'Yes sir. A Muslim family. The lady was a widow.'

'Um...huh,' he said, 'I remember Muslims living in that house. They lived a quiet life. I think they left...oh...about twenty or so years ago, may be more. You are going to ask me where they went, eh son.'

'Yes, yes, uncle.'

'And I am going to tell you I don't know, because that is the honest truth. But...but...all is not lost. They had a cousin living on Sarat Bose Road, just around the corner, house number eighty. I don't know if the cousin is still there, but go and ask.'

'Uncle was there a girl in that house, about twenty-five years old?'

'Yes, there were a few ladies. But I didn't know them personally.'

As I turned to leave, Spotty stood up and growled. I quickened my pace.

Unlike Lake View, Sarat Bose Road was a busy main thoroughfare dotted with shops and eating-places. Number eighty was set back between a tailor shop, Deva Tailors and Madras Tiffin restaurant.

Along a narrow alley, I picked my way with care, overstepping green moss and accumulated water. Even before I knocked a man's unshaven face appeared at the kitchen window. 'Who are you looking for?'

'Is *sahib* at home?'

'Yes, wait please.'

A young man of about twenty appeared at the door, casually dressed in jeans and loose shirt, eating a half-peeled banana.

'I am trying to trace a family who used to live at eleven Lake View Road. They have moved on, but they had a relative living at this address. I am looking for that person.'

The young man seemed disinterested, 'I don't know anything, talk to Suresh,' he said and went back in.

As I waited for Suresh, I could hear laughter inside, someone playing a guitar, creating a riot of harsh metallic twangs that rose and fell sharply. I listened intently, comparing him to Roby. It was easy to discern the fundamental difference. Unlike Roby who produced easy on the ear rhythmic sound, this person was aspiring to be a rock guitarist. I was still listening when another young man came to the door, dressed in striped tracksuit bottom and a stained t-shirt. 'You're looking for me?'

Once again, I explained everything in detail.

'My landlord is Muslim, maybe he is the cousin,' he said, 'I can give you his telephone number.' He invited me in, pointed at a door on the right, 'wait in there.'

The room was dark. Windows shut to block out day light. Only a small pedestal lamp in the corner provided some luminosity. The air was thick with an odour I recognised instantly. It was hashish. Same stuff I had seen Munna smoke. A boy and a girl were sitting on the only sofa in the room. A thick hand rolled cigarette in boy's fingers. He inhaled the cigarette deeply, held the smoke in for a few seconds and then exhaled.

'Sit down,' the girl said.

I stayed standing.

'*Are bhai*, sit down,' the boy said this time, kicking a bean bag towards me.

I lowered myself on the beanbag. The boy put his hand out, offering me the lit cigarette. I hesitated but took it so as not to offend. I took a puff, coughed almost immediately, and passed the roll-up to the girl.

'Good stuff, eh,' the boy said.

'Yes, it is.' I did a thumbs-up.

The girl too held the smoke in; fingers wrapped expertly around the cigarette, exhaled and passed it for another round. After two or three rounds, we fell into deep thoughts, each at the centre of their own universe, and at the same time nowhere. I remember staring fixedly at the C of Carlsberg of an empty beer can on the carpet, my head floating as if hollowed out of all unnecessary debris. The guitar chords appeared to gain exceptional vibrancy.

'Here you go mate, his name is Asghar Khan,' Suresh was standing over me, giving me a piece of paper.

Again, it started raining; an intermittent patter of raindrops. I carried on walking, getting soaked, did not care, for I was exhilarated with the progress made so far. I wanted to run back home and tell Sanju, I am nearly there; one more push and I will be at Saira's doorstep.

Now that I had a name and telephone number, I wanted to call Asghar Khan there and then. Outside a noisy tyre repair workshop, men in greasy clothes pumping hydraulic jacks, I dialled the number on my mobile phone.

'Hello this is Khan.' The voice was business-like.

I explained the reason for the call, detailed the chain of events that had led me to his tenants on Sarat Bose Road.

Khan went silent. Only his breathing was audible.

'Hello? Hello?' I said.

Still he did not speak. I thought of hanging up, call again later. Maybe I have sent him crashing into a cavern of nostalgic memories.

Suddenly Khan boomed, so loud I had to pull the phone away from my ear 'She was my cousin. Why are you looking for the *kuti*, bitch?'

Bitch? I was speechless. 'I am ... only helping a friend ... Mr Khan,' I lied without thinking of consequences.

'Who is the friend? What's his name?'

'Sir....my friend doesn't want anyone to know who he is until he has found his aunt,' I said and realised instantly I had made an error by inventing the relative. Such a person would also be his relative.

'Nonsense, I don't believe it. In any case, I haven't seen her for many years. I can only tell you where she lived fifteen, twenty years ago.'

'That's no problem. If she has moved on, I can ask the neighbours, someone will know where she has gone.'

'Why should I be telling you anything? I don't know you. Who are you?'

'We are only interested in finding Saira Banu. That is the only reason why I have called,' I said, trying to remain calm and polite

'*Accha, accha,* but I am not telling you anything on the phone. You say you are Kalu. You better come and see me, and bring an ID with you.'

'ID ...?'

'Yes, an ID.'

'I will show you ID,' I said though I did not know what it

244

was or where to get one. The exhilaration of a few minutes ago was now deflating rapidly.

'Calm down you fool, speak slowly,' Sanju said. I was trying to tell him about my conversation with Asghar khan. *Harami* swore at Saira, how dare he?'

'You will have to go see him,' Sanju said.

'Why? He thinks I am some kind of a fraud, wants to see my ID.'

'Because he will give you the information you are looking for.'

'What makes you so sure?'

'Human nature,' he said.

I didn't think it would work, but went anyway, expecting Khan to scream and swear, as he had done on the phone.

I arrived at the pizza restaurant that also did deliveries, on Jawaharlal Nehru Road. It was a small cosy place with neatly arranged tables and chairs. Walls decorated with framed pictures of snow covered mountains. A speaker hooked to the wall was playing English pop music. A family with young children was at the far end. A baby's pram pushed to one side.

'I have come to meet Mr Khan,' I said to a waiter.

'Yes please. I call,' he said and went in through a yellow revolving door.

A man of about forty years of age came out and raised his eyebrows, 'what can I do for you?'

'My name is Kalu. I have appointment with Mr Khan,' I said, wiping my clammy hands on the trouser.

'Which Khan?' he said impatiently.

'Asghar Khan.'

'Why didn't you say so? Wait here.' He slipped back in

through the revolving door.

This time the man who came out was about seventy years of age. Large build and almost bald, except for a line of hair running from ears to back of the head, deep set, tired eyes. Smartly dressed, he had the manner of a successful businessman.

'So, you are Kalu,' he said, 'this way.' He led me through the yellow door into a storeroom with several stacks of cartons and drums. On the wall were three framed pictures, one of Asghar Khan himself. Through a screen, I could see men rolling dough, working at incredible speed, behind them an open oven. We crossed over to the open back yard. Four mopeds stood in a row by the fence. Three plastic garden chairs stood against the wall under a cloth canopy, the only shelter from the beating sun. An overflowing ashtray sat on the table, odour of baking pizzas gushing out of an exhaust grill in the wall. I felt very hungry.

'We can talk here.' He placed a mobile phone on the table. 'Sit, sit,' he said, and then yelled to someone inside, 'Bring two cokes and my cigarettes.'

A young boy in t-shirt plastered with tomato sauce and baking flower, came out and placed two cans of cold Coca-Cola and a packet of cigarettes on the table.

'I thought you will not come,' he said.

'Why did you think that?'

'I thought you were a Banu. That's why.'

'Khan *sahib* I have not come to bother you or cause any distress. All I want is Saira's address so I can give it to my friend.'

'Your friend is a relative of mine, yet he doesn't want to come to me direct. Why?'

'He is a little embarrassed.'

'Embarrassed.... Embarrassed? Not embarrassed. He is

afraid, shitting himself. He knows I'll break his legs, both of them, *bahnchoot* Banu.'

That shook me. I wasn't expecting this kind of reaction. It felt as if I was intruding into someone else's fight.

'And listen to me. I tell you this. That woman will rot in hell,' he said and his face turned red as if he was going to lash out.

'Khan *Sahib*, I don't know what Sairaji has done. It is not my business. All I want is her address. Then I will go away, won't cause you any more bother,' I said politely, trying to keep him calm. That was the only way I would get anything out of him.

As if he hadn't heard. 'I was married to her,' he boomed and slammed the table. The ashtray rocked and the can of coca cola tipped over the edge of the table. It rolled on the ground towards a gutter, fizzing noisily as it went. 'Only three months we were married when she decided to end it. She said she had made a mistake. I tried hard to make her see sense, but will the *kuti* listen?'

I was panicking, fearing all was lost. Just then, the younger Khan I had met earlier came out. 'Abba I am going to Park Street. I'll be back in fifteen. You can go home now. I don't need you anymore.' He straddled a moped, kicked the engine alive and drove off, kilting dangerously in a show of bravado as he turned a corner.

'My son,' Khan said, following the speeding figure, 'he thinks I am an old man.'

So that was the son, though I couldn't see any likeness with the father. 'But you look young,' I said, flattering him, it might calm him down, 'may be sixty.'

'Yes, yes,' he said, 'but I know my age.' His hand moved to the cigarette packet on the table, stopped an inch short, fingers tapped the table. 'I am trying to give it up,' he said.

A little girl in lilac dress and pink hair ribbon appeared riding a tricycle in the alley. Khan looked at the child and said, 'how have you got caught up in this messy business?'

For a split second, I thought he was addressing the little girl. He continued, 'anyway it's at home in my diary. Call me tomorrow.'

'Call you tomorrow …?'

'If you want the address,' he said.

'Oh, yes, yes. I will call you tomorrow. Is ten o'clock alright?'

He exhaled long and hard, waved a hand in resignation as if to say ten o'clock is alright, any time is alright, what the hell does it matter?

I was numb in the brain as I left the pizza restaurant. *Phew*, what an experience.

Sir, visualizing Saira in a marital bed with that monster was eating me up. I could not sleep thinking about it. At midnight, I got out of bed and pulled out the plastic carrier bag containing takings from last few days. I spread everything on the table and separated the bankcards from paper money and coins. Dropped the coins in a jar, split up the paper money into individual denominations, rubber banded each bundle and returned them to the plastic bag. Finally, I slid the bag in the secret compartment in the pillow. I woke with a stiff neck next morning.

I telephoned Khan as promised, at ten o'clock sharp. Surprisingly this time he was very forthcoming, gave not only the house number and street name but also directions to a house. It belonged to Saira's brother-in-law. 'From Sealdah take the train to Kanchrapara. Take the bus to Krishnadevi nursing home and hospital. Then you are to hop on to another bus. Get off at Chottobazar on Kabi Guru Rabindra Path. You understand? Good and good luck my friend.' After a few moments' silence he continued, this time there was sadness in his voice, 'and one more thing. I don't have long to live. If you do manage to meet Saira, tell her I kept my promise.'

'*Bilkul*, I will tell her,' I assured him. I waited for him to say what the promise was. But he stayed silent.

'Are you alright?' I asked.

'No. I have bad heart. Doctor said I have a year maximum. If Allah is kind, he may let me live a little longer.' He put the phone down after that, left me feeling discontented, for I wanted to know more about him and Saira. It seemed he really wanted me to meet her. It also appeared he was a deeply hurt man. Perhaps he was still in love with her, even after so many years. *Good luck my friend.* The words had sounded strange coming from a man who had shown so much contempt for her only few days ago.

I did not waste time, sir. The very next day I was at Sealdah station. The ten thirty to Kanchrapara took off at eleven thirty. Sitting squeezed between two grim-faced gentlemen in starched white shirts I settled my gaze on the newspaper a man was reading opposite. The newspaper had no interesting headlines. I turned my attention to the open countryside, littered with clusters of houses. Ponds covered in green hyacinth, men on bicycles, country lanes snaking through green fields, farm trucks and tractors, clouds of dust in their wake.

Come out of Kanchrapara station and you are in centre of the town. You will find buses waiting for newly arrived passengers from Kolkata. The place reminded me of Haridwar, the same confused madness, people running around shouting, spitting, shoving. Only the language was different. Here people spoke Bengali. Chottobazar was at a cross-section of three lanes. A *paan-wallah* sitting cross-legged in his shop, spreading white lime on betel leaves. I asked him for directions.

'*Accha*, you are looking for Mitra Vilas, *hah*. What number?' he said.

'Number ten.'

'Take the path by the pond, on the other side turn right and then left. Be very careful of the slippery path or you will fall down in the pond,' he warned, as if it was a regular occurrence.

I followed the directions to Mitra Vilas as meticulously as possible. Half a mile on, I came across a village square. Boys were playing with an old bicycle. They saw me, whispered and sniggered. A small dog began yelping as it saw me approach. Up the street, I came across an old lady in pale grey sari, a small figure with arched back. As I levelled with her, I saw she was pushing a baby buggy, a very old wobbly contraption; wheels screeching painfully. A shopping bag was sitting in the small space where a child should have been. As it went over a rock a loaf of bread slipped out of the bag and fell on the track.

I ran, picked up the loaf and snuggled it carefully between tomatoes and green *brinjals* in the bag. 'Here you are. It's going nowhere now, *mataji*.' I reassured her.

Instead of being reassured, she looked at me in horror as if I was going to attack her. To make matters worse the boys with bicycle came running. '*Kali billi boo, boo. Kali billi boo, boo*,' they began chanting and teasing the poor woman. I had to step in and shoo the boys away.

'Mataji, don't be afraid, no one will harm you,' I said and

moved on.

Number ten Mitra Vilas was a small two storey house, brick built but not plastered. The owners had planted a few banana and papaya trees on a patch of land in front and the side. A roughly built high wall separated this house from the next. A trailing plant was clinging to the wall. Under the branches hung a wooden letterbox, further down an electric cable ran lengthwise to the rear of the house. A striped tablecloth fluttered from the railing of the small balcony on the upper floor.

I stood across the path, my heart palpating, finally I had found her, or so I thought. There was also a possibility she no longer lived in this house. If she had moved on, how was Asghar Khan to know? I gave myself a pep talk: do not be foolish Kalu, stay calm. If Saira answers the door personally explain everything calmly, she will understand.

When the door opened, just a few inches, the face peering out was not of a woman, but an old man with pale complexion and deep-set wrinkles, bushy eyebrows like pubic hair and eyeballs behind the dark framed reading glasses looked hideously large.

'*Namaskar, babu,*' I dived quickly into the rehearsed story, apologising for the unannounced visit; made it known I had come all the way from Kolkata. The old man listened patiently with a cupped hand behind his ear. When I had finished, he said, 'but Saira Banu doesn't live here.'

My heart sank. I thought all was lost. It was a wasted trip.

'Do you know where she lives?' I asked.

In reply, he gestured with his hand, 'you better come in,' and opened the door wider. Sun's rays hit his tall, skinny figure. He had no shirt on, just a vest and baggy white pyjama hitched high above the waist, the drawstring hanging loose to the crutch.

I was about to step inside when I heard a familiar sound behind me, squeak of wheels, metal rubbing against metal. I swung around to look. You can imagine my surprise, sir. For whom do I see coming up the path under a banana tree? It was the silver haired lady I had helped earlier with the loaf of bread. She saw me standing and as before froze in fright.

Behind me I heard the old man say, 'this gentleman has come from Kolkata. He was asking about Abida and Saira.'

'Oh, hoh, hoh,' she began wailing, 'don't let him in ... don't let him in ... he is a thief ... he is a thief ... he is a thief ... don't let him in ... thief.'

What is she saying? I never robbed her, the bitch. I wanted to protest forcefully. But I didn't want to start a commotion in this strange place.

'Sukta, Sukta, everything is alright. Sukta, be quiet, be quiet. He doesn't mean any harm. *Shanti koro.*' the old man tried to pacify her.

She continued wailing. 'Who is he who is he who is he.'

'He is looking for a friend who used to live here. That's all. He is not a thief.'

'Looking for a friend not a thief not a thief not a thief.'

'Yes, he is alright.'

She calmed down a little, but still refused to cross my path. The old man came out and took her arm, 'come let's go in.'

I waited at the steps with trembling heart. Phew, that was close.

The old man returned with a remorseful expression on his wrinkled face. 'Don't be offended son. Come in.'

'We can talk here,' I said, fearing another outburst from her indoor.

'Alright then. I can explain about my wife. She's got a mental condition. Has been like this for a few years. Very difficult to live with her.'

'I am sorry.'

'She was robbed recently by some youths. She doesn't trust strangers, even me sometimes.'

'I won't take too much of your time. Could you tell me about Saira, where can I find her?'

'Yes, yes we knew Saira and her sister Abida very well. Sukta and Abida were teachers in the same school. They were good friends. What do you want to know?'

'Tell me everything.'

'Abida, her husband and Saira used to live in this very house. About twenty years ago Abida passed away. Her husband moved to Chennai. Good man, very good man. He let Saira stay for as long as she wanted to.'

'She was Muslim,' I said. I wanted to be certain we were discussing the same person.

'Yes, yes, the Muslim lady,' he said and then lowered his voice as if sharing a secret, 'she changed her religion though, converted to Christianity many years ago. She said Islam was not a religion for her. It's true. She had a dark secret of her earlier life, which she would not discuss with anyone. I think it was something to do with broken marriage and all that, family problems.'

Of course, I knew all about the broken marriage and the broken heart. But in my mind that was not good enough reason to forgo one's religion. I wondered if she had suffered in some other way, met or fallen in love with a Christian.

'What kind of family problems?'

'As I said, she was a private person and disliked talking about her past. But it is well known she had been disowned by her family. Her father had committed suicide and the family had blamed her for his death.'

'When did you see her last?'

He patted his cheeks pointedly, to draw attention to the sagging skin. 'Old age was catching up on us all. She developed arthritis of joints and many other problems, could not cope on her own, so they took her to live in a home. That was the last we saw her, about five or six years ago.'

'Did she ever talk about Raju?'

'Not to me. Who is Raju?'

'It doesn't matter.'

I thanked the old man and left Kanchrapara with the address of the old peoples' home.

Back home I found Sanju playing with the Sanyo voice recorder, switching it on and off idly, and he looked pale and distraught. I thought the Sanyo had broken down again. 'What's the matter?'

'Madam has died,' he said.

'Madam who?' I thought he was referring to someone from his college.

'Madam from Bangalore.'

I realised he was talking about Madam, his benefactor. 'Are you going to Bangalore?'

'What for? I have nothing there now. I will go back home, to my village,' he said.

'How long for?'

'For ever' he said, 'I am not coming back.'

'But what about your education, aren't you going to finish it?' The thought of Sanju going away filled me with despondency. He was such a good friend, like a brother. Who would listen to my whinging, and give saintly advice now.

'*Yaar*, how will I pay the college fee? I can't even afford to pay Baldev. He is going to kick me out,' he said with tears in his eyes, and then he astounded me by saying, 'you can have my laptop. It's of no use to me anymore.'

'What will you do in the village? Your mother doesn't want you.'

He shrugged his shoulders. 'I will think of something.'

'Listen to me. You must finish your studies just as your father would have wanted and go into politics – remember you said you wanted to become Prime Minister.'

'I will be lucky if get a job as peon in Prime Minister's office,' he said bitterly.

'You leave it to me. I will sort things out for you. Now let's go and have a beer. We need some relaxation, both of us.'

I took him to one of those places, which no one admits to ever visiting. Yet people pack these places to the ceiling, day and night. I am talking about illegal beer dens in famous Sonagachi. If you ever go to this square mile of bustling red-light district you will be accosted by ladies dressed like wedding party guests. If you look carefully, you will see the dresses are same age as the girls, held together with pins and rough stitching. They hover in doorways and windows, catcalling and making suggestive gestures. There are girls from all over India, including Nepal and Bangladesh. It was a wonder Sanju came along with me without a protest. Any other time he would have refused to set foot in a place like this. We sat with a Kingfisher each, watching a live show of girls, some naked, dancing on a podium. At one point, two white girls came on stage, wiggling their hips and boobs. Sanju's eyes popped out of the sockets. 'Oh baba, where have they come from?'

I explained they were probably hippies and back packers from Europe. 'They do this to make some extra money for their travels through India. It is a well-known fact. Touts and pimps never harm them. Any incident involving a European will mean instant police raids, mass arrests, mayhem, until the culprits are caught. If they can't find real culprits, they will round up a few known pimps and put them in jail.'

'That's out of order,' Sanju said.

'Police are under instruction to act fast when Europeans are involved. Or they get their backsides kicked. If the girl is Indian, no one cares. That's life.'

I asked Sanju if he wanted one of these girls. 'I have money, don't worry about that,' I said.

He looked at me horrified.

'Relax *yaar*,' I said, 'have some fun while you can. You are young only once. You won't be able to do this once you become Prime Minister.'

I saw him smile for the first time in three days.

Have you heard of Sonagachi Modidji? It is the biggest red-light district in whole of India. Some say it is biggest in Asia. You can have girls of all ages, as young as nine. Imagine fifty, sixty years old men with fat bellies having sex with children. Did you know that sort of thing happens all the time? Did you? If not, then why not? Do you think these children work as prostitutes of their own free will? No, like me, they are abandoned children. Men, even women, come along, offer them sweet-talk, food and a home. The home turns out to be a brothel.

Do you remember the speech in the *maidan*? You said every child in India is like your son and daughter. So how will you feel if you saw your own ten year with a man old enough to be her grandfather?

Chapter 23

Having just returned from the morning ritual at the temple Baldev was washing his feet under the tap, a pious look on his face.

'Uncle, can I have a word?' I said.

He nodded while still chanting a prayer.

'Sanju has a problem,' I said.

He stopped chanting and his face darkened. 'Has he found somewhere else to live?' he said. I realised he was thinking of the loss of status for his establishment.

'He will no longer be receiving money from home. Can you help him?'

'Help? How?' He looked at me sharply and his hand went to the fountain pens in the top pocket.

'Don't charge him rent for a few months, until he has sorted himself out.'

'Don't charge? What do you think I am running a charity? I didn't get where I am by not charging rent. Who gave me anything for nothing? I came to Kolkata with just hundred rupees in my pocket – hundred rupees – it didn't even buy you a roti and dal those days. No - I didn't beg or ask for favours – I worked with these hands – shed sweat and blood labouring in factories.' He put his hands out, showing me his crab like fingers, 'these hands have hammered steel in the truck factory.'

I let him rage and rant for a while. 'Think about it, a student of Presidency College, what prestige he is bringing to your establishment.'

'*Accha*, two months' rent off. After that he must pay or get out.'

'I will pay after that. But Sanju is not to know. You tell him you are letting him stay rent free until he has sorted himself out.'

He was suspicious. 'What's in it for you?' he asked as if he was missing out something lucrative.

'Nothing. He is a friend. This is what friends do for each other. But you won't understand all that.'

'You scoundrel, get lost.' As I was leaving, he called after me, 'I will give him three months. After that you pay or your uncle pays, I don't care who.'

Rent was taken care. Now I had to find a way of raising money for his college fee and money to live on, a far more daunting task. For a whole week, I watched Sanju getting more and more depressed until finally he stopped attending lectures. I was as depressed as Sanju. I did not want to lose a friend and I was thinking of my letter to you sir. Who will do the typing? Will the project die a sudden death? All the hard work put in by me and Sanju wasted?

On the eighth day he received a message from Bangalore asking him to return forthwith as madam's sister needed a servant for her household. Next day I found him packing a suitcase.

'Are you mad?' I pulled him away. 'You want to work as a domestic servant. Wash dishes and sweep floor.'

'What can I do?' he said nearly in tears again.

'Didn't I say I will think of something?' I calmed him down, asked him to stay put for a few days.

I was thinking, thinking what to do until one evening I

caught up with Nandu-*da* and his friends idling in the restaurant with tea and cigarettes. It just came to me then. Why don't I ask Nandu-*da*? An eminent lecturer, he would have contacts at the university.

I told him about Sanju's problems, about the political science degree. If we don't help him, he will be forced back to working as a domestic servant.

'We can't have that,' Nandu-*da* said, slapping the table, 'he must be helped to continue his studies.'

His friends agreed too. One said he would contribute five hundred rupees, another said he would match it. Most were willing to contribute.

'No, no that's no solution. We need to speak to someone in authority within the ministry of education or some charitable organisations,' another of his friends put in, 'does anyone have contacts?'

There was a brief silence. 'I know someone high up in the education department,' Nandu-*da* said, 'why didn't I think of it before? You leave it to me Kalu, I will take care of it.'

What a relief that was. It was like a ton of weight lifting from my shoulders.

Next day, as planned, I woke up early in the morning. Stepped into the new trouser I had got stitched from a tailor in New Market. On impulse I had bought a shirt too, white with thin grey stripes. The tailor had said it goes perfectly with the trouser, what all trendy people are wearing these days. I was not sure. Thought he was mocking me, smirking inwardly, but I bought it anyway.

I looked at myself in the mirror. Will people take me for a rich *sahab* or son of a rich *sahab*? I unbuttoned the top half of the shirt and did the arrogant self-assured gesture, like rich peoples' children do; as if they possess every inch of ground under their feet. But it didn't feel right, sir. I felt a fraud. People will stare at me. Look at the country boy trying to rise above his station.

Sanju came down to my room. 'How do I look?' I posed for him, stood erect with arms stiff by the side.

He burst out laughing. 'Huh *bara sahab*. You look like a *chutia*, fool.'

'Why, what's wrong.'

He pointed at the leather sandals I was wearing and sniggered.

'What's wrong with my *chappals*?'

'You fool *chappals* don't go with the dressy trouser and shirt, you need shoes, proper shoes.'

We did a swop. He lent me his shoes, and I gave him my sandals. As I was tying the shoelaces, Roby the *paadmaru* came in. We had lately nicknamed him *paadmaru* because of his habit of farting at inappropriate moments.

He saw me in the new clothes and winked. '*Accha, accha*, I know. You are going to meet Tanya,' he said.

I let him believe that's where I was going.

At Mahanayak Uttam Kumar metro station, I got off the train and took a bus. The old man's words in Kanchrapara were still fresh in my head. 'Saira lives in a care home in Tollygunge. If she is still alive that is,' he had said. There was hint of sadness in his eyes. Even as he was writing the address, I could sense grief in his shaking hands.

A man sitting beside me on the bus was clearing his throat repeatedly, as if attempting a lion's roar and failing miserably. He took his Adam's apple between his fingers, gave it a hefty tweak. 'Very serious condition,' he said.

'What is it?' I asked.

'*Baba* what to tell you, I have got infection, a form of cancer. Doctors tell me there is no cure.'

'You should take it easy.'

'*Baba*, it's alright for you to say take it easy. I have to shout all the time. It stresses my voice box.'

'What work you do?' I asked.

'Fish business. I sell fish - all kind - *hilsa, chitol, rui, tilapia, puti, boyal*, everything, big ones, fresh catch only, *hanh*, mark my word.'

'So why does it affect your voice box, *dada*?'

'How can I sell fish in the market without shouting? Eh, you tell me. If I don't shout the customer goes to the seller on my left or the right, but not to me.' He attempted a chuckle but managed only a series of coughs, 'do you smoke?'

'No, never.'

'Good.' He patted his chest with a closed fist. 'See what's happened to me.'

The bus shuddering on potholed road stopped periodically, disgorging passengers or taking on new ones. An hour later, as it swung into a narrow lane a signboard came into view attached to the wall of a three-storey building. It said Tolly Park Home. I had arrived at my destination.

I stood by the roadside to take stock and strangely felt no apprehension, as if I knew with complete assurance just what was to come. A man squatting under the owning of a shop, taking shelter from the midday sun, was watching me curiously as I searched for the entrance to the building. '*O babu* the doorway is at the rear. You take the side alley and turn right at the canal,' he shouted.

A reek wafted from the drain carrying murky black sludge, as it clashed with warm muddy water flowing in the canal. I walked along the narrow unpaved path, past a long line of residential shacks, taking in the smells and sounds of life, a child crying, splash of water, someone having a bucket bath, crackling noise of a radio being tuned somewhere, a hint of acrid smoke from a coal brazier mixed with ammonia of urine. The aroma of cardamom from a steamy chai blended with silky smoothness of cooked rice. The bite of sizzling *tarka* dropped on a pot of steaming dal.

The entrance was an ordinary wooden door painted dark brown. An old lady was coming out, leaning on a walking stick, behind her a young man, who could be her grandson. I stepped aside to let them pass. A sign attached to the door said *All Visitors Must Report to Warden*. It was in English. I wondered how many people around here were able to read anything other than Bengali.

I pressed the buzzer. 'Come in,' a woman's voice crackled from a hidden speaker. In the ramshackle surrounding where it seemed time had stood still for thirty years, they were using the most modern of technologies. I pushed the door open and stepped inside into a cool calm interior. In the small lobby the only furniture was a table. On my right was the closed door to a lift. A short woman in blue uniform emerged from a door marked Warden. I asked if Saira Banu lived here, while dreading her reply: Saira Banu does not live here, or she refuses to see visitors, or she is dead.

'Saira Banu,' she parroted after me.

'Yes.'

'First tell your name, who you are,' she asked sternly.

I gave my name and address.

'She is in room five. Through these doors, go to the end of the corridor and turn right. Her room is second on the left.'

I went through the swing doors into a narrow corridor, a row of rooms on both sides. An odour of unwashed clothes hung in the air and I could hear occasional bronchial coughing and sound of daytime television. Room five was in the quieter part of the building with wider corridor but no windows. I stopped, took deep breaths and knocked three times. My heart pounded as I waited for a response

'The door is not locked.' I heard a muffled female voice.

I pushed the door open. The lady facing me was seated on a padded chair below a window, an open book in her lap. Her silvery grey hair shimmered in the sunlight, hands slender and elegant but with loose skin. Black eyes and light brown complexion, exactly as I had envisioned. On her feet under the white sari were orange slippers with silver thread embroidery. On a table lay several bottles of medicine and water jug.

'What do you want?' she asked and put the book down on a side table.

She was so attractive and serene. I just could not take my eyes off her.

'Speak, why are you here?'

'Are you … Saira Banu?' I asked.

'Well yes, who were you expecting?' she said as if I had asked a foolish question.

I took out a folded piece of paper from my shirt pocket and offered it to her without saying a word. She looked puzzled. I pushed it further towards her and shook it, urging her to take it. She studied me up and down. What she probably saw was a boy, first growth of moustache on upper lip, as tall as a grown man but with awkwardness of youth. The shirt and trouser meant for an older man, the kind of thing a mother might buy for a boy going to high school, imagining that somehow her son will grow into them.

She took the paper and gave me another look before leaning back and unfolding it.

She had hardly read a line when she exclaimed in a shrill voice, 'Raju.' Her eyes locked into a stare, hooked in that middle and mysterious distance one sees in painted portraits of Kings and Queens of years gone by and then she whispered, 'who gave it to you?'

'I found it,' I said.

As if she hadn't heard. 'Do you know Raju?' she asked.

I must have mumbled something incomprehensible for she asked again, 'do you know him?'

'Err … yes, I have met him,' I said.

She turned pale and very still. I panicked, thinking she had become ill. 'Are you alright?' I asked.

'You better tell me who you are and why you are here. Or I will call Rajaram.'

I guessed Rajaram was a security guard. 'I will tell you *mataji*. But are you alright? Will you like some water?'

She shook a finger asking me to sit down. I did as asked, and began telling her everything. The only lie was that I had found the wallet on the street.

'How did you find me?'

I told her more, again truthfully, about my visits to Ballygunge and Kanchrapara. How I got lucky and found Asghar Khan.

'You have met Asghar?' she said with a loud gasp.

'Yes.'

She looked into my eyes, searching, as if trying to work out how much I knew. After a while she dropped her head back on the chair.

'Would you like to rest?' I asked.

'No, no. Tell me about Raju,' she said.

I told her his home was in Kalighat. He had become a schoolteacher after leaving the army and he never married. 'Would you like to meet him?' I asked cautiously.

She laughed at that, her laugh so high and girlish I felt instantly relieved.

'Meet him? You are too young to understand this. True love never dies. But how can I take him away from his current life? That will be cruel. I will be happy just to rest my eyes on him for a few moments, a final time, before I leave this earth.'

'I will talk to him. Maybe you will meet him very soon.'

She giggled again in that girlish way. It made her look years younger.

On the train, going back home, I sat sandwiched between two old ladies. They were of similar age and build as Saira. Strange, I have just left one Saira behind and now I am with two more. I felt doubly joyed that she had said she would like to meet Raju. Her words were almost identical to Raju's. He had also said he would like to meet her one last time.

I had learned so much about the two lovers. Then the realisation hit me that I was the only point of contact between them, a privileged position. From then on, I wanted more than ever to arrange that meeting.

CHAPTER 24

Late in the evening, going up to my room I saw Pratibha bent over an oil vat, par boiling chopped potatoes. Her stomach in sideways profile looked bloated. I took a closer look. There was no denying, she really was pregnant.

I was wondering if Sanju had noticed it too when my mobile phone jingled. I took it out of the pocket. Read the text message and dashed into Sanju's room. 'Sit down. I have something to tell you.'

'I am sitting already you fool,' Sanju said.

'I have just received a text message from Babu.'

'What does he want?'

'The photo, of course. He says he has been very lenient. Now he has given me a week. This is the last warning, he says. This time he wants me at Howrah station on Monday morning.'

'What are you going to do?'

'I will have to convince him somehow the photo is lost for good. He doesn't have to worry as I cannot blackmail him.'

'Will he believe you?'

'Probably not ... you know people who are crooked believe everyone else is like them. They don't trust anyone. I don't know what to do.'

'My advice is do nothing. Let him believe you have the photo. It's in safekeeping.'

'But he has made life hell for me. I piss in my pants every time the phone rings.'

It was not easy to ignore Babu's ultimatum, but I had no choice. I tried to keep myself busy, looked for things to do, stay away from home as much as possible.

A few days later, I went to Kalighat. Raju was sitting by the window, a book in hand.

'Where have you been?' he cried, 'I thought you wanted to learn to read.'

I told him something important had come up.

'What can be more important than learning? I even bought some books for you,' he said and called Champa, 'bring those books down from the shelf for me.'

Champa came in with two thin books and glared at me as before. 'Baba, why are you wasting time on this boy. Will he ever be able to learn to write and read?' she said scornfully.

'That is the whole point Champa. The harder the task, the more worthwhile it is.'

'Bah,' she said and stomped out. I broke the news about Saira. 'She has been found.'

He bolted upright on his chair and just as quickly fell back again. 'You have? .... Saira.'

'Yes, she is fine, *dada.*'

'Where did you meet her?'

'She lives in Tollygunge.'

'Tollygunge, I thought she was in Dubai or some faraway place. Tell me more.'

'She lives in a nursing home.'

'Nursing home?' Worry lines suddenly appeared on his face. 'Did you tell her about me?'

'Yes, I did. I also asked her if she would like to meet you.'

'And ... what did she say?'

'She said, yes.'

He lowered his eyes and focussed on the book in his hand, at an open page.

'You want to meet her, don't you, *dada*?'

'Yes, yes, I do, but….'

'Why are you hesitating Raju dada?'

'This is not right. People have families, attachments. It can complicate things.'

'She said the same thing. But if you want the honest truth, I think she is keen to meet you.'

He went quiet. I held the silence too, listening to his erratic breathing, waiting for him to say yes. This went on for a minute. Finally, he said, 'but not straight away, I am having some treatment. After Durga Pujo.'

A week later, I went back to Tollygunge, to break the news to Saira: meeting will take place after Durga pujo. I wanted to make sure she was committed.

She was sitting on the same chair with eyes closed. A maid was combing her hair. Looking around I noticed a collection of Rajasthani dolls and puppets arranged decorously on the shelf and sideboard.

'Oh, Kalu *beta* you have come,' she said, pleased to see me and dismissed the woman grooming her.

'How are you?' I asked.

'I am well son.'

'Are you wondering why I have come?'

'Yes, tell me,' she said waving her slender hand, asking me to come closer.

'I met Raju dada the other day.'

'Oh, tell me, what did he say?'

'He said he wants to meet you.'

'What ...' she exclaimed very loud and placed a hand on her chest, as if I was conveying a marriage proposal. 'When is he coming?'

'After Durga Pujo, is that alright?'

She laughed and her eyes moistened. I supposed they were tears of joy. 'What does he look like? Tell me, tell me.'

'Handsome. Just like a film star,' I said.

'Get away.' She chuckled again. 'How can he be like a handsome film star at this age?'

'No but he is,' I said teasing, pleased I was able to amuse her.

'Ahh, he was like a prince those days. He used to take me to the cinema, every week a different film. So much fun we had,' she said.

She asked me for some water. I filled up a glass from the jug and handed it to her.

'But first I want to ask you a question?' I said.

'Yes son.' She took a sip and looked at me with cute inquisitive eyes.

'It's about Asghar Khan. Were you married to him?' I asked cautiously, worried she might be offended. Thankfully, she appeared more surprised than affronted by my direct question.

'What did he tell you?'

'He said you were married but....'

'Yes, we did get married, only because my family put so much pressure on me. You know what it is like. What terrible mistake.'

'Why did you go to Dubai?'

She shut her eyes, as if searching for an answer in the deep well of old memories. 'I had to go away for I had become pregnant ... a baby boy. Asghar found out and came to Dubai. He said the child was his and he was going to take him away from me. I could not resist. I knew he was right. I had married him, and I had left him, broken the pledge to love, obey and honour in true Muslim tradition. I was certain he would provide for him better than what I could have done on my own.'

'Have you met your son lately?'

'No. It would not be fair on him. I made Asghar promise he wouldn't tell him about me.'

I felt strangely privileged, knowing I had met the son she was talking about. But I didn't tell her anything.

Later when I was leaving, about to step out of the room, she called me back. 'Show me your hand,' she said.

I put my hand out, surprised, was she going to reveal some more secrets of her past life. She took my hand in hers. 'You are a young man,' she said, 'what are you doing so far away from home, with an old woman like me?'

I was dumbfounded. The question stirred up deep emotions in me. Feelings I always kept locked in the heart suddenly erupted. I wanted to bring them all out. I wanted to tell her I wished she was my mother, wished I had a family complete with brothers and sisters, wished I had been to school and college. But I couldn't bring myself to say anything. Tears started rolling down my cheeks.

'*Arre beta* why are you crying? This is not a crying matter. I asked only,' she said.

I composed myself. 'Excuse me *mataji*, I don't know what came over me.' Unable to look directly into her eyes I turned my attention to the puppets on the shelf.

'They are beautiful, aren't they,' she said and asked me to open the wardrobe. I pulled one of the doors open. Instead of saris on cloth-hangers, I was staring at several cardboard boxes.

'Take one out, go on,' she said.

I pulled a box out and raised the lid. I was surprised to see six or seven Rajasthani puppets, similar to ones on the sideboard.

'You know what they are? Have you heard of *kathputli*?'

'No,' I said.

'It's an old folk tradition of story-telling with hand operated puppets.'

I picked one up and examined it. It had been fashioned out of a piece of long wood, one end shaped into a head, eyes, nose and mouth carefully painted. Dressed in colourful fabric, several long strings attached to various parts of the body so each limb and head was manoeuvrable individually.

'Take out another box,' she said.

I pulled a box out at random. This one contained only three puppets, old and delicate with faded fabric and peeling paintwork.

'Be careful with those,' she said, 'they are hundred years old. I got them from a performer in Shadipur, Delhi. They belonged to his grandfather who was also a *kathputli-walla*.'

'How many have you got?' I asked.

'Now about fifty, but at one time I had over two hundred. I have given them away because I have nowhere to store.'

'I have never seen a *kathputli* performance,' I said.

'That's the tragedy Kalu *beta*. People are not interested in traditional art anymore. *Baas* all day long they are playing games on computers, mobiles phones, this and that.'

She asked me to bring down the box marked PJ 9. The four

puppets in this box were very different. They were dressed with shirt and baggy trousers up to the calf, lots of red, green and yellow, clownish in appearance with a long hooked nose and, laughing faces and eyes.

'They are called Punch and Judy,' she said, 'I got them from an English family from Liverpool who were travelling all over India performing to school children. What fun I had learning to operate them.'

Chapter 25

One evening, after a long stint at Victoria Memorial and the *maidan*, I caught the last train of the day to Shyambazar. From there it was a twenty-minute walk home. Out of the station I veered left on to Shankar Das Lane and then right into deserted Temple Street, a narrow lane of densely packed houses, cars parked on pavements. Under a lamp post I glimpsed my own shadow as it moved swiftly away from me. I had just passed a house with a mango tree in front when I heard someone shout, '*are bhai kahan ja rahe ho intni rat me.* Where are you going this time of the night?'

I looked behind me. Two big men were coming towards me.

'*Arre bhai*, stop a minute. We want to talk to you,' one of them said.

I guessed instantly who they were and speeded up, hoping to create a distance. They had quickened their pace too. I turned right into a side lane. Still they were behind me. On my left I saw a boarded up house, its side gate unhinged. I jumped over the low boundary wall and sprinted across to the gate leading to the back garden. The gate gave in easily. Tall fencing enclosed the rear garden. It was too high to scale with ease. I started searching for hiding places. The back door to the house was slightly ajar. I dashed in. Once inside I slammed the door shut and searched desperately for a lock or latch. There was not any. I stood with my back pushed against the door; arms outstretched gripping the doorframe. In here, in here, I heard them whisper on the other side and then I fell forward, crashing head first, into a windowpane. I blundered on in the dark. Felt a hand on my shoulder. '*Bhai* stop,' someone said. The face was on my right. On impulse, I picked up a glass vase from a table and smashed it on the head. The vase broke. Its neck with jagged edges was still in my hand. I pushed it at the face. The man screamed in pain and I saw blood on his chin. I became aware of another man on my left.

'What do you want?' I said, 'leave me alone.'

He gripped my jaw in his powerful hand, forcing my mouth wide open. 'Boss wants the photo, you understand.'

A movement in the dark told me there was someone else in the room. I saw a woman cowering in the corner, two little children clinging to her. '*Bab re bap*, what are you people doing here?' she squealed in fear.

I felt a sharp pricking sensation on my left shoulder and caught the glint of a long knife. 'Run, call the police,' I yelled at the woman.

But she was too terrified to move. Bells began ringing in my ears. A knee struck my groin followed by several punches to the face.

Suddenly a ray of light entered the window, lighting up the faces and part of the room. Startled by the intrusion they stopped and looked nervously at the door. Then just as suddenly it was dark again. I took advantage of the confusion and made a dash for the open door. They caught me on the steps. I turned around and began throwing wild punches.

In the struggle, the knife man tripped on something. 'Aahh, *saala, madarchoot*,' he screamed as he fell.

Realising he had stabbed himself in the fall I started kicking him, going for the patch of blood. The second man rushed me head on. We grappled for a while and then fell on the hard surface. I was on my back. The man astride me raised a clenched fist. Biggest bunch of knuckles I had ever seen, a chunky ring on the middle finger.

'This is boss's message, listen carefully, he says send the photo now or *tumhari chockri*, the girlfriend, will get it.' And then he pulled his fist higher ready to strike. God, now he is going to kill me. In that instant the only thought that came to me was of my absent mother, a woman I had never met or spoken to.

CHAPTER 26

I was in bed shielded by light blue curtains. Beyond the curtain, I could hear ethereal voices, the squeak of rubber soles on linoleum, beep of electronic machines. Three men in white shirts came and stood over me, one reading a chart on a clipboard with the intensity of a dyslexic. He had greasy hair pasted flat on his head, like nineteen fifties film stars. 'How many fingers?' he asked and raised two fingers and then cunningly switched to four. They smiled and nodded at my answers.

I sat up on the bed and tried to swing my legs over the side. A shooting pain in the abdomen made me stop. My head was throbbing as if someone was hammering a nail in the skull. I raised a hand to my face. Why are my fingers bandaged? My eyes focused on a tube attached to the nose. There were several plastic tubes, one taped to my wrist.

'Take it easy … easy. Don't move.' A nurse came running and attached a mask to my face. 'This will help you breathe. You mustn't strain yourself. Do you understand?' She was very loud. I am not deaf I wanted to say.

The intense medicinal stench and strange noises were intriguing me. I did not know how many days I had been there.

The next day when I woke someone was sitting beside me. Dark face with short curly hair, his black eyes focused on me, eyebrows curled as if he was waiting for a reply to a question. It took several seconds to recognise Sanju.

'*Weh*, how are you?' he asked.

'Where am I?'

'*Weh*, you don't know where you are … you're in hospital.'

'Hospital? I am in hospital?'

Sanju pointed at the monitors on trolleys, charts and diagrams on the wall. A gas cylinder on the floor and several plastic tubes criss-crossing the room, 'You are most positively in a hospital.'

'Why?'

'You were beaten up … bad, bad. They found you in that strange house on Temple Street. Why were you there? Who did this to you?'

And then it all came gushing back. I remembered the walk from the station and the two men.

'How will I pay for the hospital treatment?' I said.

'Baldev brought you here, don't worry.'

Baldev spending money? Not possible. He will want it all back, every rupee and then throw me out of the room. My head started throbbing again.

The next time I awoke, I could hear loud noises, cranking trolleys, sighs of stricken patients, patter of relatives, speeding nurses. I was feeling besieged when I became aware of voices nearby – urgent, fluxing into each other. I picked up two words – internal and haemorrhages. The rest stayed outside my mind's reach. One of the voices was familiar.

'Doctori, can you explain what you mean,' Baldev was saying, addressing a man in white shirt.

'… Pneumothorax and extensive internal haemorrhage … the two most pressing issues … the knife incision to the lung was at 45 degrees. When this happens, air enters the space between the membranes surrounding the lungs. The lung suffers trauma and in extreme cases this can be fatal.'

Baldev opened and shut his mouth, gasped helplessly like fish out of water. 'But, but doctori, you'll make him fit again, want you?' he said, nodding vigorously, as if willing the doctor to say yes.

'We're working on it. But we're not out of the woods yet.'

'What are the ...' Baldev said, trailing off mid-sentence, gesturing with his hand - you know what I mean.

'Fifty, fifty.'

'Woh,' Baldev grimaced, as if he himself was a stab victim, 'can't you do better, doctori?'

'We are doing the best.'

Seeing I was awake, Baldev rushed over to me. 'How are you, son?'

'I don't know?' I said, fearing he was going to ask me to vacate the room.

'*Re*, you'll be alright soon,' he said and picked up the nurses' clipboard, studied the chart and figures as if he understood everything and then sat down heavily on the chair. 'What happened to you, son? You want to talk about it with me? I am here to help.'

How could I tell him the truth?

'You don't want to talk to me. You want to talk to Pratibha. I can ask her to come.'

'I'll tell you. But not now ... they were not trying to kill me,' I said.

'Not trying to kill you *re*?' he screamed pointing at the bandages with furious shake of his hand, 'you call this not trying to kill you.'

A nurse entered the room with a trolley. Baldev pounced on her, 'nurse, if you make him better within a week, I will give you a big box of *mithai*, my *mithai* is best in whole of Kolkata. You ask anybody.' With bunched fingers on his lips, he gave a loud smack.

The nurse laughed. 'Only if you give me six boxes of *chum chum* and *sandesh.*'

'Done,' he said, 'you make sure he is home next week.'

That night I had a dream. I am in an alley where lights are reduced to pinpricks due to thick fog. Dying figures are stumbling past me. A child is standing at the street corner, crying for his mother. The child's crying grows shriller until it becomes wailing of wild animals. More people are arriving, in their hundreds, staggering and falling, some half upright in doorways and against lampposts; their mouths are open, out of their throats the song of death is pouring out in gusts. Suddenly I hear a woman's scream. Her arms are outstretched. 'Stop it, stop it,' she is screaming. The singing stops. 'Where is my child?' she howls. The child is right there, in front. Why can't she see it? 'Where is my child, where is my child?' she is howling louder and louder and louder. Her face has no eyes... just two black holes.

Next day they transferred me to a ward with five older men. The men were recovering from surgeries to internal organs. I hated the odour and the wailing. An orchestra of fractured coughs and painful grunts, as if they were all protesting, demanding relief, not from pain but from this life. All day long patients were coming in, wheeled on clanking trolleys.

CHAPTER 27

'Pratibha, Pratibha that was the hospital,' Baldev yelled.

'What do they want?' She was sweeping the back yard with a long-handled broom.

'It's Kalu. He has been taken into Intensive Care.' Baldev came stomping to the yard, his greasy shoes on the swept floor.

'Nooo ... don't come here with your dirty feet,' she cried, hit his legs with the broom, the bangles on her wrists jingled noisily, 'did they say why?'

'They said I should inform his relatives. I am going there right now,' he said and dashed into the bedroom. Dancing on one foot he pulled out the grease stained shoes one after the other and pushed his feet into a clean pair. He bumped into Nandu on the way out.

'Oh, Professor sahab. You come for fish pakora? Good, good.' He yelled at the cook behind the counter, '*Reh*, make sure you give Professor sahab the best fish that came this morning.'

'In such hurry, hurry, where are you going?' Nandu asked.

'It's Kalu. He is very ill, in intensive care.'

'What? I saw him only the other day. He was absolutely alright,' Nandu said shocked.

'Yes, Professor. What to say. He got beaten up.'

In the hospital a nurse guided Baldev to room six. 'He is on respirator. You can go in but you mustn't speak to him,' she said sternly.

Baldev was horrified. 'Why? What happened?'

'He has been diagnosed with severe lung infection, maybe pneumonia.'

'Pneumonia ... it can't be, nurse, I was here two days ago. He was looking like he was ready to come home.'

'I don't know about that. You will have to speak to the doctor. He will be here later today,' she said brushing him aside and moved on to another patient.

Baldev opened the door and went inside. Kalu was lying on the bed listless covered in a thin sheet. Electrodes taped to his arms, chest and legs, intravenous drip attached to his forearm, eyes taped shut. An oxygen pump hummed relentlessly. The room smelled of strong medicines. And then he realised Kalu had company. Two policemen were standing in one corner.

He ignored the policemen and stood for several seconds staring at the face of a boy about whom, he now realised, he knew so little yet had grown to like immensely. If pushed, he would admit to seeing Kalu as part of the family. For the first time in a long while a lump appeared in his throat. He murmured a few words, 'son, you have to fight.'

'One minute,' the senior policeman came up to him, 'are you a relative of the patient here.'

'I am a friend, not relative,' said Baldev, 'what do you want?'

'Just a few questions, sir, would you mind coming this way?' He took Baldev out of the ward to the stairwell. Boxes of dirty linen and other hospital paraphernalia lay scattered. He took out a notepad from his pocket. 'May I ask your name and how you know the boy?'

'Baldev Ramlal Behari. This boy rents a room above my shop. Very good boy. Who would want to beat him up like that? ... *Ram, Ram, Ram.*'

'Where was he before he came to you?'

'How do I know? What is all this anyway? Who has done this to the poor boy?'

'We have to make enquiries. What can you tell us about his family?'

'He told me he is from Uttarakhand. That's all I know.'

'Is that all you know about your tenant?' the policeman said in a sarcastic tone.

'Why are you harassing me? Instead of wasting time you should be out there looking for the real *badmash* culprits.'

'So, what do you think we are doing right now?' the policeman said moving closer, scrutinising Baldev's face.

'Why're you looking at me like that … I did it? Is that what you think?'

'Did I say that?'

'You better not or I will report you to your chief,' Baldev said stamping his feet and turned away. He kept on walking until he was out of the main gate.

'Why did you come back without speaking to the doctor? You coward I want you to go back at once,' Pratibha screamed and dropped on a chair exhausted. 'Even he thinks you are a coward,' she said looking down at her swollen belly.

'He thinks I am coward, nooo, never,' Baldev cried, fell on his knees and clamped his ear to her stomach, 'I can't hear him.'

I was sitting up eating a biscuit. Again, they had transferred me to an open ward. It was as noisy as a train station, relatives crowding the aisles, fussing over patients on beds, feeding them roti and dal, fruits and all kinds of Bengali sweets. Nurses were running up and down with scary looking instruments.

I was feeling depressed as hell, wanted to be out of the hospital when I saw Nandu-*da* in his favourite kurta with embroidery on collar and sleeves, scanning the big ward, as if searching for someone. He saw me and nodded.

'Are you alright?' he asked pulling up a chair.

'Getting better, Nandu-*da*,' I said, 'I am so surprised to see you.'

'I had to come when I heard you were in hospital.' He studied the bandages on my body. 'Baldev told me you got into a fight.'

'Yes, what to do,' I said.

'*Arre* this looks serious. What happened?'

I did not reply.

'You can tell me, we are friends, remember,' he said with the customary shake of his head and half smile.

His smile and body language, the mere presence was enough to put me at ease. 'Nandu-*da*, we are poor people. If we don't fight, we go hungry.'

'*Arre, arre arre*, Kalu I know all about that. You don't have to tell me.'

'Then you understand Nandu-*da*.'

'Sometimes it is wise to let them take what they want. No point risking life for a few rupees. Is it?' he said.

'*Bilkul*, what you are saying is right,' I said. I wanted to let him believe it was a case of everyday robbery. Then he said something I was least expecting.

'Do you remember the conversation we had at the airport?'

'Yes ....' I remembered it like it was yesterday.

'Do you still want to meet your mother?'

'Yes,' I said, excitement building up in my stomach.

'Then you will have to tell me everything about you. Are you prepared?'

'I will do absolutely anything.'

'You will have to go back to your childhood; as far back as you can remember. Think you can do it?'

'Yes ... yes ... yes,' I said. It was not just the prospect of meeting my mother, but also to be able to tell someone the pain and anguish I had suffered all my life. I picked up a glass of ice cold water, took a sip. This time it hit the tonsils and threw me into goose bumps and into a memory from the past in Haridwar: we are in a dark cold room, bored, nothing to do. All the nannies have gone down for some kind of meeting. We open a medicine chest. Bhagu takes out a jar of red tablets. These will give you a high, he says winking, you will love them, they will make you happy and you will fly like birds. So we take one each. I am sick within minutes, my teeth start clacking, and I am rolling on the floor. A nannie comes and curses, slaps me across the face. You want to die, go do it somewhere else. She gives me warm salted water to drink. This will empty your stomach, you son of a bitch. Maybe I should let you die, as your mother wanted you to. My mother wanted me to die. I believe her. I feel so unloved I start crying. She slaps me repeatedly. I cannot stop crying.

'Are you alright?' Nandu-*da* was leaning over me, stroking my forehead.

'Yes, yes, I am fine,' I said.

'Then we will make a start as soon as you are fit.'

Next day I walked out of the hospital without anyone noticing.

'Oh, my God,' Pratibha yelled seeing me come in through the back door.

Baldev cried, '*Re*, only two weeks and you think you can sing and dance already.'

Pratibha put down the tray of filleted fish and rushed forward to embrace me.

'I was feeling better, so decided to come home,' I said.

'Are you sure?'

'Oh yes.'

I had lied because the missions I had in mind were of far greater importance. Arrangements were to be made for Raju, Saira's meeting, and I had to start a search for my mother with help from Nandu-*da*. I could not tell all this to Baldev and Pratibha however kind and helpful they had been to me.

Sanju and I went to Vishram Das Cars on Rabindra Sarai to book a hire-car. We did not want any old ragbag, like Maruti or Ambassador. It would have be a prestigious foreign car, maybe a Honda CRV or late model Hyundai. I paid half the money in advance, in crisp notes, and gave instructions to pick us up at eleven o'clock sharp. Both Raju and Saira had been informed. We were going to meet Raju at twelve in the afternoon. Expected time of arrival at Tolly Park Home was two o'clock. Take it slow and steady. Leave Raju with Saira for as long as they wanted. Then later in the afternoon or evening take him back home. What could go wrong?

Twelve days to go, I was passing time by staying mostly in my room, for I didn't want to bump into Babu's gorillas again, not until I had completed the business. Meanwhile I was keeping the Sanyo busy, recording my story as quickly as I could. At one time, it frustratingly stopped working. However, it was only the battery. Nandu-*da* had taken Sanju to meet some influential people at the university. He was reassured something would be sorted out; meanwhile he should keep attending lectures. I was getting bored, counting each hour and day. To pass the time I started going down to sit in front of the television, watch rubbish soap operas, like *Gunahon Ka Devta, Sasural Genda Phool, Kitani Muhabbat Hai.*

On the eighth day, I had returned to my room after watching a repeat of *Kehsi Yes Yarian* when my mobile rang. I took out the phone from my pocket, my heart sinking rapidly, expecting to hear Babu's booming voice gloating at what he had done to me.

At first, there was silence at the other end then the caller said, 'it's me, Shanta, Tanya's friend.'

'Hello Shanta, how are you?' I almost yelled in relief. I had met Shanta at the Club.

'Do you know,' she said.

'Know what?'

'Tanya had an accident on the way to the office. She was hit by a car.'

'How is she?'

'She is in hospital. Bad ....'

I ran upstairs to tell Sanju.

'*Weh*, what kind of joke is that, Kalu. It's very bad joke,' he said.

'No joke, she had an accident.'

'No …. Let's go,' Sanju said and started buttoning up his shirt, 'but you are not well, maybe you should stay home.'

'Not possible,' I protested. On way to hospital, I confided to Sanju about what Babu's men had said in the house in Temple Street. Return the photo or my *chokri* girl will get it. 'Do you think Babu has done this to Tanya?'

Sanju thought about it for a moment and replied somewhat unconvincingly, 'it could just be an accident.'

The fat woman at the reception desk gave us directions to Acute Trauma Unit. 'Follow the green arrows,' she said.

We walked through a warren of narrow corridors and swinging doors, bumping into trolleys, uniformed medical staff and relatives wandering lost like us.

Shanta was already there, standing at the door marked ATU along with three other men, all looking very solemn. They were Tanya's uncles and a cousin.

'Go see her,' Shanta said, pushing the door open, 'she has several fractures, internal bleeding and concussion. She will be sent for MRI scan.'

Tanya was lying partly covered by a sheet. Her heavily bandaged left leg, hoisted up with a contraption over the bed. Bandages covered her head and side of the face, a mask over her nose and mouth. She looked so fragile and small. Strong medicinal odour hung in the room reminding me of the hospital I had once visited in Haridwar.

She saw me and removed the mask from her face. 'Kalu,' she whispered.

'How are you?'

'It hurts.' Her face drew up. Then she smiled.

'You'll be alright.'

'I am sorry.'

'What for?'

'I should have been more careful crossing the road.'

'What nonsense. It's not your fault. We all know these car drivers are maniacs.'

'Will you miss me?'

'No.'

'No … why not?'

'Because you're going nowhere… and I am going nowhere.'

'I am going to die.'

'No you won't. Stop talking rubbish.'

'Please,' the nurse snapped, 'don't distress her.'

I moved aside as the nurse wrapped a rubber strap to Tanya's arm and pressed a button. The strap inflated quickly then began deflating very slowly. She appeared unhappy with the reading. 'I will have to do it again, nothing to worry about,' she said reassuring Tanya.

Dissatisfied with the second reading she left the room and returned with another nurse and a doctor.

'Is everything alright?' I asked.

'Are you next of kin?' the doctor asked, a tall man in blue shirt.

'Friend,' I replied.

'Could you wait outside please, we will call you when we can.'

I came out. The uncles and cousin were sitting on a bench in the hallway.

'How is she?' Sanju asked.

'Not good,' I said, and a conflict started raging in my head. Poor Tanya. It's my fault. What if she dies? She can't die. Yes but what if she should die? She can't die, I am telling you. Don't be a fool. People recover from worst injuries. But what if she should die? She won't. She's alright. But what if she dies? She will not, she won't, she won't. Now shut up. What if she dies?

The door opened suddenly, startling everyone. A man in brown overall came out walking backwards. Then we saw the wheeled stretcher on which Tanya was lying with her head propped up. She saw us, made a weak gesture of recognition. They wheeled the stretcher rapidly down the hall, one man pulling and the other pushing. People stood aside to allow the stretcher to pass.

'Where are you taking her?' One of the uncles asked.

'Radiology,' the porter replied.

We followed the stretcher, like a funeral cortege, through several swing doors, right and then left again, medical staff criss-crossing their path, thick manila folders in hands. A patient walking around lost in nightgown. At the end of the hallway, we stopped for an elevator. The door opened slowly. The stretcher went in first and then everyone piled in, squeezed tight. Out of the elevator, the porters stopped suddenly in front of a door, began manoeuvring the stretcher forth and back, like an articulated lorry in a narrow lane, until they were half through the door. 'You can't come in here,' the porter said, 'waiting area is on your right.'

'How long will it take?' the uncle asked.

'Don't know *sahib*. Give it two hours.'

I sat down on a long metal bench fixed to the floor, beside

an older man reading a newspaper. There were quite a few people waiting, some shouting into their phones, others reading magazines or staring into nothing.

An hour had passed. Still we were waiting. Sanju and Shanta returned from a walk. They started staring at pictures on the wall, reading the notice board or studying the contours of the floor.

The door flew open again. This time it was Tanya's stretcher, pulled by same two porters. 'How is she?' the uncle with the gruff voice sprang to his feet.

'Can't say *sahib*, we been asked to rush her to intensive.'

ICU was a short distance down the hall. They rushed the stretcher in, its rubber wheels screeching on the linoleum tiles. The doors crashed shut behind the stretcher. I did not go in. There was lot of activity inside, scrambling feet and shouted instructions. The uncles had barged in demanding to know what was going on. I heard someone say, 'cardiac … ten milligram … stand back everybody.' I knew it was not good. Shanta, her hair in disarray, was weeping. Sanju was comforting her.

Two minutes later a doctor came out. 'She is resting, not in fit state to talk. You better go home and take some rest. We will call you if her condition worsens.'

So that was it.

Back home I went straight to my room, telling Sanju I needed to rest. Fifteen minutes later I was down again. Baldev was debating politics with some men. I slipped out quietly and walked to the taxi stand a quarter of mile away.

'Howrah station,' I said to the driver and settled back on the rear seat. At the station, I queued up to purchase a ticket for Bangalore. The next train to depart was 23.30 sleeper. It would arrive at 09.05 in the morning.

'Train full,' declared the man behind the counter.

'It's very important. I have to get to Bangalore,' I said.

'You don't understand *bhaiya*. How I can give you ticket when there are no seats available?'

'Five hundred rupees extra,' I said firmly, not caring who was listening.

He ducked under the counter, began shuffling papers around and then sat up and typed something on the keyboard. A ticket slid out of the printing machine.

'This ticket is in the name of P Deshpande. You tell them you are Deshpande,' he said keeping his voice low.

Still three hours to departure, I went to the café, ordered a *masala dosa* and let it sit on the table. I had no appetite.

'Mr P Deshpande,' the train steward said checking names on a long list, 'you are on bogey number five, seat twelve, upper berth.'

I sat on the berth with legs outstretched. Unlike other passengers who had suitcases and holdalls, I was travelling unburdened, not even a handbag. While others slept, I was wide awake, thinking of Tanya, praying for full recovery.

At nine thirty in the morning when the train finally stopped at Bangalore Cy Station, I jumped out and ran to the taxi depot.

'Main Road, Indira Nagar,' I instructed the driver.

An hour later, navigating his way through heavy traffic the driver entered Main Road. 'Which number?' he asked.

'Number twenty, the music store.' I paid him and waited on the pavement until he was out of sight. I walked back the way we came and stopped a little distance short of the *Romani*

Orthodox Church. The panelled fence and the metal gate, Father Petre's green door, everything appeared the same as if I had never left. I went closer, staying level with the perimeter hedge, so I would not be spotted from inside. The cameras were still located in their usual positions. Instead of taking the main path, I stepped over the low wall, keeping out of the camera's line of vision I unlocked the gate with the set of keys still in my possession. Once inside I shut the gate with a light touch and walked silently to the entrance of my former home. With another key I opened the door and went in to a familiar smell and sight. Garments were hanging on hooks, shoes and sandals lay scattered on the floor. This time of the morning I knew only Babu was likely to be home. I tip toed to the living room door, peeped through a crack in the doorframe. Babu was sitting at the table, eating a paratha, breaking a piece, dipping it in yogurt and then in his mouth. Deep concentration on his face as if he was reading a book or newspaper, but there was no reading material in front.

Confident he was alone I pushed the door open and barged in as if I still lived there. He looked up in surprise, yelled, '*abe saala,*' and sprang to his feet, knocking back the chair, accidently spilling some yogurt on the floor.

'It's me,' I sang and threw my arms in the air, as if I intended to give him a pleasant surprise.

'Kalu,' he cried. I had never seen him look so startled. He regarded me up and down. I guessed he was looking for evidence of injuries on my body. I had taken care to hide the bandages under the garments. I could do nothing about the bruises on my face though. He looked beyond me, checking if I had companions. 'Are you alone?' he asked; face dark with suspicion and alarm.

'Babu *da*, I have come to ask for forgiveness. I have made a big mistake,' I said. I had never called him Babu *da* before, which is a Bengali way of addressing an older brother.

He went to the sofa and sat down, crossed his arms, made a face to show he was not impressed. I stepped closer, fell on my knees and touched his bare feet, while staying alert to any sudden movements from him. 'Babu da, please forgive me. I want to come back and work for you again. This time it will be different. You will see.'

'It's too late. How can I forgive you for what you have done?' he said. The hard look of a taskmaster returned. He reached for the packet of cigarettes on the coffee table. I noticed he had changed the brand. This one was Kent king size.

'You must, Babu *da*, you must,' I said, 'I want to apologise to Father Petre too. Is he here?'

'He is away for a few days,' he said and lit a cigarette.

'Oh, then I will ask for his forgiveness when he comes back.'

'That will do you no good,' he snapped, 'in any case I make the decisions here.'

'Then you tell me I can stay,' I said sniffling and scrubbing my nose with the back of my hand.

He stared at me hard.

'Babu *da*, let me stay.'

'You understand the difficulty I had explaining to Lal Bahadur. He was not happy. I could have lost my job because of you,' he said.

'Please excuse me, I will make up to you,' I said, 'we will be just like before, happy.'

He was quiet for a few moments, staring into me, as if trying to read my mind. I knew what he was thinking: I have come to make a deal, a good sum of money in exchange for the photo.

'Have you brought the photo?' he asked.

'Yes, yes, I have. You can have it,' I said.

He looked surprised for a split second, very brief, and then he was normal again. 'Give it to me,' he said and put his hand out.

I was tempted to ask him why he had picked on Tanya. Did he know his gorillas had nearly killed her? But I let it pass. 'Babu da first tell me I can come back and start working, just like before, as a team with my friends Gokul and Bhushan.' I also wanted to know if Bhushan was still in the house or had they done away with him.

'*Achha, achha*, alright, I will speak to Petre. Now give me the photo. Come on.'

I laughed inwardly. He must take me for a fool to fall for that. 'It's with a friend. He is waiting for me in Ashwin café outside. I will go and get him,' I said.

'With a friend,' he cried stubbing the cigarette in the ashtray.

'There is no problem. He doesn't know what all this is about,' I said.

'You stay right here. I will send Mukund.' He got up and went to the kitchen. 'Mukund,' he yelled banging on the connecting door to the church and came back to sit on the sofa.

'*Saala* Mukund is so slow, thinks this is his father's house,' he said irritably.

Mukund appeared, walking very lightly as usual, with bowed legs, as if he was treading shards of glass. He saw me and immediately shuffled on his feet, a shadow of surprise passed his face. '*Hanh sahib?*' he said addressing Babu.

Babu did a hand gesture to indicate I had an errand for him.

'Mukund *bhai*, my friend is waiting for me in café near the music store. Can you go and fetch him? He is a short man in white shirt. Name is Tublu Dasgupta. You won't miss him,' I said.

'Go, go, hurry,' Babu said.

Before Mukund left I gave him another instruction. 'While you are out, pick up a box of *ladoos* from Ganesh Sweets. They are for Babu da only.' I handed him five hundred rupees.

'*Abe, saale*, you trying to bribe me with sweets,' Babu said, 'it won't work.'

'It's nothing, just a token,' I said, 'it feels so nice to be back.'

Mukund left us promptly. When I heard the front door close I announced, 'I need to go to toilet,' and went out to the long hallway. I opened the bathroom door noisily and banged it shut without going in. I stood very still, listening and watching Babu through a crack in the doorframe. He had already picked up his mobile phone and was dialling a number. He placed the phone to his ear, waited and then started speaking in low whisper. I could not hear what he was saying, but there was urgency in his manner.

I got to work swiftly, putting my head around every door, checking if anyone was in. Confident Babu was alone I walked to the kitchen through a connecting door. Nothing much had changed here either, except a new Microwave oven. I crept across the kitchen to the door to the living room. Babu was sitting upright now, his attention to the door through which I had gone out. He did not know I was behind him, six feet from the sofa, looking down at a small thinning patch on the crown of his head. I stood very still.

Babu's mobile started ringing. He had placed it on the coffee table. Babu bent down to pick it up. I wrapped a handkerchief around my right hand swiftly. With the other hand, I pulled the knife out of my pocket, flicked it open and transferred it to the right hand. Babu had picked up the phone. I raised the knife, took six strides forward. Babu was about to press the answer button. I brought my hand down hard and pushed the blade in his neck, aiming for the base of the skull.

He gave a frightening scream. His right hand shot up to the neck. I pushed the hand out of the way and plunged the knife in again, this time a few inches to the right. The blood began flowing from the cut in hesitant spurts. I moved to the left and plunged the knife in two more times. He tried to get up, still screaming. I pushed him down by the shoulder and drove the knife in again, this time lower down his neck. His head fell forward. The phone slipped to the floor, rang a few more times before falling silent. The blood was now flowing steadily, spreading to the leather sofa. I drove the knife in one more time and then fell backwards as if pushed with force. I sat on the floor breathing hard. Two minutes, three, five, I could not tell how long I had been sitting on the floor. I got up and walked around the sofa, facing him. The body had now slumped forward. I picked a hand to chest height and let it go. It fell as if there was no life in it. I did it two more times. Each time it fell in exactly the same way.

I sat down on a chair. My hand felt numb and listless. I looked at it and the blood-soaked knife, surprised I had actually done it. As I un-wrapped the handkerchief from my hand and wiped the blade clean, I saw my fingers shaking horribly. I grabbed a dusting cloth from the kitchen, wrapped it around the blood-soaked handkerchief and the knife. Making sure I had not left anything behind I went to the back garden. As I had done a few months ago, I climbed over a fence into the neighbour's rear garden and then stepped into the back alley. A little way up was the open gutter. I dropped the bundle in the black sludge and watched it roll slowly until it disappeared.

Back on the road, I hurried to the taxi stand. It was a struggle not to break into a sprint. I happened to look inside a taxi passing by me. Seated on the back seat was Father Petre. Before I could react our eyes met, a brief fleeting glimpse. A look of recognition and surprise on his face, and the taxi was gone.

The bastard, Babu, had lied about Petre being away for a few days. My heart thumping horribly, I looked back to see if the taxi was turning around. It wasn't. How long before he discovers Babu's slumped body? I started running. Instead of going to the taxi rank I turned right into a side street.

CHAPTER 29

I had managed to catch the night train to arrive at Howrah early next morning.

'You bloody fool, where have you been?' Sanju screamed, 'do you realise the car will be here very soon.'

'Yes, yes I know,' I said as if it was no big deal, 'are you ready?'

'Of course I am bloody ready. Where have you been?'

I had a dilemma here Modiji. Should I tell Sanju? I decided not to. For the first time I had to lie to my friend. Not for my sake but for his, spare him the gory details.

'Didn't I tell you I was going to the hospital for check-up? They insisted on keeping me overnight for observation.'

'You didn't tell me?' He was still very angry.

'*Yaar*, calm down, I must have forgotten. What's the big deal?'

I went to my room and changed the shirt, slipped into the brown trouser which still had creases intact. I was thinking of Raju, he too must be getting ready for a very important day of his life. I swallowed a Tapal Aspadol with a cup of tea before going down.

Baldev was sitting cross-legged at his cash desk, a new set of black, blue and red flick top pens visible in his breast pocket. He was accepting money, handing out change while the assistant weighed and packaged the sweets.

He did not notice the shiny black Toyota estate stop in front of Baldev Sweet, driven by a man in white shirt and short cut hair style. Sanju and I slipped onto the back seat.

Raju's door opened at the first knock. He was waiting, dressed in a crisp check patterned shirt, beige trousers with turned up bottoms and polished oxford shoes, like a Bengali *bhadrolok* emulating an English gentleman.

'Are you ready Raju dada?'

'Yes, yes, let's go.' He had a nervous smile as he came out on to the path, treading carefully so as not to soil the newly polished shoes.

Once settled in the car I introduced Sanju. 'He is a student at Presidency College.'

'*Achha*, student, Kolkata University. What are you studying son?' He seemed very impressed.

'Political science,' Sanju replied.

'Wants to become Prime Minister,' I quipped.

'*Achha, achha*, very good. I will vote for you,' Raju said with a raised finger, laughed and then fell silent.

On the car radio, they were discussing upcoming Kali Pujo.

'Already talking about Kali Pujo,' I said, 'Durga Pujo has only just finished.'

'Yes, all this *dhoom dham* gives me headache,' Raju said, 'and what waste of money.'

'Why is it waste of money *dada*, it's actually good for the economy of the city. Creates employment for poor people, even if it is only seasonal, gives them something to look forward to,' Sanju said.

Raju said nodding, 'it's the noise and the crowd I can't stand.'

'*Dada* you complain of noise at Durga Pujo and Kali Pujo but do you ever complain when you hear a poor man's child crying because it doesn't have food to eat or cannot find shade from the sun?'

Raju appeared stung by the accusation. 'Son,' he said, 'you don't tell me about the suffering of the poor man. I have spent twenty years living and working with them. I have been teaching their children. I have seen the misery of the poor man when he sees the rich and middle classes singing, dancing, and feasting. He only gets the leftovers. The rich make a big show of feeding the poor once a year in order to lighten their guilt. Oh yes, I know all about that son, after all I am one of them.'

'But surely the money raised by donations in the end goes to the poor. You can't deny that *dada*,' Sanju said.

'Yes it does. But it is a drop in the ocean and not a permanent solution. Much better to use the money to educate the poor. They can then break the cycle they are stuck in. Learn to stand up for their right and force social change. Education is the only solution I say, education.'

I kept a watch behind us, checking if anyone was following us. Anyone looking at me was a potential threat. How long before they catch up with me.

Sanju cleared his throat but did not contradict Raju. I knew it was only because he did not want to be disrespectful to someone his senior, a masterji.

'Education is power,' Raju continued, 'proper education. You are at university. Why do you think your parents have sent you there? It's because they understand the importance of education. Which family do you belong to son?'

Sanju went red in the face and I could sense his discomfort.

'Dada look something is happening up front,' I pointed at a crowd milling around a bulldozer. An incidence was indeed taking place. Cars had slowed to walking pace while the honking had increased in reverse proportion. A few cars mounted the already congested pavements, in an attempt to overtake, infuriating the shop keepers. A scuffle broke out between a driver and mango-sellers.

'What is happening?' I asked our driver.

'The usual, *sahib*,' he replied, 'a procession or something like that, who knows.'

As we inched closer, the reason for the holdup became clear. Police were raiding an illegal *busti*, slum, dismantling it. Bulldozers were flattening everything in their path. Hovels constructed with bamboos, tarpaulin and tin sheets were falling like playing cards. Children screaming, mothers were running with babies in arms, men were trying to salvage what they could, a loudspeaker was warning people not to obstruct police in executing High Court orders. A police cordon was keeping the onlookers at bay; resistance was met with swinging *lathis*. It seemed certain a riot would breakout.

Sanju was getting restless. 'We must go and help,' he said. He was half out of the car. I pulled him back in. 'Don't be a fool. There is nothing you can do.'

Raju, sinking uncomfortably in the seat, was wiping his forehead with a handkerchief and shaking his head, as if he had made a mistake by coming with us.

'Do something, get us out of here,' I said to the driver.

With window rolled down he started asking people directions. Someone pointed at a dirt track wide enough for a car. He swung the car around and barged in. Cyclists dismounted to let us pass; stray cows had to be coaxed out of the way. Inches from a wall or boundary fence we kept making progress, bumping in and out of potholes, taking sharp turns.

'Are you sure Saira is waiting for me? If not take me back

home,' Raju said patting his thigh nervously.

'She will be waiting Raju dada, I promise,' I said. His eyes were darting left and right out the window as if memorising landmarks.

Finally, we entered Tollygunge. Raju whispered, 'I haven't seen her for so many years you see, I was wondering what she looks like.'

I did not know how best to describe Saira, whatever I said would be inadequate. 'You will meet her soon anyway, why not wait.'

'Yes, yes you are right,' Raju said, 'how much longer?'

'Not long.'

An hour and five minutes later, we stopped under the sign *Tolly Park House*. 'We are here,' I announced, and Raju began fidgeting again, this time with the shirt's buttons.

We took the dirt path, past storage sheds and labourers' hovels.

This time the caretaker came to the door personally.

'*Namaskar didi*, we have come to meet Saira,' I said.

'Saira?' she studied each face in turn, 'come in.'

Raju got his feet tangled on the steps. Sanju grabbed his arm and helped him over the threshold.

'I'll show you to her room, this way,' the caretaker said impatiently and set off at a brisk pace.

'Wait for me.' I made Raju sit down beside a desk with stacks of leaflets and followed the woman. Her enormous posterior under the sari swung ungainly. Past the lifts and stairs, we entered an enclosed hallway, air reeking of unwashed bodies suffused with pungency of fried fish.

We were in an older part of the building, darker, dirtier and uninviting. 'But this is not the way to her room,' I said.

She did not reply but stopped abruptly, pointed at a sign that said Visitors Room above a double door. 'She is in there,' she said, and without waiting for a response disappeared round the corner.

I waited until the sound of her tapping shoes had faded. Now I was all alone, not a sound from the Visitors Room. I wondered if Saira really was in there. Could she have changed her mind? I peeped inside the room through the glass porthole. A few high-backed chairs stood arranged roughly in semi-circle. There were a few side tables, each with a vase and dry flower arrangement. On the walls were framed pictures of holy men and saints, Swamy Vivekanand the most prominent among them. The room appeared unoccupied until I looked side-ways. There she was, sitting by herself on a high-sided chair. She looked so graceful in a bottle green sari with small flower patterns, a black shawl slung on her shoulders and she was wearing matching green sandals on her slender feet.

I pushed the door open and went in.

She looked up startled and then raised a hand bidding me over. 'Oh, Kalu is he here?' she asked whispering fervently, as if I was her confidante.

I mimed the words: waiting outside.

'No,' she squealed, 'what does he look like?'

'You will see him in a minute,' I said, 'shall I bring him in?'

'Wait, wait, wait.' She stood up and looked down at her feet, patted her sari to make it fall in place. Once satisfied she sat down with her right leg tucked slightly under the chair, crossed the left leg over the right, the sari fell to the ankle, just touching the sandals. She straightened her shoulders, head at

304

slight angle. 'Now,' she said.

Back at the reception desk Raju was sitting slumped on the chair, legs bent at the knees at right angle, feet side by side, as if waiting in line for an important job interview. 'Is it time?' he said in a whisper.

I took his hand and walked him to the Visitors Room. At the door I squeezed his shoulder. 'Be gentle with her, she is nervous. Good luck.'

He opened the door. Took a few steps in, looked to his right and stopped. Saira sprang to her feet. Neither said anything for a few moments, like a movie clip frozen in time. Then she threw her arms up in the air. 'Raju,' she said in a trembling voice.

'Saira, is that you,' he said, his voice loud and gruff. He moved towards her, hesitating at first and then hurrying.

She clasped both hands tight to the chest, shy and demure, waiting for his arms. He ran the final few yards, placed his arms around her waist, pulled her towards him. Her feet left the floor. She was crying now, sobbing hysterically.

Raju, a strong and silent type, consoling her, 'don't cry Saira, don't.' His shoulders too began rising and falling rapidly.

THE END

TRANSLATION

Hindi	English
Alu puri	Fried pan cake with potatoes curry
Beta	Son
Bhakts	Followers, devotees
Bahnchoot	A swear word
Bilkul	Absolutely
Bakwas	Nonsense
Bade bhai	Elder brother
Bibi	Wife
Bania	Shopkeeper
Bhutta	Corn on the cob
Band-walla	Musician
Batua	Wallet
Chor	Thief
Chamar	A caste in India (considered very low)
Chutia	A swear word
Chappal	Slipper, footwear

Curd	Yogurt
Darshan	Meeting, audience
Didi	Nannie, older sister
Dadima	Grandmother
Dhobi	Washer-man
Dalit	A caste in India
Ghat	River bank
Gaandu	A swear word
Gaadi	Car, wheeled platform
Gamacha	Towel
Haramzada	A swear word
Havan	A religious ceremony
Halwai	Baker of sweets
Khana ghar	Dining room, canteen
Keema	Mincemeat
Kathputli	Puppet
Kuti	Bitch
Lungi	Mens' wrap around
Lathi	Stave, stick
Lomri	Fox
Maidan	Open space, garden
Masi	Aunt

Ma bap	Mother father
Namaste	Greetings, hello
Natakbaz	An actor
Oh, hariram	Oh, my God
Phoketmar	Pickpocket
Pharishta	Angel
Pandit	Priest
Paan	A condiment for eating (betel nuts, brown paste, wrapped in edible leaf)
Rasagulla	A syrupy sweet
Sarak ka kuta	Street dog (wild)
Slokas	Religious hymns
Samp	Snake
Sadhu	Someone who has renounced the world
Saala	A swear word
Sarkar	Government
Tamasha	Funfair, party
Tilak	Paste applied to forehead, (religious symbol)
Yateemkhana	Orphanage
Yaar	Friend